D0041601

PALM BEACH

Also by Mary Adkins

Privilege
When You Read This

PALM BEACH

A NOVEL

MARY ADKINS

HARPER

An Imprint of HarperCollins*Publishers*

PALM BEACH. Copyright © 2021 by Mary Adkins. All rights reserved. Printed in the United States of America. No part of this book may be used or reproduced in any manner whatsoever without written permission except in the case of brief quotations embodied in critical articles and reviews. For information, address HarperCollins Publishers, 195 Broadway, New York, NY 10007.

HarperCollins books may be purchased for educational, business, or sales promotional use. For information, please email the Special Markets Department at SPsales@harpercollins.com.

FIRST EDITION

Library of Congress Cataloging-in-Publication Data has been applied for.

ISBN 978-0-06-301137-3

21 22 23 24 25   LSC   10 9 8 7 6 5 4 3 2 1

For Katie Beth Ongena,
a mother who set the bar from day one

CHAPTER 1

The most international thing about Palm Beach International Airport were the Italian loafers of the tanned men in baby-blue shorts and white polos who hurried off the plane from first class while Rebecca and Mickey passed Bash, wailing, back and forth between them in economy.

"I tried that," Rebecca said as Mickey scrambled to pull up *Sesame Street* on his phone. She offered the woman standing in the aisle next to her husband an *I'm sorry* smile. Bash—short for Sebastian—hadn't cried for the entirety of the three-hour flight from LaGuardia, but he had for most of it.

"Honey," the gray-haired woman said, "we're back in the sunshine now. Here, nothing matters."

It was only Rebecca's second time in Palm Beach—the first, two months earlier, had been to find an apartment to rent. Over seventy-two packed hours, she and Mickey had been shown every high-story condo in the downtown area, her two requirements being: it had to be within walking distance of a coffee shop where she could write, and it had to have a view of the water. (If she was going to be lucky enough to live by the ocean, she might as well be able to see it before she brushed her teeth.)

"Do you live here?" Rebecca asked the woman, assuming that

retirement had brought their fellow passenger to Florida's southern coast, as it had for so many.

"Going on three years," she said. "What about you all? Family vacation?"

"We're moving here," Rebecca said, absently rubbing Bash's back as he continued to scream.

"You'll love it. Everyone loves it. What's your husband do?" the woman asked, glancing at Mickey, who had found a way to distract Bash with his sunglasses. Their eight-month-old's wails stopped as he pried apart the earpieces with his tiny fingers. Ray-Bans, Mickey's birthday present from her. A hundred and twenty bucks, Rebecca thought with an inward sigh. She started to reach for them, but the line to deboard finally loosened and began to inch forward, and Mickey nudged her before she could answer the woman.

She checked the seats to make sure they weren't leaving anything behind—no bottle nipples, no singing toys, no balled-up diapers—and slung her carry-on over her shoulder, feeling the woman still waiting for an answer.

"Oh, um," Rebecca said as she yanked the travel stroller (world's smallest, Guinness Record!) down from the overhead bin. "He's a caterer."

"A *caterer*?" Mickey said. They stood in the Hertz line, saddled with bags—a striped one, a nearly identical polka-dotted one, a diaper bag covered in teal elephants.

They'd hauled all of it, along with their three seventy-pound suitcases, strollers (two), car seat, and pack-'n'-play portable crib onto the shuttle bus that they'd taken to the rental car building, where several people with far less baggage had beaten them to the desk.

On the to-do list: buy a car. They'd never owned one, or needed to—Rebecca had lived in New York for eleven years, Mickey for fifteen.

"Fine, a butler," she said. "I don't know. What are you?"

"A house manager," Mickey said. Rebecca laughed, and he grinned.

It was a winning quality of Mickey's—that he didn't take himself too seriously, or all that seriously, period.

For an actor, that had been surprising to her.

In those early days she'd been struck by how mild-mannered and accommodating he was, content to relinquish attention to others—how on earth was he a *musical theater actor*? Actors, she'd believed, were all a bit narcissistic, or at least self-involved, by nature.

Not Mickey. He didn't perform modesty; he was genuinely humble. It had taken a month before he'd dropped that he'd been a lead on Broadway—and been nominated for a Tony for it.

"Wait, you have a *Tony* nomination?" She'd actually stopped in her tracks, as the saying went. She didn't remember how it had come up, but she remembered they'd been walking down the sidewalk.

"Yep," he'd said.

By that point he knew about every high-profile interview she'd ever produced at *Good Morning America* before she'd quit to freelance. She'd probably dropped Beyoncé's name three times. (One encounter with Beyoncé definitely warranted three mentions.)

"What else have you been keeping to yourself?" she'd asked, and he'd winked.

But soon she'd learn that there was more, a kind of more that he didn't fail to disclose because he was humble as much as because he didn't care about it enough to share. Like so many working New York actors, for years Mickey had catered between (and even during) shows to pay his bills.

The thing people who weren't in the acting world typically didn't understand—what she hadn't understood until she'd started dating Mickey—was that working actors, *successful* actors, moved in and out of other work for decades, some their whole lives. The ones who stayed in the business managed to do so because they filled the gaps—those intermittent, sometimes interminable periods between acting jobs—with money gigs. Some catered or waited tables or tended bar. Some taught. Some became part-time yoga teachers, or personal trainers, or life coaches. Others gave up, moving to Texas or Ohio to take up real estate.

But the lifers kept showing up to auditions. As the audition sides—the one to two pages of lines they had to memorize to land the role—changed from "20s student" to "30s divorcée" to "40s bedraggled parent," the gritty ones didn't give up. They weren't so much chasing the dream any longer as stepping in and out of it.

Catering shift, audition, catering shift, callback, show for six months, catering shift.

Rinse and repeat.

The difference between Mickey and most of his fellow caterer-actors was that he was so good at it—so reliable, attentive, and discreet—that by no intention of his own he'd risen to the top of New York's catering world. By the time Rebecca had met him, he was a go-to guy for Manhattan's billionaire class . . . which meant she wasn't the only one who'd brushed sleeves with stardom.

"Oprah likes seltzer with extra lime," he'd told her once, and seen her eyes light up.

"Tell me someone else's," she'd said.

"Steven Tyler?" he'd said.

"Let me guess. Diet Pepsi?"

"TaB."

"No!" She'd told everyone she knew.

Even as he'd waited on heads of state, poured tea for first children, and helped Barbra Streisand discreetly remove a forgotten sales tag from her blouse, he'd never identified as a caterer. It was money work, a necessary evil, the price of being an artist in one of the most expensive cities on earth. To both of them, his catering was a side gig; Mickey was an actor.

Over their early months together, Rebecca learned to talk theater. She said "break a leg" or "merde" (French for *shit*) rather than "good luck" before his auditions, and she knew not to ask about them afterward. She became comfortable reading lines with him, an activity they spent hours doing because Mickey was dyslexic and therefore committed to memorizing even when he wasn't obliged to; to read in public had been a nightmare since grade school. She learned to set up the ring light and iPhone stand to film his video auditions, to say "rolling," "action," and "take three."

But not anymore. As of that moment in the Hertz rental center, Mickey was a career caterer . . . or house manager, the title Freddie Wampler, media mogul, had given him.

It hadn't been the plan, of course. But one morning eighteen months earlier, out of the blue, Mickey had woken up raspy, his voice dry and airy. At first it hadn't seemed like a big deal; he'd lost his voice before. Whether due to overuse or a cold, he'd go on vocal rest for a few days, drink hot tea (until he learned that that made it worse), and wait for it to come back. If he was in a show, he'd call out, and was never offstage for longer than a week.

But this time was different. He felt fine, with no cough or congestion, and he hadn't been in a show at the time, so it wasn't immediately consequential. Just the missing voice. When it hadn't returned in five, then six days, he'd scheduled a visit with an ENT, Dr. Dyre—a man whose services were so in demand by New York's swamp of professional singers that he didn't take a single insurance. Mickey had seen Dr. Dyre only once before; he was the kind of doctor you could afford to visit only when things were very bad. His name suited him.

High in his white Madison Avenue office—white walls, white furniture, white countertops—Dr. Dyre had inserted a tiny camera down Mickey's throat and diagnosed him with a vocal hemorrhage: the vessels on his vocal cords had become inflamed, and one had erupted, causing blood to accumulate. It was a fairly regular occurrence for people who belted from a stage over many years, and the doctor had prescribed Mickey more vocal rest: no singing or speaking at all for seven days.

The first few days, Rebecca would forget that he couldn't speak. She'd ask him a question and wait, only to remember after several seconds passed in silence. By the end of the week, they'd fallen into a new dynamic: yes or no inquiries, easily answerable with a nod or shake.

"Do you want spaghetti squash for dinner?" Shake.

"Okay, rice noodles, then?" Nod.

"Will you be ready to go in ten minutes?" Nod.

But after a week, not only had the hemorrhage not improved, but the bleeding had actually produced a polyp, which could only be removed surgically. Three months later, he'd undergone a microlaryngoscopy, which the surgeon had warned him carried a 1 in 100 chance of a permanent hoarse voice. But what choice did he have? It took an afternoon, in and out. Not covered by health insurance, it had cost twenty-seven hundred dollars, which he'd put on his Visa. He was to refrain from singing—and, of course, auditioning—for six weeks.

In the process of removing the polyp, the surgeon mentioned in passing, he'd caused a "small amount of trauma, the size of a dime" on Mickey's left vocal cord that he hoped would heal.

Mickey had been in the business long enough to know that a dime was a planet on the scale of neck organs.

As soon as he'd come out of surgery, he'd had a bad feeling.

His voice hadn't been the same since.

"Jesus. What are the odds?" Rebecca had asked rhetorically, regarding him with such genuine pity that he'd had to look away.

But Mickey had been told the odds: 1 in 100. It just so happened that he was the unlucky one percent.

He'd stopped trying not to speak at that point, going about his life as before—minus everything he loved about it other than Rebecca, and now with a chronic rasp.

By then they were married. Rebecca had moved out of her beautiful Manhattan apartment to live with him—her studio was too small for two adults, while he had a rent-controlled sizable one-bedroom in Queens. It had only made sense.

Although her beloved antique yellow desk had lost a leg in the Penske truck on the drive across town, which she'd feared was a bad omen, her career as a freelance journalist had begun to thrive. In one month alone, she was assigned a piece on the burgeoning music scene in the Middle East for *GQ*, an exposé of the Body Shop for *Vanity Fair*, and a piece on gay divorce for *New York* magazine. For the *GQ* piece she'd gotten to go to Dubai, skiing down an indoor ski slope in the middle of July.

Her favorite subjects to write about were corruption and income inequality—the toxic greed of the über-wealthy—but she wasn't picky. Especially if an assignment allowed her to travel, she took it.

Meanwhile, Mickey couldn't audition because he now sounded like John Mayer, or Sting—not exactly the easy, lilting tenor of Tommy in *Brigadoon*. He'd cater, and come home, and try to believe that his career wasn't over. He was only thirty-six.

Then, early in March, Rebecca had had Bash. As winter lingered and the days remained short and cold, their rent had gone up by 4 percent, and life was reduced to missing pacifiers, the endless chug-a-lug of the breast pump, and prayers for poop—a good baby poop in the afternoon or evening meant a solid stretch of baby sleep at night, up to five hours even.

Bash woke to feed at eleven p.m., two a.m., four a.m., or more. In their apartment, which now seemed smaller than ever, they tried to take turns, but it was impossible to sleep through the crying and soothing and toilet flushes and bottle rinsing, and Mickey got his only uninterrupted slumber on the subway. On every ride to cater, he snoozed on the Q train. As for Rebecca, her body gave in at random moments. One night, she awoke on the toilet, her cheek stuck against the tiled wall.

Money had become tighter as they'd put purchase after purchase on their credit card, each item seeming crucial for their survival: a second baby carrier, when they discovered the one from their registry turned out to be for bigger babies; a newborn insert for the car seat for when they Ubered to the pediatrician for checkups; wipes, diapers, wipes, diapers.

Mickey, catering seven days a week, was on his feet for so many hours that his toenails had turned blue the way marathon runners' do, and his daily step counter plateaued at 18,000. The hemlines of his black H&M pants grew threadbare, and the pits of his white shirts yellowed bronze.

His primary work by that point was for Freddie Wampler, fifty-four-year-old multimillionaire Democratic donor, who, with his wife, Ingrid, split his time between New York City and East Hampton in the warm months, and Palm Beach in the winter. During the Wamplers' annual northern stint, they kept a rigorous social calendar for their eponymous foundation: in a sizable gathering room on the eleventh floor of the foundation's Fifth Avenue offices (fewer high-value items for guests to spill drinks on than in their Park Avenue home), Mickey spent multiple evenings a week pouring wine, offering cheddar biscuits to stacks-of-bones women with taut foreheads (who would decline them), and using an environmentally questionable number of paper towels to hand-dry champagne flutes.

One night, pressed against the greasy door of a cab headed back to Astoria in the wee hours of the morning, he and two friends who'd been on the same shift had passed a swiped bottle of top-shelf liquor back and forth.

"How are you going to afford a kid in this city, man?" one, a dancer, had asked.

"We'll figure it out," Mickey had said, while inside a boulder had begun to form in his gut.

As a freelancer, Rebecca had had no maternity leave, and she didn't have the energy to pitch. It was the spring before the presidential election, and she added phone banking to her daily activities of running and reading—calling up registered Democrats in swing states to remind them to vote, repeating over and over, "Can I get your promise to vote this fall?" with Bash attached to her chest.

Then summer had come.

Hauling the stroller up and down the stairs to the subway platform had been treacherous enough in the New York winter, but in a July heat wave, it became downright insufferable. The sweat would pool in Rebecca's cleavage and run down her shins as they waited for the train. She'd blow on Bash's small, red face above the torrid concrete, worried that he was overheating.

One evening in the fall, just after Bash had turned seven months old, Freddie Wampler himself (rather than Celeste, his event planner, who was Mickey's usual point of contact) had approached Mickey.

"My house manager in Florida has decided to retire, and I need someone to run Palm Beach right away, early December at the latest." He'd spelled out the offer in the concise way that a man like Freddie Wampler would: a salary of $125,000 plus moving costs. December 1 was six weeks away.

Mickey had worked with house managers before but had never known anyone to be offered the job.

For him, it seemed like an easy call. He wasn't performing, and wouldn't be any time soon. There was his ballooning student loan debt, and the credit card debt at which he was barely chipping away. Still, he was surprised to find Rebecca elated by the idea. His mother, living in Boston, was not, but they promised that she was welcome anytime, and their living by the beach wasn't a bad perk in Fran's view.

As soon as Mickey accepted the offer, it seemed, things had started looking up. Bash began to sleep through the night. The fall temperatures cooled Astoria, and leaving the apartment became enjoyable again. Rebecca wrote a piece for *The Atlantic* that got the attention of her J-school classmate Henrik Bloom, now an editor at *New York* magazine, who'd offered her an online column—a column!—on wealth inequality.

Being offered the column was like someone knocking on her door and saying, "You know that topic you're obsessed with? You get to write about it for money." A dream come true after eight years logging sixty-hour weeks producing morning show fluff and four years hustling to land assignments as a freelancer.

Within the space of a month, they packed up their belongings, giggling over how the fancy relocation company Wampler had recommended was going to be shipping their secondhand glassware and IKEA chairs, probably at an expense much higher than what the items were worth, and now, here they were. Floridians.

Mickey still hoped it was temporary. The idea that he'd given up his acting career for good wasn't something he was ready to accept. (He was still paying off his vocal performance BFA from Carnegie Mellon, for God's sake.) But as the Hertz rep handed Mickey the keys to the Nissan Rogue they'd rented for the month, Rebecca felt her whole body exhale.

CHAPTER 2

Rebecca had never visited a beach town during the winter holiday season, and being here in early December felt incongruous: people in flip-flops hauling surfboards and bright coolers past doors adorned with Christmas wreaths and windows displaying menorahs. The miniature plastic Christmas tree she and Mickey had stored year-round in New York, folding it up and sliding it under the bed, looked puny and out of place in their new condo, and that seemed right: Christmas didn't belong here. West Palm Beach Christmas felt more like a nod to the holiday than an actual celebration of it, the same way a city outside of the United States might acknowledge the Fourth of July.

A couple of blocks from their condo, Rebecca was exploring the neighborhood with Bash in the stroller when, between two residential buildings, she came upon a tiny French bakery tucked away in an otherwise empty alleyway.

She went inside, and a bell dinged, announcing her entrance. A token Santa hat drooped on the countertop, and sparkly green tinsel hugged the register. It was empty. She ordered a black tea and took a bistro table along the back wall. She pulled out her linen wrap designed to cover a nursing infant, draped it across her chest, and lifted Bash underneath. Before her sat a stack of free local publications she'd grabbed off the counter.

It had been a whirlwind move. Rebecca's request that their home be walkable to coffee (her shorthand for "I don't want to have to get in the car to find a quiet place to write") limited them to the downtown West Palm area, a single square-mile patch with a dozen or so condo buildings sprinkled among restaurants, shops, a couple of parks, and a high school. The neighborhood was also close enough to Palm Beach, the realtor had said, that Mickey would be no more than a five-minute drive or twenty-minute walk across the bridge to the Wamplers', aka the ultra-wealthy part of town.

Looking at apartments had affirmed their decision to leave New York. The size of them—1,200 square feet on the low end! The smallest one they'd visited had twice the square footage of their Queens place. The light, the proximity to the water! They'd chosen the third unit they'd seen, which was also the most expensive, on the twentieth floor of a luxury doorman building with views of Lake Worth and the Atlantic beyond.

Now they lived high above a blue horizon, and every morning for the past seven days she'd taken Bash on long morning walks by the water. They would return glowing and sun-kissed despite the sunscreen she lathered on both their cheeks. To promote his verbal development, she was supposed to narrate their lives, talk to him about anything and everything. "Tell the baby what you are thinking!" the parenting books and magazines instructed. So when he was awake, she would speak to him: *Here is a building. There is the library.*

Most of what she uttered were short statements of fact: *I see a bird. I see water,* and it surprised her, how happy the simplicity of it made her. Her old twentysomething self, full of ambition and easily bored, would never have guessed how much joy she could find at thirty-four as a new mom pointing out tree stumps.

She loved Bash so damn much; so many of the things she'd rolled her eyes at once upon a time now made sense. The "I never knew love before I had her!" and "I never want him to grow up!" posts by girls she had gone to high school with—these had bugged her, and made no sense, before she became a parent. First, to say that any love you experienced as a nonparent wasn't real love was insulting. Second, why on earth wouldn't you want your child to grow up? The alternative was tragic.

But after having Bash, she understood that it was a new kind of a love, rooted in the bones, fierce and frightening. Things that used to scare her—a threatening sound in the night, a shadowy figure in the dark—now set her on the offensive. Where she used to cower, she braced herself for a fight: *I dare you to come near my baby.*

She surveyed the room of empty tables. It was part relaxing and part eerie. In twelve years in New York, she had never found herself alone in any public place, except for once in a subway car at three a.m. As Bash nursed, she flipped through the glossy brochures featuring local homes for sale and a stunning number of estate sales, skimming as she thought about her next column. She hadn't decided what to tackle yet.

Rebecca had officially been a biweekly columnist for nine weeks. She'd written four of them already, and she still felt the impulse to pinch herself.

She'd been fascinated by wealth—not covetous of it, but fascinated by it—since she was a girl growing up on a Tennessee farm. Her father owned land and some cattle and worked for his brother's cattle-processing company. Her uncle's massive, tristate operation outfitted her cousins in Abercrombie & Fitch and J.Crew while Rebecca wore the same Old Navy jeans until she outgrew them, sometimes splurging on Gap with her babysitting money. Even as a kid, it had seemed so arbitrary to her, who got the fancier clothes and cars, whose families left the country during school vacations rather than driving to the Alabama gulf during hurricane season to take advantage of lower rates.

She was only a little jealous. Mostly she was fine with what she had, which, she later realized as an adult, had still rendered her quite privileged. But she had been struck as a child by the disconnect between good fortune and desert. Her cousins stole candy from Winn-Dixie while their mom was distracted and stuck their chewed gum under the table and copied anyone's homework who would let them.

Rebecca let them. She didn't like conflict.

Living on a farm, she'd seen things she still thought of in flashes. In first grade, her father had sold a calf in front of her. She'd watched as the calf was tied up, crying for its mother, and shoved into the back of a stranger's pickup. She'd observed silently, but soon after, she'd begun having nightmares.

Later that year, when a few of her classmates stumbled on a dead squirrel at recess, one that had suffocated after getting its neck stuck in a torn plastic water bottle, she couldn't control her outburst. Rebecca had been a spectacle, sitting alone on the dirt crying while her peers backed away. Her teacher had taken her inside and tried to calm her before finally calling her parents to pick her up.

To soothe her, her mom and aunt had tried to convince her that it wasn't that bad. Animals die. Things die. It's the circle of life.

But what Rebecca had heard was: you're crazy.

So she had toughened herself up with knowledge, acquiring a shield of facts and a rigid political viewpoint. By fourteen, she was a vegetarian, and by sixteen, a vegan. Her parents, who weren't especially political, weren't sure how they'd wound up with a daughter so obsessed with progressive values. Twice in high school, her mother had sat her down to express concern that perhaps she was too serious. (This was after Rebecca had watched a documentary on the endangerment of whales and become so determined that she and her parents should save them that it was all she'd talk about. "I have no idea how we're supposed to do that from Bell Buckle, Tennessee," her father had responded.)

But, in fact, Rebecca found great satisfaction—even joy—in educating herself on the workings of the world and using that information to shape and structure her life. It had driven most of her public school teachers crazy ("I don't *know* why the civil rights movement only gets one week," one teacher had told her in response to her questioning, "*I* didn't write the curriculum"), but her tenth-grade newspaper teacher Mrs. Lake had encouraged her to pursue journalism, and she'd headed to Northwestern–Medill Journalism School.

Then came eight years as a producer at *Good Morning America*, a job she took because it was the only one in New York she had been offered. It was a good job, well paying, in the toughest city in the world. She was a minion, but one with a badge, and access. And who did she know who was thrilled with their job, anyway? It wasn't like her journalist friends working in "real" press were doing meaningful work–they, too, were made to chase ratings, or clicks, and to prioritize sensation. Year after year, she'd prep guests behind-the-scenes–Bono, Melinda Gates, The Rock–engaging them in frank, fascinating conversations about their work and values, only to watch them go on air and be asked to rank chocolate milk shakes or compete in a lip-syncing contest.

The week she finally snapped, it was over a famous influencer. While protests sparked by police brutality raged in Ferguson, Rebecca had been charged with getting the influencer ready to talk about her new celebrity-lifestyle app. Watching in the darkness as this shiny-haired woman, on air, explained how she was a "friend guiding you through your A-list life," Rebecca thought: I can't do this anymore.

The next morning she'd given notice. It would be hard to get by as a freelancer, but she had connections to editors from Medill and eight years in the industry. At least she'd control her workload.

Her first–and only–serious assignment to land after having Bash: a piece for *The Atlantic* on the hypocrisy of Silicon Valley start-up culture, how it fancied itself a bastion of social goods like community and democracy while flaunting policies that perpetuated inequality. (A popular vacation lodging site, for example, had announced a commitment to combat racism and discrimination by its hosts, until its lawyers got their fingers in the matter, at which point the company changed its tune: "We can't actually control what people do," it essentially said. "We're just the middleman.")

That was the article that had prompted Henrik Bloom to call her up. By the next week, she was writing about the buy-one, give-one business model and its detrimental effect on local economies, about the gut biomes of America's poor and the long-term health implications of lacking key nutritional bacteria, and about how white high-school dropouts still made, on average, 33 percent more than Black college graduates.

She loved the dig, the quest to find a fresh perspective on a timeless story growing more relevant by the day: the massive, yawning gap between the well-to-do and the barely-getting-by.

She opened the glossy social register for Palm Beach and scanned the listings of upcoming charity events in town: several fundraisers for various forms of cancer and a couple of soirées funding, vaguely, the arts.

The listings were generally simple, not flashy: a photo of donors in evening gowns beneath a short blurb of text, details for registering. But then she came across one that caught her eye. As the *Sesame Street* episodes they pulled up on the iPad for Bash would say, it was "not like the others."

The announcement took up half a page: a cartoonish drawing of a high heel next to—half its size—clip art of a terrier.

Wine and WOOF!, a doggy fashion show and luncheon held at a local private club called the Stuart House, benefited a local dog shelter.

Tickets to the event ranged from four hundred to twenty-five thousand dollars, with donor levels named "Top Dog," "Leader of the Pack," and "Tail Wagger."

"The most anticipated midday event of the season!"

She reminded herself that she was a wealth columnist now, and living in the New York elite's winter wonderland. Palm Beach was, as the cabdriver who'd driven them to the airport had put it when they'd told him where they were moving, "the sixth borough."

Rebecca checked the date—it was two days away, on Saturday. Mickey wouldn't be working and thus could take Bash.

She grabbed her phone to text Henrik. Now she just had to convince him to pay for her ticket.

Across the lake and half a mile west, Mickey mopped the deck of the Wamplers' yacht, wondering how his wife and son were doing back over the bridge.

Already they understood (it was impossible to miss) that Palm Beach was divided into two parts: the east and the west. Palm Beach proper, which sat snugly between the skinny strip of water known as Lake Worth and the Atlantic Ocean, was where the billionaires and their ilk lived. Oversized clocks on stilts reminded everyone that time to acquire more was running out. Canopies of palm trees bent over the swept and smooth streets, shading the shiny cars that passed underneath onto Worth Avenue to visit the high-end shops: Hermès, Prada, Gucci.

Mickey stood on the boat looking out over the lake. Yachts, some twice the size of the Wamplers', peppered its bank.

"Mickey!" called Chuck, the grounds guy. "Can I get you to help me with these Chinese fan palms?"

Mickey rested the mop in the bucket and headed up the manicured hill toward the house.

His first five days of work had been easier, frankly, than any catering work he'd ever done back in the city, including for the Wamplers. The pace of life was slower here, and expectations, it seemed, followed suit. His primary responsibility so far had been overseeing the descent of myriad decorators and designers and their hired help, teams brought in to stage the place for the island's

annual Holiday Tour of Homes, which raised money for something; Mickey didn't remember what.

Every morning people showed up with poinsettias and garland
and silver candelabra, marching in with cardboard boxes of three-
foot-tall nutcrackers and gold-leafed angels while Mickey stood
by, making sure they didn't track wet footprints, knock over any
vases, or scratch a pristine wall.

He unloaded the pots of giant Chinese fan palms—the kind gei-
shas use to fan emperors in old movies—from the truck, and when
they finished, Chuck asked, "Would you mind grabbing Mrs.
Wampler? I just want to confirm where she wants the bromeliads."
Mickey could see that in the back of the truck there were more
potted plants, equally dramatic—fiery red cones peeling open to
expose a hot yellow center.

Mickey changed his shoes at the door and climbed the stairs to
Mrs. Wampler's sitting room, where he could hear the TV inside
playing softly. The door was ajar. He rapped gently on it.

"Yes?" Her voice sounded tired.

"Chuck has a question for you," he said, peeking in. She stood
and stretched, then yawned.

"Thanks, Mickey," she said. Then she approached him, reached
down, and squeezed his crotch. Hard. A full hand grip.

She walked away, saying nothing, just gliding down the hallway
in no hurry while he stood, stunned, for several seconds before
following her downstairs and outside.

Mrs. Wampler had employed Mickey for dozens of events, if not
hundreds. She'd hired him to work parties that she hosted alone
without her husband, small affairs in their New York penthouse,
meaning that only the two of them—she and Mickey—had been
present in the kitchen for hours at a time while he prepped and she
issued directions.

In fact, back in New York he'd catered her monthly Billionaire
Wives Poker Night: BWPN. (They actually called it that. There was
a ten-thousand-dollar minimum bet for a seat at the table, and the

winnings went to the winner's charity of choice: St. Jude's and the Nature Conservancy had been among them, but so had CEOs for French Culture.)

Nothing like this had ever happened in any of those instances. It was so unexpected, so out of the blue, that in the minutes that followed, he wondered if he'd hallucinated it.

While Mrs. Wampler instructed Chuck on the flowers, Mickey's mind cascaded into doom. He saw everything as it would now play out: he was not going to reciprocate Ingrid Wampler's advances, so he was going to lose his job. Even if he did—not that he would—he didn't see things ending any differently. It was a lose-lose situation.

He hadn't even been there a week. Was this why they'd brought him down? To be her pool boy?

For the rest of the day, she behaved as if nothing had happened. Unsettled and reeling, Mickey ordered kitchen supplies for the chef, arranged for the back deck to be restained, and booked a new fountain restorationist, whom it took two hours and seven phone calls to find, since the current one had left rust-colored rings along the rococo structure's base. His only further interaction that afternoon with Freddie and Ingrid was serving them lunch—a mint pea soup and an arugula salad.

"Maybe it was a one-time thing," Rebecca said. "Was she drunk?"

They sat on their oversized balcony high above West Palm. To their left was all of Palm Beach and, visible beyond it, the silver ocean. Seven stories down, on the thirteenth floor, the building's Olympic-sized pool was flanked by orange pool chairs, few of them occupied at this hour. The setting sun behind the building cast a pink glow on the pool below.

Their chairs catty-cornered, Mickey's legs were draped over Rebecca's, and an open bottle of rosé sat between them on the small, outdoor side table they'd picked up at Target—their first priority upon arriving, to make the balcony usable. Bash was already in his crib asleep.

"I don't think so . . ." he said. Ingrid hadn't seemed drunk, and he hadn't smelled any trace of alcohol.

"Is this the first time you've ever been sexually assaulted at work?" she asked.

"I wouldn't go so far as to call it sexual assault. Maybe harassment," he said.

"Tomato, tomahto," she said. "If the genders were reversed, we wouldn't question calling it assault."

He shrugged. It was a fair point.

Personally, Ingrid Wampler's bizarre aggression didn't upset Rebecca as much as she might have expected. Perhaps because Mickey seemed relatively unfazed by it, she found it more curious than distressing. In all of the stories Mickey had told her about serving the über-rich, this, strangely, was the most human one of his clients that had ever come across to her—impulsive, reckless.

But as she sat, she also thought it was one more example of why she needed her career to take off. Mickey shouldn't be strapped into work that he loathed, that he found degrading. Once she made enough, he could take time to find something he enjoyed—singing was now out of the question, but he could always teach, right? She didn't know if he even wanted to be a voice teacher; she just wanted him to have choices. She also wanted him not to get assaulted at work, or be in a workplace where he was viewed as inferior and thus exploitable.

"I'll just wait and see what happens," he said.

She shrugged.

"I mean, I have to, right?" he said.

She frowned.

"You don't *have* to. You could quit," she said.

But they both knew he wasn't going to quit. They'd just moved. Their rent was twenty-seven hundred a month.

"What time is your thing tomorrow?" he asked, changing the

subject. Rebecca's editor had approved her attendance at the fundraiser the next day, forking over the money for her to go ("not to become a regular thing"). They'd never left Bash with a sitter before, and they didn't know anyone in Florida, regardless.

"Eleven thirty," she said. "And you're good to babysit Bash?"

"It's not called babysitting when I'm the dad," he said, kicking her foot.

"Sorry," she said, then smiled a little. "That was the second most offensive thing to happen to you today."

"Ha-ha," he said, sipping his wine. He was off for the weekend since the Wamplers would be in New York; he wouldn't have to face Ingrid until Monday.

"For a building with over four hundred units, there are never many people in the pool," Rebecca observed, gazing down. A woman in a swim cap swam laps, a slow side stroke, her limbs pale and long. A white-haired man in Umbro shorts and compression kneesocks was sprawled out on a lounge chair reading a thick hardback with a red, white, and blue cover.

"Off season?" Mickey said.

Already they'd learned that everyone in Palm Beach—and, Rebecca guessed, much of South Florida—spoke about time dichotomously: whether it was "on" or "off" season. "On season" began over Christmas and lasted through Memorial Day. "Off season" was the rest of the year.

"Maybe," she said. "Or everyone is just old and stays inside."

"When should we start teaching him to swim?" Mickey asked, perking up.

Mickey couldn't swim himself, though he'd grown up near the water in Boston. His mother hadn't taught him, and while he'd spent sporadic weekends with his dad, who'd take him fishing or to watch soccer at bars, or sailing in his small boat off the rocky Massachusetts coast in the summer, Peadar had never taught Mickey to swim either.

Their relationship had been defined by distance in all senses of the term—his father had been an Irish student studying in America for the semester when his mother, Fran, a lithe, twenty-year-old tap and ballroom dancer, had gotten pregnant with Mickey. Eventually, Peadar married Fran in order to stay in the United States, but it was a marriage only on paper, and he didn't live with them in their Boston three-decker. But the fall that Mickey started sixth grade, Peadar Byrne departed to Ireland for his yearly visit home, met a woman there, and called Fran to say he wouldn't be returning. The woman had two boys of her own. One was Mickey's age.

To be discarded in favor of another mother and her sons (one his age!) was unbearable. Even in his eleven-year-old mind, he knew the feeling it unearthed in him was never going away. He was left with a mountain of grief under which he'd spent the next twenty-five years.

Probably as a result of his own father's deficits, Mickey's favorite fantasy was all the things he'd do with Bash: softball, camping. Teaching him to swim was high on the list.

"We need to get him walking, or at least crawling, before we throw him in the water," Rebecca said.

She closed her eyes for a moment to feel the warm breeze on her skin.

"We're going to miss the gym," he said.

Their Queens apartment had had floor-to-ceiling windows on the street side, and from the living room they could see into a new and high-priced gym across Astoria Boulevard where classes were held—kickboxing, Zumba, hip-hop.

Mickey and Rebecca would pull the kitchen stools up to the window, their knees touching the glass, and stare into the night at the bright, spacious room across the street at all the earnest gyrating in spandex while Mickey narrated, intimately familiar with the lingo from all his years as a child waiting in the back of his mother's dance studio, ". . . and five, six, seven, eight . . . Thrust, jump, spin, *kick!*"

Rebecca would double over, her lips stained with red wine, and he would love her so hard that he wondered if this was a preview of what it might feel like to have a heart attack: a tightening in the chest, an ache so deep it felt like it must have started from beyond him, somewhere preordained.

"Oh, there's plenty to see here," Rebecca said. "Just wait."

The building was shaped like a U, and their interior unit offered the open ocean view to the left, at the U's mouth. But if they looked in any other direction, they could see the sliding glass doors of all the other interior units—dozens of lives on display, as long as the blinds were open. Sitting outside during Bash's morning and afternoon naps, Rebecca had already gotten to know the habits of several residents: the woman who frantically vacuumed for hours at a time (Rebecca suspected she might be taking uppers—no one cleaned with that much energy); the businessman who came home for lunch and played video games in his T-shirt and boxers, then threw his suit back on and dashed out; the older couple who ate a two-hour breakfast while swapping sections of the newspaper then had missionary sex on their four-poster bed.

Suddenly a screech croaked through the air, and Rebecca leaped up, reaching for the handle of the sliding door. But the sound wasn't coming from inside, nor was it a baby. It was a chorus, cackling and wild, as if witches on broomsticks were descending on their courtyard.

Other residents trickled onto their balconies to investigate the noise.

Because darkness had settled within minutes and the light of the new moon was dim, it took them several long seconds to register the birds—hundreds of them, giant and circuslike, had landed en masse and were perched in the palm trees surrounding the pool.

"Parrots?" Mickey said as his eyesight adjusted.

"Do you think they escaped from somewhere?" Rebecca asked. She'd never seen parrots like these in the wild. These were tropical.

Mickey was already googling it.

"No . . . looks like they're South Florida parrots," he said, reading his phone screen. "It's a thing."

As quickly as they'd stormed in, they grew still and silent, shadows weighing down the branches below, which bounced in slow motion under their claws.

"I think they all just went to sleep," Rebecca said.

They sat in silence for a moment. Maybe weird things like this happened in Florida.

"So what is their house like?" she asked. He'd been so eager to tell her about the incident with Ingrid that they hadn't discussed the property itself.

"Just like their Hamptons house," he said.

"Not bigger? Huh," she said. "Seems like you could get more space in Florida."

"I don't mean size. I mean it's the same house," he said. The first thing that had struck Mickey about the Wamplers' Florida estate was that it was identical to their Hamptons home. From the cabinet knobs to the chandeliers to the banisters, it was indistinguishable. "It was built to be the same house. The only difference is the art, and the walls are a different shade, I think."

Rebecca stared at him, her jaw slack.

"What?" he asked.

"Can you imagine," she said, "thinking your life was so perfect that you wouldn't change a single thing about it if given the chance?"

But Mickey hadn't viewed the identical homes as an indication of deep satisfaction on the Wamplers' part. Instead, he attributed them to what it often came down to with the .01 percent: expediency. There was nothing the über-wealthy loathed more than having to learn a new system. Much of life was an inconvenience—you didn't have to be wealthy to know that much. The difference was that the very rich had the option to eliminate much of that inconvenience; they could afford to design an existence in which they didn't have to concern themselves with its administrative aspects.

So that's what they did. Why learn to operate a new showerhead if you don't have to?

Anyway, it made his job easier. Everything was stocked in the same place.

"Maybe she was on Ambien," Mickey said, changing the subject back to Ingrid. "Or sleepwalking. Ambien makes people do crazy things, right?"

"Right," Rebecca said, smirking. "Like eat peanuts."

CHAPTER 3

Four years earlier, they'd met because of a book at a Midtown vegan restaurant where she ate at least twice a week; he'd been there a few times.

He'd just come off his dream role–Guy in the national tour of *Once*. For an Irish-blooded musical theater actor under forty, there wasn't a better part. He'd nailed it night after night, city after city, signing autographs for stringy-haired girls and doe-eyed boys in transitioning arts districts across America, unpacking his avocado knife in Hyatt Places (or Days Inns, when he wanted to pocket more of his per diem). He'd learned the tricks of travel as an ensemble member on his first tour, *Les Mis*: he brought his own pillow in a bright blue pillowcase (so not to accidentally leave it behind), and a tablet preloaded with movies for long bus rides through rural stretches with no Wi-Fi. He zigzagged through the heartland belting Glen Hansard's ballads to misty-eyed auditoriums, performing love so convincingly that he almost convinced *himself* he wasn't lonely. His proud mother, Fran–first runner-up for Miss Rhode Island and owner of the Shake It! studio for thirty-two years–made it to nine out of the eighteen tour stops to cheer him on.

Here was the thing: in all of those hundreds of hours of travel, Mickey hadn't read more than one book. He wasn't a reader. The only reason he'd even read *Banana: The Fate of the Fruit That Changed the World*, after finding a discarded, water-damaged copy in his dressing room in Cleveland, was that *Birdman* hadn't successfully downloaded for the drive to Columbus.

That the single book Mickey had read in fifteen years—a history of the banana, of all things—was the book being read by the woman at the other end of the bar in the Hell's Kitchen restaurant, a woman whom he'd noticed there before and wished for a reason to talk to, had struck Mickey as uncanny. She had long, dark hair with a bright silver streak tracing her left cheek. It seemed to shimmer under the restaurant's twinkly lights when she turned her head. He couldn't look away.

"Great book," he'd found the courage to say.

Rebecca had lifted her gaze across the space she'd intentionally placed between them out of courtesy. Given his notable jawline and a day's scruff, plus a short-sleeved cotton shirt with an embroidered pocket, she pinned him as a Brooklynite. Williamsburg.

"I actually thought it was a different one," she'd said. "I just realized that the book I meant to order is called *Bananas*, not *Banana*."

"Ah, multiple bananas. That one is probably . . . longer." He had the slightest Boston accent.

She'd laughed. "The plural *Bananas* is about how the United Fruit Company screwed Central America."

"That's in this one, too, don't worry," he'd said.

For the next hour and a half they'd talked.

"I like your hair," he'd said at the bottom of their second drink. "This part," he said, touching the streak.

"You like my evil streak?"

"It's evil?"

"It's called a Mallen streak. I used to dye it. In literature they're associated with evil characters . . . you know, like Cruella de Vil."

"All I remember about Cruella de Vil is that my mom loved her. She's the fashionable one, right? Who wears the furs?"

"Yes, furs she kills puppies for."

"Shh," he'd said, exaggeratedly eyeing their neighbors in the vegan restaurant. She'd liked that he was funny.

As they'd gathered their things to head to another bar, she'd held up the book. "So did you like it or not? Should I keep reading?"

"Nope," he'd said. "Lost interest by the third chapter."

"So you didn't finish it."

"Oh, I finished it."

She'd raised her eyebrows.

"I like to see things through," he'd said, grabbing his coat from a hook under the countertop.

"Even if you don't like them?" she'd asked, signing her bill.

"Yep," he'd said, signing his own check. "I'm a masochist that way."

She'd known she'd marry him that night. After chatting at the bar, they'd spent the next six hours in each other's company, migrating from the restaurant to a whiskey lounge and concluding the evening in her West Side studio with a breathtaking view of the Hudson River and the southern Manhattan skyline. At the whiskey lounge, a drag queen had made them balloon hats. Back at her place, they'd worn them as she'd grabbed her phone and navigated to the Cure's "Feels Like Heaven." Wearing only their balloon headpieces and underwear, they'd danced to the Cure in the moonlight.

Leaving the restaurant, as they'd woven their way through the tables to the exit, she'd asked, over her shoulder, "How would I know if you like something or not then?" She was flirting, and she knew it.

"You probably wouldn't," he'd said, grinning. "Unless I told you."

"Not with me," she'd thought aloud as they'd reached the sidewalk. "If I didn't like you, you'd know."

The smallest difference, mutually acknowledged, but what is it that causes an avalanche under chaos theory—a grain of sand?

The next morning, Bash awoke before the parrots.

Rebecca took him out onto the balcony and pointed to the closest one—a tall, lime-green creature with bright orange and yellow streaks perched impossibly on a sagging palm frond nearly perpendicular to the ground. His humanlike eyes closed, he looked regal, like a slumbering noble.

At 7:25, the birds awoke all at once. With one squawk, then two, they flapped to life, their vibrant colors stunning in the early light in a way they hadn't been the night before.

Again, their collective cackling erupted to a deafening volume, and Bash began to cry, frightened. She covered his ears, too intrigued to go inside, and within minutes they'd all flown off.

"They just came to sleep," Rebecca said to Bash, who was too little to be fascinated by any of it.

They had several hours to kill before Rebecca's luncheon, and so the family took the Nissan to the outlet mall, just a fifteen-minute drive away (everything was so close compared to New York where you couldn't get anywhere in under forty-five minutes). It was your standard half-indoor, half-outdoor outlet mall—Sunglass Hut, Ann Taylor Loft, the Gap.

Neither of them was a big shopper—living gig to gig they'd never had the luxury—but now, Mickey was making good money, and their northeastern wardrobes of jeans and sweaters weren't going to cut it.

"Okay, here's how we'll do this," Rebecca said. "Thirty minutes, seventy-five dollars, you win based on number of items."

"I buy for you and you buy for me?" Mickey said.

"God, no!" Rebecca said.

"Come on," Mickey said. For someone who'd initially been confused by her love of games, he'd taken to them and was now as enthusiastic as she was.

"Okay," she said. "But save receipts." She'd definitely have to return whatever he picked out. The only piece of clothing Mickey had ever bought for her had been a hot pink bandage dress with a plunging neckline from Express. He'd been so proud of himself that she'd declined to tell him she wouldn't have worn that even in her twenties. Or teens. She'd finally stuffed it in a Goodwill donation bag two years ago.

An hour later, they sat at a table in the food court sipping Diet Cokes and snacking on Sour Patch Kids (Rebecca's weakness) as Mickey pulled an olive cotton sheath dress from a Banana Republic bag and handed it to her.

"I actually like this," Rebecca said, holding it up, openly surprised.

"And these," he said proudly, procuring tan slides from a Rack Room Shoes bag.

"I didn't know Rack Room still existed," Rebecca said, the logo jarring a flashback: the discount Keds from the clearance rack her mother bought for her every fall before school started. The slides were workable. "Nice, again. Two for two."

Then it was her turn.

"Also from Banana," she said, "four T-shirts and two pairs of shorts."

Mickey groaned.

"Just try them," she said.

Mickey hated shorts. He didn't believe men should "bare leg," and although he only ever said it in a playful way, he didn't wear them even in the peak of a New York summer.

But now they lived in Florida.

"Since you can wear whatever you want to work," she said.

"Not *whatever* I want . . ."

"Surely, 'summer business casual' includes shorts."

He'd been given a surprisingly flexible dress code: "summer business casual" in neutral tones during the day, and a black suit and tie in the evenings.

"I doubt it," he said. There was no way he was going to wear shorts to the Wamplers'.

"Well, you can wear them on your days off," she said, sipping the last of her soda.

After a visit to a Children's Place to buy Bash a tiny swimsuit and swim shirt, they headed back home, making an impulse stop at Chick-fil-A before they hit the highway.

"We're not supposed to eat at Chick-fil-A," said Rebecca, who could hardly find anything vegan on the menu anyway.

"Yeah, yeah," Mickey said, pulling into the drive-through line. "But we're Floridians now. I wear shorts and you hang out at doggy fashion shows."

She laughed.

"I'll take a diet lemonade," she said.

The luncheon was scheduled from eleven thirty to four thirty, which meant she'd either have to leave early to get home and nurse Bash, or use her portable pump. She'd packed it in her navy tote but assumed she wouldn't need it. She told herself that five hours of a doggy fashion show was too many, but in truth she'd never been away from Bash for so long.

As she parked the rental among the Mercedes and Teslas and Aston Martins, she already missed him. He didn't even *do* anything yet: he cooed, sucked smashed fruits from $1.99 pouches labeled "organic," sat upright, and occasionally tipped over. That was about it. When she was alone with him for hours, she was both bored and smitten, restless and aware that there was nowhere she'd rather be. It all made no sense and all the sense in the world.

Her phone alarm sounded—a reminder to take her pills. She dug the bottle from her purse as the engine died.

After giving birth, her emotions had gone haywire. She would sob at the sight of a three-legged dog, a text from a college friend, a diaper commercial featuring a child's love for his fish. It terrified her, to be so vulnerable, so emotional. Her doctor had suggested a "very low dose" of Lexapro, and she'd felt no hesitation filling the prescription.

Overnight her old self was back, a miracle of modern medicine. She'd told anyone who would listen: if you feel any uncharacteristic sadness after giving birth, don't wait to tell your doctor! No shame over taking drugs! Fuck pride.

She popped both her birth control and Lexapro as she locked the Nissan, thinking of her dad's old joke whenever they'd pull up in her uncle's sweeping circular driveway: "Better lock the car— rough neighborhood!" Then she joined the stream of women making their way into the gargantuan and pink building, a sprawling oceanfront property that she'd learned was owned by a Russian oligarch who rented it out for events.

She checked in, got her press badge, and followed the crowd into the ballroom, which was set up with long tables covered in white tablecloths and dotted with empty wineglasses, three per place setting.

This was no Hilton ballroom. With massive white marble columns, dozens of chandeliers, and dark wood floors, it was indeed elegant, but there was also something strikingly pretend about it. It reminded her of one of Mickey's musical theater sets, the kind that could be struck in under ten seconds. A column might topple if you leaned on it.

She found her seat near the "runway," a four-foot-tall platform that bisected the room, and left her bag on her chair, grabbing her reporter's pad and pen and venturing into the crowd to mingle.

Tacky, she jotted down. It was 11:42, and the ladies were buzzing as they poured in.

So many blondes: platinum, golden, single-process, highlights so thick and overdone they might as well be single process. They outnumbered all other hair colors 3:1.

Blonde, she wrote and underlined it twice.

And thin!

Rebecca had always been slim. Part of it was natural, and part of it was that she'd been mindful of calories since her mother gave her her first pocket calorie counter from Eckerd drugstore at age eleven. She tried not to think of thinness as a virtue, but it was so ingrained that she'd found the value impenetrable, and so her solution was simply to accept that she'd loath her body when it was heavier and like it more when it wasn't.

Post-baby, she'd lost all the weight she'd gained in pregnancy with the exception of seven pounds. She fucking hated those seven pounds.

The designer attire of the women around her, their Botox and fillers and four-inch heels and fine silk—none of this touched her. But standing among them, the brush of her stomach against the cotton dress that Mickey had picked out left her self-conscious.

Helium balloons printed with doggy paws were tied indelicately to the backs of chairs, and in the corner of the room, a petite woman in a tuxedo manned a table selling plush, stuffed dogs of various sizes and breeds. Rebecca spotted a Dalmatian and a chow next to a pile of golden retrievers. Perusing the stuffed animals was an older woman clutching a crystal handbag that read GUCCI.

Rebecca made eye contact with a woman around her own age and smiled.

"Hi, I'm a reporter covering the event," Rebecca said. "May I ask what brought you here today?"

"Oh, the dogs," the woman said gravely, "the sweet dogs. I come every year. I don't miss it." And then she turned to find someone more important to talk to, leaving Rebecca with her pad.

It was a refrain she'd hear for the rest of the day. No one said the food and wine, or the socializing, or, of course, the opportunity to see and be seen. It was, they insisted, about the dogs.

Lunch consisted of a wedge salad drowned in blue cheese dressing that hardly a soul touched, branzino, and roasted potatoes.

("No eating wedge," Rebecca wrote.) During the meal, a local news anchor in a soft pink button-down with rolled-up sleeves (no pretenses here) emceed the event, pacing the stage with a cordless mic, his clean-shaven, rosy cheeks and shiny forehead broadcast on a jumbo screen behind him.

He alternated between pushing items in the silent auction—a seven-day vacation on a personal yacht, a month on Lake Como in Italy—and pulling on patrons' heartstrings with stories about pups that had been rescued by the shelter, their images broadcast to the room.

Frito had been hit by a car.

Juniper abandoned in the woods.

Casper beaten and left hungry.

As the emcee called out the bids, ticking up and up, she couldn't help but wonder how much money a local dog shelter needed. Palm Beach had eight thousand residents—mostly seasonal. West Palm Beach, one hundred thousand—fairly large for a U.S. city, but still only a fifth the size of Atlanta or Miami. Casper, Juniper, and Frito had all been adopted. And at this point, this event had already raised several million dollars.

Her seatmates were a group of friends in their forties who showed just enough indifference toward Rebecca to trigger cringey high school memories. After saying hello and introducing themselves, they ignored her for the rest of the afternoon, dismissing her questions and avoiding eye contact while they giggled among themselves.

As a reminder to herself as much as anyone, she kept her reporter's pad on the table, proof that she was there as a reporter and for no other reason. Her press badge, hanging on her neck, she clung to absently. She didn't need acceptance; she belonged to a separate category.

As the servers cleared the plates, and the emcee told them all to get ready for a killer fashion show, Rebecca realized her chest was becoming achy and heavy. She'd need to pump soon, or leave.

She remained seated for the first round, clapping along as canine after canine that had been adopted by socialites in attendance emerged, walked by their tight-skirted owners, to delighted shrieks and applause: a Chihuahua, a chow, an ambiguous terrier. When a flawlessly groomed shih tzu trotted onto the runway, Rebecca had a hard time envisioning it as a stray.

The dogs varied in formality: one was decked out in bejeweled satin, one in bandanna-themed country wear, another sported patriotic knits.

As a three-legged wolflike breed made its way down the runway, drawing a collective "aww" from the room, Rebecca stood and ducked into the hallway, wandering until she found a gilded bathroom. There was no sitting area, leaving her to pump in a stall. It wasn't the first time.

She sat on the toilet and hooked herself up to the little machine, balancing it on her lap as she texted Mickey.

How's it going? Leaving soon, she wrote.

We're good! See you soon, he wrote back.

She opened the Notes app on her phone and began to toy with angles for her piece.

There was something in the mismatch between giving and need. A monthlong stay on Lake Como, bids climbing past a hundred thousand dollars . . . and to benefit what? Not children's education or hunger, or the trees or oceans, but rescue dogs in Palm Beach.

How many of those could there even be?

After several minutes, the pump clicked off, and Rebecca carefully sealed the bags of milk, which she'd need to put on ice. She could ask one of the many servers for some cubes on her way out.

"Absurd." A woman's stern and commanding voice floated over the stall wall as Rebecca quietly packed up her equipment. "An embarrassment."

Rebecca grew still, listening. The woman was clearly speaking on the phone, not to a companion.

"It makes a mockery of philanthropy in the community, and I won't pretend otherwise if Gina asks on Tuesday."

When enough time had passed that Rebecca was certain the woman had hung up and retreated to her own stall, Rebecca emerged.

But there she was—five foot eleven at least—applying fuchsia lipstick in the ornate mirror. She appeared to be in her late sixties or early seventies and did not share the air or appearance of the hundreds of others in attendance. They wore pink; she wore black Belgian loafers with small tassels, straight black pants, and a cream silk blouse. Their heads were regularly doused in bleach; her silver hair was coiffed and smooth, a stylish lob that, to Rebecca, said: I'm a serious person, and possibly the most important one in the room.

She appeared entirely unfazed by Rebecca's appearance. As Rebecca washed her hands, she tried to catch the older woman's eye in the mirror, but before she'd reached for a thick hand towel, the elegant cynic had dropped her lipstick tube into her low-profile clutch and glided away.

CHAPTER 4

What will you do for Christmas?? his mom's text read.

Mickey stood in the Wamplers' entryway awaiting the evening's dinner guests. He had his phone on hand because Freddie, who was late getting dressed, had asked him to text when the guests arrived.

It was December 23. Fran had always spent Christmas with them, and though this year they wouldn't be able to fulfill their annual tradition of watching the Rockettes in *The Christmas Spectacular*, she had wanted to come down anyway, but Mickey had told her that he'd be working long hours and that it would make more sense to come in the new year, when he could see her more. She had agreed sadly.

Working! We will FaceTime you! he quickly wrote back then pocketed his phone, thinking, *Rebecca will FaceTime you while I'm here serving duck.*

The Wamplers' guests were the Stones from down the street, along with the U.S. secretary of the treasury. Already, he'd discovered that guests at the Wamplers' Palm Beach home were unlike guests at foundation events back in New York. At the New York philanthropy headquarters, event guests often included the employees of nonprofits funded by the foundation—the assistants and social media managers and outreach coordinators, people in their twenties who made five figures and got haircuts with Groupons—plus the grantees of the nonprofits themselves. The latter were typically people of color, usually Black grade-school students from outer boroughs. They were always expected to perform in some way: recite a poem, do a dance, tell a story. This made the foundation people and their personal guests feel warm and proud.

Mickey had had to learn tricks for dealing with the understandably clueless requests of the "plebes" (as he and his fellow caterers affectionately called the nonprofit workers making forty thousand annually, who had more in common with Mickey and his buddies than with their hosts). If someone asked for white Zin (it happened more often than you'd think) or a Corona, he'd kindly say, "We don't have that, but could I pour you something similar?" Then he'd come out with one of the world's most expensive rosés (because why own anything less?), a blend of Grenache and Rolle grapes from eighty-year-old vines in Château d'Esclans, Provence, served in crystal formerly belonging to the last czar of Russia.

Here in Palm Beach, however, Mickey was learning that the guests were far less socioeconomically diverse. They came in two varieties: fellow billionaires, and people serving in the administration. The presidential administration. Of the United States.

Occasionally a foreign dignitary also appeared.

Mr. and Mrs. Stone were in their seventies, older than the Wamplers, and greeted Mickey with polite nods before following him into the grand foyer while he texted Freddie.

As Mickey exited to fetch their drink orders, he heard Mr. Wampler enter and promptly begin to educate them on the story behind a sculpture in the foyer, a prancing boy. Mrs. Wampler had not yet come downstairs.

"The artist is Navajo. She modeled the child on her own, whom she lost as an infant due to inadequate medical care on the reservation . . ." he said.

Cocktail hour would last only twenty minutes—Mr. Wampler wasn't a fan of standing around—so Mickey moved as quickly as possible.

When he returned with the drinks, he found them as he'd left them, points in a triangle four feet apart, while Freddie continued to lecture on the artist and her career. In the regular world, this amount of space between people chatting at a dinner party would have seemed strange, but here, distance was tasteful, in proportion to the surrounding space. Tastefulness was equivalent to distance of all kinds: physical, emotional, personal.

Standing back and folding his hands awaiting instruction, Mickey considered how rarely he'd ever heard the Wamplers and their guests discuss anything like what he, Rebecca, and their friends talked about: their children, their fears, the things from their day that were funny. As if all that security graduated the heart from humanity's basic occupations. Even the joys.

Soon after Ingrid Wampler appeared, cocktails slid into dinner right on schedule, and it was time for Mickey to summon the truffle man into the dining room.

The truffle man was a mushroom dealer from the Netherlands who periodically showed up in Palm Beach. His time was in high demand in a town where billionaires per capita was around one in three, and it had been Mickey's responsibility to ensure that he made time for a visit to the Wamplers by phoning his cell repeatedly until he picked up. The man would sidle up to each guest at the table and brandish a glossy wooden box displaying his latest stash, like an upscale pot dealer.

Mrs. Stone, the first to be presented with the box, glanced back and forth between it and the table. Spotting the slightest hint of uncertainty, Mickey knew what was needed. Within seconds he was sliding an escargot fork alongside her place setting, and, in the same motion, as if they'd choreographed it, she lifted the fork to spear a dusty, charcoal lump as Mickey discreetly distributed forks to the others, as well.

Mr. Wampler, ignoring the fork, plucked a truffle with his fingers and popped it into his mouth. Mickey, with well-honed subtlety, exchanged an amused glance with the truffle man.

In the kitchen, moments earlier, they'd debated whether the tiny forks were necessary. The Wamplers' chef, an embittered and withdrawn man who'd been with the family for decades, had been certain that they weren't, and the truffle man had agreed—fingers were fine where he came from, just how it was done. Mickey had known someone would expect a fork, though, and so he'd gathered them against the mushroom dealer's wishes. He'd stood by with the tiny utensils in hand when he'd noticed Mrs. Stone's eyes searching.

The meal proceeded as usual, the entrée followed by a salad course, a crème brûlée with tangerine glaze and poached sun-dried raisins, and, finally, espresso and port in the library. As the evening drew to a close, Mickey was tending to the table with the crumber, running the narrow silver blade over the starched tablecloth, when he looked up to find Mr. Stone hovering over him.

"Thank you," he said. "What's your name?"

"Mickey, sir," Mickey said, unaccustomed to a personal inquiry from a guest.

"I haven't seen you here before," Mr. Stone said.

"I just started," Mickey said.

Mr. Stone nodded and headed in the direction of the nearest guest bathroom.

Returning to the library to check on the group, Mickey saw Mrs. Wampler tilt her teacup back at an angle that meant she was finished. All week he had been cautious around her, keeping as much distance between them as he could without drawing attention to it. Nothing else out of the ordinary had happened, and as the days passed, he'd allowed himself to hope that the coast was clear. Maybe she *had* been on something. Maybe she'd already forgotten.

He took Mrs. Wampler's cup and saucer, vaguely aware of Mr. Stone's eyes on him as the man reentered.

Finally the guests stood, and, with their hosts close behind, followed Mickey to the front door. Mickey opened it, letting in the warm December air. Mr. Stone approached and stopped before Mickey, who was a full head taller than him. Mr. Stone's bald, freckled head glistened in the moonlight.

"Come work for me," he said. "I'll double whatever he's paying you."

The man spoke at full volume, clearly as much to Mr. Wampler as to Mickey. Mickey chuckled and glanced over at his employer.

"I would understand if you couldn't turn that down," Mr. Wampler said slowly, looking serious enough.

What was happening? Mickey looked from one man to the other. "I don't know what to say . . ."

"Think about it," Mr. Stone said, swiveling on his heel to follow his wife out onto the front patio and into the night. "Good night, friends. Thanks again."

Mickey's gaze lifted to meet Mrs. Wampler's. She did not appear pleased. No, that was an understatement. If Mickey had to name the expression on her face, he'd call it horror.

Mickey was making $125,000 working for Freddie, which meant he would make $250,000 with Mr. Stone. He pedaled furiously up the bridge, already thinking about the job in the present tense. *I now make.*

He could not fathom earning that much money. He hadn't been able to fathom making a guaranteed six figures, period, especially not by catering—at the peak of his acting career on Broadway he'd barely broken that after agent fees, manager fees, and union dues, and, even then, it wasn't an annual salary. Acting, even the best work, was a career broken down into monthslong contracts; you were lucky if a great role lasted a year or longer, but you certainly didn't bank on it.

He was being offered a quarter of a million dollars a year to fill water glasses and run a letter opener through envelopes. Sure, the work involved more than that, but still—it was a lot easier than a long day under a helmet in a factory line or flipping burgers in a greasy Sonic.

A thought struck him—perhaps Mr. Stone hadn't realized what he was proposing. Perhaps he'd thought he was offering to double a five-figure salary, not a six-figure one, and would rescind the offer once he figured that out.

As if reading his mind, his Apple Watch vibrated on his arm, a 917 number. He recognized the area code as being from a New York cell and rolled to a halt, lifting his wrist to speak.

"Hello, this is Mickey," he said.

"Mickey, Cecil Stone."

"Hi, Mr. Stone," Mickey said, straddling his bike on the cusp of the drawbridge. To his left, cars passed every few seconds—purring luxury sedans hardly making a sound. Above him, the sky was clear and wide.

"I just spoke with Freddie. I told him I'd be offering you two fifty. No ill will on his part, by the way. He understands that I'm an old man and pickier than him about my help."

In the twilight, Mickey stood still. The stars shone up from the still, calm lake between the island and mainland, and their light bounced around the masts of boats that looked, in the gleaming night, smaller than they actually were.

"Why me, sir?" he asked. "If you don't mind my asking."

"Sure," Mr. Stone said. "The fork for the truffles. You can read my wife's face. In my world, that's priceless."

Rebecca had her hand in a steaming carton of SkinnyPop and was reading a book called *The Wonder Weeks: How to Stimulate Your Baby's Mental Development* when he entered, breathless, just after nine thirty.

"You're not going to believe this," he said. "Cecil Stone came to dinner."

She blinked.

"Should I know who that is?" she asked.

"No." He was frenetic, his skin blotchy from the race home. "But he offered me a job. The same job I do for Freddie. For—are you ready?—two fifty."

"Two hundred fifty?"

". . . thousand dollars."

Rebecca frowned. "That's ridiculous," she said.

"I know. Completely."

"To do *what*?"

"The same stuff."

"No way," she said. "For that money, he wants more than a house manager." She looked at him meaningfully.

"I don't think so," he said. "He has a wife. And he liked that I gave her a fork."

"Huh?"

"Doesn't matter. He lost his help, and rich people don't do well when they're left to fend for themselves. They're like toddlers."

"Can you not refer to yourself as 'the help'?" she said.

"Whatever, estate manager," he said.

"Freddie *just* moved us here. Sooo . . . that's not cool, right?" she said, tossing a handful of popcorn into her mouth and holding the bag out to him.

"I'm good. Freddie doesn't seem to care." Mickey slammed a glass into the refrigerator ice machine, and Rebecca flinched at the sound. Bash was asleep. "It's like there's some hierarchy or some-thing, and Mr. Stone is his elder so he just goes with it . . ." Mickey let the cabinet door shut loudly.

"Hey, shh," Rebecca snapped. Their Florida apartment was three times the size of their New York one, and Bash was in his room at the far end, but she hadn't really grown used to the space yet.

"This place is so weird," she muttered, then asked, "How did he make his money?"

"I don't know," he said. "The stock market? Isn't that how every-one makes their money?"

"Eventually, but not usually at first."

"Why do shopping malls ring a bell?"

"Shopping malls? No," she said. "Shopping malls are dead."

"Well, he's no spring chicken."

She grabbed her laptop. "What's his name again?"

"Cecil Stone." He took his first sip—glorious, icy sweetness—and wedged himself between his wife and the arm of the couch. He rested his arm around her shoulders as she read aloud, "In the early 1990s, through his hedge fund CPS Investments, he engineered a merger between Harbor Real Estate Investment Company and Gareth Outlet Group, which he bought out of bankruptcy. As the new owner of a conglomeration of shopping malls across the United States, he set about gutting them, giving rise to the term 'vulture capitalism.'

"He laid off hundreds of workers, combining departments to run operations on minimal management, ceasing all maintenance op-erations from fixture replacement to regular cleaning, and selling all of the company's physical locations to himself. He then charged the company rent and, when it failed to turn a profit, ninety-six thousand people lost their jobs.' Mickey, no."

He pressed his lips together and sighed.

"You don't have a problem with my working for Freddie," he said.

"Freddie is a Democrat," she said, which of course he knew. But she was making a point. "He signed the Giving Pledge."

"I don't know what that is."

"Yes, you do, because we've talked about it. It's what all the decent mega-rich guys sign. It's a promise to give away at least fifty percent of their money. You know who I'm sure hasn't signed it? Cecil Stone, the vulture capitalist."

When Mickey and Rebecca fought, she won because she had words. Sometimes he had trouble finding his words.

"Working for someone doesn't mean endorsing what they do," he said carefully.

She looked amused—an expression that made him feel stupid, which stirred his anger.

"Stop making that face," he said.

"Of course it does," she said, "when you have a choice. If you didn't have a choice, it wouldn't, but you're making perfectly good money working for Freddie."

"Rebecca, it's double the pay."

"We don't need more."

"Double. The. Pay."

She rose. "More money just because. Very capitalistic of you," she said.

"We don't know that we aren't going to need it. We have a kid. What about college? What about school?"

She laughed, standing over him. "Now you want to send Bash to a fancy private school because we've had a steady household income for . . . two weeks?"

Mickey got up and went to the fridge to get more ice.

When they argued, he knew there were things never to be broached—the comment that can't be withdrawn, that cuts to the core of an insecurity.

He didn't say: *You don't understand money because you've never struggled.* Rebecca didn't have student loans—her parents had paid for college. She'd supported herself ever since, but she also knew that the money was there if she needed it, that help was only a phone call away.

Mickey did not have this safety net. Fran had never had extra income lying around; he'd even transferred *her* some cash a few times over the years when he was flush from an acting job. Peadar had paid child support . . . sometimes. When he didn't, Fran would hound him for it, but she felt it was toxic to talk about Peadar's delinquency around Mickey, and she never bothered to pursue legal recourse for the same reason. Eventually, Peadar had just stopped paying.

Rebecca was back on the laptop, reading. She groaned.

"I knew shopping malls couldn't be the source of all that money. He's a newspaper guy. He bought a bunch of them through a fund called Starr Capital."

"That makes sense. They were talking a lot about media at dinner," Mickey said.

"Listen to this from a blog I just found," she said. "'He sent his henchmen, Wharton grads with coke habits who'd never set foot in a newsroom, into America's most beloved media institutions—our local papers—and ordered them to decimate the papers from the inside out. Stone's strategy of buying companies in distress, milking them for all they're worth, then discarding the carcasses has single-handedly destroyed the hometown newspaper in the United States. Local reporting is a relic. Just ask anyone in Minneapolis-Saint Paul (the *Twin Cities Star*), Louisville (the *Louisville Register*), or Tampa (the *Tampa Sun*), all of which shuttered their doors after Stone, who laid off over ninety percent of their workforce and pay-squeezed the remaining ten percent until they hit the dust. The list continues to grow as he adds properties to his morbid portfolio, cows being led to slaughter.'"

She glared at him.

"Oh, come on. Henchmen? Slaughter? Sounds like a reputable source."

"*I'm* a journalist."

She resumed her googling, and he sipped in silence. When she got like this—righteous, indignant—it was best to let her fizzle out on her own.

"I don't understand why there's not more about him on the Internet," she said. "There are only a couple of pages of hits and no photos, and yet he's one of the country's twenty wealthiest people? That creeps me out more than anything."

She continued her search while he brushed his teeth, and when he emerged from the bathroom, she said, "I still haven't found a single photo."

"I'm going to lie down," he said.

"You haven't accepted the job, have you?" she said.

He didn't answer.

"Mickey! You didn't even wait to discuss it with me?" Now he was the one to shush her.

"I didn't say yes," he said softly. "But I heavily implied it. It's a no-brainer."

Rebecca sighed.

"I have to take the job," he said, trying another tactic. "Mrs. Wampler made clear today that she's not done with me."

"What do you mean?" Rebecca asked. "How did she 'make it clear'?"

"I can just tell," he said, picturing the woman's expression earlier in the night upon overhearing the job offer. "Christmas Eve is tomorrow, anyway. It's not like I'm going to give notice on a holiday."

"Night," she said coldly as he kissed her forehead and headed into the bedroom.

After eleven, Rebecca tiptoed to the kitchen, where she made some tea and settled back into the living room to research. The harder it was to find personal information about Cecil Stone, the more determined she became to learn about him, or at least why there hadn't been more written.

Every article she landed on provided only the same generic bits of information. He was vastly wealthy (yes, duh); he was private (clearly); and he'd fathered a couple of children, who were also conspicuously absent across the web. She found a few mentions of him as a guest at high-profile social events, but they weren't accompanied by photos.

Finally, toward the bottom of page four of a search involving his son's ex-wife's maiden name, Rebecca found a marriage announcement in the Palm Beach Social Register. Dated 1992, it reported his small, family wedding to his fourth wife, Astrid Martin of Jackson, Mississippi. Held at his lakefront Palm Beach home, it was officiated by the mayor of Palm Beach and attended by his children—two adults and one little girl who looked to be nine or ten.

She zoomed in on the photo of Stone and his bride, who wore a lemon skirt suit with the puffy sleeves and shoulder pads of the era, and towered over her groom, who was balding and nondescript, of average height and build.

It was the first photo she'd found of him, but he wasn't the one who caught her eye.

As soon as it flashed onto her screen, Rebecca recognized the woman, but she needed to be sure.

Enlarge, enlarge, enlarge... even hazy and pixelated, it was clear. Mrs. Astrid Stone was the silver-haired lady from the luncheon.

Into the wee hours of December 24, Rebecca read everything she could find on Astrid Stone, née Martin.

She'd attended Wellesley and graduated in 1964, majoring in art history.

After college she became a secretary in the office of the New York financial firm D. L. Harmann & Co. and three years later married D. L. Harmann, her first husband.

Six years later, when she was twenty-seven, they divorced.

In 1978, at thirty-one, she appeared on the television game show

Tic-Tac-Dough, a trivia game based on tic-tac-toe in which a winning contestant was invited back to play again and again until they lost. Over the course of seven weeks, Astrid Martin defeated thirty-six opponents, a record for the show. All in all, she took home over $300,000, the 1978 equivalent of $1.2 million.

She'd taken her winnings and invested them in a vineyard in Oregon.

Astrid Stone was an art collector and a patron of arts education. She apparently had a massive collection, which she kept on rotation in museums in cities "not on the East Coast." Every decade or so, she'd auction off several high-value pieces and donate the proceeds to an arts education nonprofit.

She of course served on numerous boards . . . of museums, of charities both frivolous and substantive, of 501(c)3s.

But the gaps were what kept Rebecca awake, on the hunt.

One article had mentioned that Cecil Stone was her third husband. Who had been the second? His name hadn't come up in the profiles she'd read. Did she have any children? What had happened to the vineyard—and had she run it as a young divorced woman? In the eighties?

Rebecca wasn't sure why she was so captivated, but she couldn't look away. Whoever this woman was, she made Cecil Stone seem like a much more interesting character.

On Christmas Eve morning, Rebecca didn't mention anything about Astrid Martin (Stone) to Mickey. She still didn't want him to take the job, but by the time he came home that evening, she'd softened a little toward the idea. Not because she thought Cecil Stone was any better of a person, but because she didn't want to be the kind of partner who demanded her spouse line up with her ideologically on every point. It was his decision, not hers. Plus, a day of wrapping presents for Bash—a few learning toys, plus some onesies and a reindeer ornament that said "My 1st Christmas" with a round hole for a photo—had imbued her with the holiday spirit.

She may not have shared all of Mickey's views—he still ate meat, for instance (just not when she cooked), and unlike her, wasn't categorically opposed to prison as a concept. But she could respect the thought and intention behind his views; she could trust that he tried to be a decent person.

Besides, if veganism and anti-prison-industrial-complex-ism had been hard criteria for a mate . . . let's just say she'd dated plenty of men who were ideologically perfect on paper and were far from partner material. (One hadn't "believed" in soap; another had frequently "forgotten" to reply to her texts until she discovered that he didn't have a cellphone plan at thirty-two.)

When Mickey came in at ten after nine, the Christmas Eve meal she'd prepared was waiting on the table—roasted cauliflower, baby artichoke bruschetta, and mushroom stuffing. She'd even mixed his Manhattan using ice from the special tray she'd planned to put in his stocking—perfectly square cubes.

"How was your day?" she asked.

"Fine," he said, removing his helmet and shoes and running his hand through his damp hair. "You?"

"I've chilled, don't worry," she said. "Just in time for Christmas!" she joked.

He hugged her and took the drink. "Sorry I'm sweaty," he said. "Weird to sweat on December twenty-fifth."

"Take the job, it's fine with me," she said as soon as they sat. "It's not something I would do. But I'm not you."

He threw her an exaggerated side-eye. "This feels a little like a parent saying I can make my own decisions, but they'll be disappointed in me."

"No, no," she said. "I don't mean it like that." She paused to consider whether her next statement was entirely true before going on. "I won't be disappointed in you. This isn't the same thing as moving. That was a choice we made together. This is where you have to work every day. I'll respect your decision." He served himself a slice of bruschetta and nodded.

"In that case," he said, "can we go furniture shopping this weekend? There should be after-Christmas sales, and the Grand Canyon couch has got to go. I think my ass grazed the floor the other day."

She smiled. "Sounds good to me."

The next morning, it was a balmy eighty-five degrees out. Like always, Mickey was gone before sunrise. Christmas Day was no different than any other, except that he'd be home even later than usual.

This wasn't anything new; back in New York he worked Christmas every year (and New Year's, and Thanksgiving . . .) for the double pay. Rebecca had grown used to scheduling their festivities around the edges of holidays, squeezing their celebrations around others' gatherings. She didn't mind. When her friends would express sympathy—*You're spending Thanksgiving apart?!*—she'd had a hard time understanding the intensity of their reactions. What made November 29 all that different from November 28? Did it matter, the exact date on which you prepared a special meal and made a point to express gratitude?

Rebecca cooked celebratory blueberry pancakes for herself and Bash, then strolled him down to the giant Christmas tree made of sand in the West Palm city square. It towered over them like a giant's sandcastle in the shape of a pine.

Small children darted about the grass surrounding the sandy mass, and older ones shouted their way through a temporary, Christmas-themed putting green next to it. They wielded plastic golf clubs, smashing them into one another with glee.

"Won't it be fun to bring you down here to run around once you can walk?" Rebecca said aloud to Bash, spotting a truckload of fireworks being unloaded behind a fence, New Year's Eve preparation underway. Bash drooled in response.

She passed a sleek Italian furniture store—closed, of course—and eyed the low, modular sofas inside. Utterly impractical for living with a toddler.

They planned to shop for a new one over the coming weekend, and, anticipating where they might look, Rebecca remembered the day they bought their current one, tangerine and pricey (the most expensive thing they'd ever bought), the "Grand Canyon," as Mickey now called it.

When she'd moved in with him, she'd ditched her college-era futon, and their living room sofa had been the massive, leather monstrosity he'd owned for almost a decade. It was cheap, of course, and peeling, so that when you lay on it for too long, tiny flecks of leather stuck to your skin.

They'd married on a whim—eloped—on a blustery day in February. She didn't feel like inviting her parents, and so they hadn't told Fran either, electing to do it on their own. The sky dropped hail and sleet, and in front of the Queens courthouse, a line of betrothed couples stood shielding their hair and flowers and silk from nature's beating. Mickey's friend Jake was their witness, and when the clerk, a hunched woman in thick bifocals, scolded him for taking photos vertically instead of horizontally on his phone, they all got the giggles.

Afterward, they met friends for bottomless mimosas at Neptune Diner in Queens. Post brunch, they'd ventured to West Elm, where they'd purchased the bright coral sectional as a wedding gift to themselves. Comfortable for napping (his priority) and cheerful plus vegan (hers), it felt like a turning point in their lives together.

"It's funny, buying furniture together feels more serious than getting married," she'd said. "If we ever get divorced, I get the couch."

"Nope," he'd said. "We can fight over it."

After a couple of years, the couch began to sink in the back. It was impossible to sit on it for very long without having to stack cushions underneath you to keep from cramping. But they'd spent so much money on it. As it grew less and less comfortable, neither brought up the possibility of replacing it. It just didn't seem like an option.

Then she recalled another memory—New Year's three years earlier, in 2015. While Mickey worked the Wamplers' NYE party, Rebecca had rung in the new year at home with her mother-in-law, who'd come down for Christmas and stayed on. She and Fran had ordered pizza, downed two bottles of champagne between them, and, by eleven p.m., had both dozed off on the couch well before the ball dropped in Times Square. They'd awoken with cricks in their necks, their legs entangled, and with champagne headaches.

That morning, she'd gotten her first double line. And when it didn't hold, her guilt over the champagne set in, then never faded.

CHAPTER 5

Standing outside of the Stones' home less than a mile from his previous employer's, Mickey lifted the heavy knocker and let it drop once. The wind rustled his hair, and he smoothed it nervously.

The house was a buttery cream color. A Spanish colonial, its terracotta roof was perched above wrought-iron French balconies that ran along all sides of the house.

While the neighbors' boxy hedges appeared almost circuslike, top-heavy and clipped into shapes nature would never choose—the Stones' yard matched the tone of the house: seamless and understated, the splashes of color carefully curated. Coral pansies tumbled from the base of majestic palms, and waxy flowers, brick-red and eye-catching—were collected in window boxes.

The man who answered the door was in his forties and had black, plastic-rimmed glasses and a full head of blond hair in loose, confident curls. (Mickey, self-conscious of his thinning crown since thirty-two, noticed the nuances of other men's hair before almost anything else.) He wore a chef's coat, khakis, and white New Balance sneakers.

"You must be Mickey," he said, reaching out his hand. "Paul. Chef."

Mickey stepped into the foyer, where he stood eye to eye with his new colleague, who was roughly the same height as him, just over six feet.

"Follow me," Paul said. Passing through a capacious foyer, Mickey discreetly peeked at the cavernous rooms to his left and right. The decor throughout reflected the predictable tastes of an older, northeastern couple: Persian rugs, eighteenth- and nineteenth-century European art, and mahogany furnishings, sprinkled with some more modern stuff—a de Kooning, and what appeared to be a Pollock.

Mickey followed Paul down a hallway and into a bright kitchen with French doors leading onto a back terrace.

"Mister is playing golf," Paul said. He didn't say where Mrs. Stone was. "Have a seat." Paul pulled a chair out from the far end of the table and sat. Mickey did the same at the opposite end.

"He poached you, huh?" Paul said.

"Pardon?" Mickey said.

"Mister tells me you were working nearby. He offered you what, double? Triple?"

"Oh, yeah. I was working for Freddie Wampler down the street."

"Same story, different day," Paul said. "He nabbed me four years ago from a family in East Hampton. You just moved from New York, he said?"

"Yes."

"The ladies are hotter there. Down here you got to get down to Miami."

"I'm married," Mickey said, wondering if his new colleague had overlooked his wedding band or just ignored it.

"Ah," Paul said, a flick of disappointment flashing across his face. "Well, let me know if you have questions. I'm supposed to have a chat and get you going. Phil was the former you. He basically did everything. So I guess that's your gig now. What else do you want to know?"

"You could show me around?" Mickey said.

"Right," Paul said, rising from his seat and clapping his hands together. "Let's take a tour, shall we?"

The tour was truncated after several minutes by the arrival of an AC repairman to fix the unit in the cottage where Paul resided at the back of the property.

"Thank fucking God," he muttered. "I've been sweating my balls off at night."

As a woman who Mickey had noticed dusting approached them expectantly, Paul looked back and forth between her and the repairman.

"I'll show you to the cottage," he said to the guy. To Mickey, he said, "This is Anna, the house manager. She supervises the cleaning staff. If you have a question about anything, ask her. She's been here a hundred years."

She swatted him.

"So have you!" she said. Her hair was pulled back into a thick bun, and she wore a white smock with white sneakers. She looked to be about Paul's age—too young to have been there *that* long.

"I've been here more like seven going on a thousand," Paul said over his shoulder as he led the repairman toward the back door. "Uh, Anna, want to show Mickey where the linens are? Mickey, you can start setting up for lunch."

Anna motioned for Mickey to follow her into a small room behind the kitchen, where a tall bureau held an extensive collection of silver and reams of carefully folded napkins and tablecloths.

A violet lightbulb on a panel of five bulbs, all different colors, flickered above the kitchen doorway, buzzing softly.

"If that's purple, it's you!" Paul hollered from the veranda. "I'm guessing he's in the garage or his shower."

Mickey had been catering long enough to understand the system. The light board wasn't exactly like any he'd encountered before, but it was close enough. They each had an assigned color bulb, which the Stones could light up using a remote. His presence was required somewhere; it was up to him to figure out where.

Luckily the unfinished tour had covered the garage. Mickey headed back there, where he found Mr. Stone's Mercedes still warm but no sign of the man himself. He hurried inside and up the marble staircase to the second floor, listening for signs of life as he guessed his way to their bedroom suite. Beyond one open door, he could hear water running.

"Mr. Stone?" he called from around the corner. "You called for me, sir?"

"Come in." The man's voice was small, as if from a great distance.

Mickey passed through the bedroom and entered a dressing area outfitted in tartan and dark wood, then farther into the deeper confines of the suite to find his new boss completely naked, sitting on the countertop, his feet hoisted and submerged in the sink.

"Morning," Mr. Stone said.

Later, Mickey would realize that Cecil Stone was the kind of old rich white man who didn't gain defining features until one got to know him and could see past a generic first impression. At this moment, though, all Mickey registered was that his new boss possessed a sagging jowl, mild jaundice around the eyes, and a circle of gray-white tracing a shiny bald cap. (Balding—that was a feature that Mickey never understood among the über-wealthy. If he ever won the lottery himself, there was no question that he'd get a hair transplant.)

But for his seventies, Cecil Stone didn't look bad, neither overweight nor scrawny, and Mickey suspected he'd been attractive as a younger fellow.

"Feet swell on the course," Mr. Stone said, making no effort to cover up his exposed genitals. Mickey, however, was more taken aback by the man's legs, which were covered in inflamed splotches, like a bad case of the chicken pox.

"Paul showed you around?"

"Yes, sir."

"You were an actor, Freddie said?"

Were.

"Yes, sir."

"A successful one, I heard. On Broadway."

"Yes, sir."

"I hear it's not the most stable lifestyle."

"It's not, but I actually had a vocal injury."

"I see. That's unfortunate."

"Very," Mickey said, then worried he sounded unappreciative. "But it worked out for the best. My wife and I were ready to leave New York."

"Well, we're no song and dance here, but at least the pay is consistent. Paul is a good resource for you. I know you haven't run a house before, not one of this size. What do you think about butler school? You'll learn the basics and save yourself some trouble." He paused. "Although it wouldn't be convenient to go five weeks without you . . ."

It took Mickey a moment to realize Mr. Stone was suggesting training that was not local.

"Where would it be?"

"Our last guy went to London."

He swallowed at the thought of leaving Bash for that long.

"Hand me that towel?" Cecil asked, but Mickey was already reaching for it. "Or we could just have someone come here to train you. That way I don't lose you for a month."

Mickey nodded, relieved.

Drying off one leg and then the other, Mr. Stone went on.

"Yes, you should do one here. Arrange for your own training however you see fit. Just train up and train well, the sooner the better. Cost is no issue. That's all."

"Yes, sir," Mickey said, taking his cue to exit. "Thank you."

"And Mickey, uniform here is white polo, khakis, white shoes. Black tie after 5 p.m."

Mickey had worn khakis, but with a blue polo and gray sneakers, an outfit that had been more than acceptable at the Wamplers'. He scolded himself for failing to ask about dress codes. Freddie was more relaxed than most (like letting Mickey call him Freddie). "Yes, sir," he said.

He descended the long marble staircase. Thank God he wouldn't have to broach the topic of an extended leave with Rebecca. However flexible she'd been about his decision to work for Mr. Stone, he knew that being away for five weeks at butler camp would, understandably, have upset her.

Back downstairs, he found Mrs. Stone in the kitchen talking to Paul. At the dinner several nights prior, her hair had been carefully coiffed in a lob, and she'd worn a silk scarf. Now, her hair was pulled back neatly into a ponytail, and she was in an expensive-looking cashmere jumpsuit.

"Good morning," he said. She responded with a tight, distracted smile.

"Welcome," she said, then turned back to Paul. "Can you do it without the leeks?"

"Leeks *are* the dish," Paul said, shaking his head.

"No, the dish is lobster."

"With leeks." They stared at each other. "Fine, no leeks," Paul finally said. "Are shallots acceptable?"

"As long as they aren't leeks," she said, turning to Mickey. "Tomorrow is Paul's day off. We want to bring in Mexican for lunch. There's a spot on Seaview Avenue that Cecil likes."

"Yes, ma'am," Mickey said.

"But their guacamole is foul," she said. "They make it much better at a place north of here on Royal Poinciana. So we'll need you to make both stops and have the table set by eleven thirty when I return from this abysmal thank-you breakfast at the Four Arts." She floated out of the room before she'd finished her sentence, still chatting away to herself about the breakfast she was loath to attend.

"The Society of the Four Arts," Paul said, explaining, "is this ... I don't know what it is. Like a museum, sort of, with a sculpture garden that Mister and Missus donate a lot of art to."

"Is there no chef on your days off?" Mickey asked, keeping his voice low. He could cook—over the years he'd had to show up behind the burners when in a sticky situation (drunk chef, chef who didn't show, the chef who *wasn't a chef*). What he'd learned from his mom while growing up he'd expounded upon over the years by observing experts in clients' kitchens. But he preferred not to man the ship, not when his clients were accustomed to award-winning cuisine.

"They'll do takeout or I'll do enough prep that you'll be fine. Don't worry. Can you heat up food?"

"Sure," Mickey said, adding, "she doesn't seem like a woman who would be into takeout."

"Oh, she isn't," Paul said with a bright smile. "She doesn't like anything. She just pretends to."

"*Butler* school? But you aren't a butler," Rebecca said from her usual spot in the sinking sofa. She'd spent so much time being pregnant or nursing there that the imprint of her body was set into the already collapsing cushion. Next to her, the bulky but more efficient breast pump, this one the size of a bowling ball, chug-a-lugged. As loud as their old dishwasher back in Queens, it sucked milk from her nipples via tubes attached to '80s-era Madonna-style cones, which themselves were secured to her chest by a thick strip of beige elastic.

Bash lay resting in what they called "the bouncer," a fabric seat strapped to a springy frame. You strapped the baby at a 45-degree angle and rocked it with your feet. Rebecca had begun to call it "the shit whisperer" sometimes because it made him poop.

Mickey sat in the chair across from her searching "online butler school."

"Estate managers are modern-day butlers," he said. "I'll come home and do butler school at night, and you can go out and party with the locals."

"Mm-hmm," she said.

Rebecca worked at night after Bash went to sleep and before Mickey came home—that was her reward, his return signaling relaxation/wine-on-the-balcony time. It was the only part of the day when she could work on her column other than during naps, but that was when she cleaned and—sometimes—did yoga.

Every other Tuesday came often. She found that if she didn't have three columns in various stages of drafting, her deadline would sneak up on her, and she'd wind up frantically working into the wee hours of the night.

"I'll watch Netflix while you do butler school," she said.

Within a few pages of hits, Mickey found a program. Self-paced, its modules covered everything from valeting to maintaining a household budget to anticipating wayward guest behavior. The lessons had titles like "From Servant to Staff: Changing Percep-tions and Attitudes Toward Service Professionals" and "Advanced Butler Etiquette: Tackling the Stickiest Situations with Aplomb." Sub-lessons included topics like cigars, tea serving, and ironing.

"Still want to go furniture shopping this weekend?" she asked.

"Sure," he said.

"There's a Rooms To Go close by," she said. "And of course there's Restoration Hardware."

She grinned to show she was kidding. With sofas starting in the four-thousand-dollar range, Restoration Hardware, they both knew, was far out of their price range. Or at least, it had been.

"Let's take a look," Mickey said with a shrug. "Paul said there's a roof deck with a nice bar there, at least."

He turned his attention back to the curriculum. Most people completed the course within six weeks, the website promised, but Mickey planned to knock it out faster. He enrolled himself just before brushing his teeth and put the forty-five hundred dollars on his credit card, to be reimbursed by the Stones. He would begin school right away. He'd serve all day, then come home to learn how to serve better.

CHAPTER 6

His first week, Mickey pieced together his daily schedule from both the official agenda provided to him by Paul—a coffee-stained sheet of paper in a plastic sleeve that had clearly been passed down—and updates he gleaned directly from the Stones ("I expect my footbath when I return from golf").

Mickey had known that even among billionaires, there were gradations, but to witness it firsthand was dizzying. While the Wamplers' property contained a pool, a jacuzzi, and tennis and volleyball courts, the Stones' boasted all of the above plus a putting green and three pools, one to catch the light at every time of day. Their wine cellar was a vast underground as long and wide as the house itself, filled with over three thousand fine wines, most of them bought at auction by their wine rep, including a 1777 Lafitte ThJ—ThJ as in, Thomas Jefferson. The bottle had belonged to him.

His standard itinerary, which he saved in his phone's Notes app, was broken down into five-minute increments:

5:15 a.m.: Arrive, meet with house manager (Anna) and Paul

5:35 a.m.: Make coffee, squeeze OJ from fresh local oranges left at back door, set table, arrange newspapers open on dining room table (*Wall Street Journal*, *New York Times*, *Financial Times*, and the *Palm Beach Daily News*—colloquially called the "Shiny Sheet" because it was printed on paper that wouldn't smudge ink on the fingers of its affluent readers), sort and distribute both the previous day's snail mail and the current morning's email, including printing Mr. Stone's messages and leaving them on his desk. (Mr. Stone only read printouts of email. He would dictate responses, which Mickey would type up and send back in the afternoon.)

7 a.m.: Serve breakfast

7:25 a.m.: Conclude breakfast

7:30 a.m.: Clean up breakfast, polish silver

8:30 a.m.: Run errands, meet with service people tending to various parts of the grounds, freshen/replace floral arrangements

11 a.m.: Set table for lunch

Noon: Serve lunch

12:45 p.m.: Clean up lunch

1:30 p.m.: Perform administrative tasks: arranging home repairs and maintenance, arranging travel/upcoming linen and china rentals for dinner parties. Transcribe and send Mr. Stone's emails. Print out day's second round of emails.

4:15 p.m.: Change for dinner service

4:30 p.m.: Begin dinner prep

5 p.m.: If guests, greet and serve cocktails. If no guests, no cocktail hour

6 p.m.: Serve dinner

8-11 p.m.: Clean up, return home, sign into butler school.

What the daily to-do list failed to capture was the interstitial time, all the minutes spent shooting the shit. While Mickey polished and Paul chopped, they talked.

Paul had been at the Stones' going on eight years. He was divorced from a woman he'd met in culinary school, and they had one son. He'd commuted an hour from Morristown, New Jersey, to Manhattan every day to work grueling hours in a restaurant while she stayed at home with the baby, and by the time his son was two, they'd split. He then worked as a private chef for families, doing stints with two others before the Stones. He didn't mind the single life. He saw his son, now fourteen, every summer, and sporadically throughout the year after a decade of arguments with his wife over allowing the boy to travel solo.

"But my ex and I get along fine now that he's older. She was happy for me when I told her about Carla."

"Carla?" Mickey asked.

"My girl in Miami." Miami was only seventy-five miles south, a little over an hour's drive. "Well, kind of my girl. She breaks up with me every other week."

"Because you sleep with other people?" Mickey asked, grinning.

"Nah, dude," he said. "Because I'm always breaking plans. Mrs. Stone freaks out when I take a vacation. You see how she likes sparring with me. Like she needs someone to fight with and I'm her guy. Dude, if not for her, this would be the easiest job in the world. Mister does not give a *fuck*."

When the Stones were gone, they spoke frankly. Paul had set the tone, and Mickey had followed, trepidatiously at first, and then more comfortably.

"What's on his neck?" Mickey asked, hovering while Paul sliced a cucumber into delicate hexagons.

"That dark spot?" Paul said. "That one is benign. I know, doesn't look it. He's had melanoma, though. A couple times. Last time was nine years ago? Eight? Before my time."

"And his legs?"

"The legs are a mystery, man. Some kind of eczema. No one can figure out what exactly, but he takes cancer medication for it. Turns out cancer medication works on shit that isn't cancer."

"I don't know if you've taken a look lately, but I don't think it's working. They look fucking awful," Mickey said, snacking on a cucumber slice that hadn't yet been shaped.

"They've been worse," Paul said. "He had these skin guys come out, people even more specialized than dermatologists. The dermatologists of the dermatologists. One from Norway. Maybe one from Turkey? He looked all over the world, man. Not a single one could figure it out. Allergies was the final call. Like that crazy shit on his legs is a reaction."

"To what?"

"Unclear. Everything? Dude, that's when things got real crazy here. Missus was out of her mind. We cut dairy, nuts, sugar, eggplant, anything she thought could be an allergen. None of it made a difference."

"Does it hurt?" Mickey asked, picturing the scads of tiny sores on the man's dry shins.

"Nah, he says it just itches." To Mickey that sounded almost worse.

"Why does Missus like to spar with you?" he asked.

"I think she likes the battle to control me because she's bored," Paul told him. "She's not happy, dude. I don't know why. She's a hard one to pin down. I can tell she hates him most of the time. You'd think by your third marriage you'd find someone you actually liked."

"How long have they been married?" Mickey asked, surprised by "third marriage"—Rebecca hadn't included that in her pointed overview of Stone's history.

"Thirty years or something. He's her third husband, and she's his fourth wife!"

"But—"

"You mean the portrait?" Paul asked. It was precisely what

Mickey was thinking of. In the dining room was a life-sized oil portrait of the Stones. In it, they were very young, in their thirties at most.

"Exactly," Mickey said.

"Ready for this?" Paul said. "Whenever he gets a new wife, he has the guy paint over the last one."

That he could not wait to tell Rebecca.

Every morning, people descended on the property like ants. They came in droves to mop, sweep, weed, rake, cut, and tend to the encroaching waterfront by shoveling water that had seeped through the porous embankment since the day before, shoring up the sandbags to hold back the tide. (All of the houses along Lake Worth—the most coveted part of the island—were built on ground below sea level, an act of hubris even Mickey had noted with a shudder.) All of this, and they came to paint, as painting was more or less a perpetual task when it came to a home like the Stones' four-story, thirteen-bedroom manor. Men in painter's coveralls waged a constant battle against the onslaught of sand and salt, standing on rickety ladders to brighten the house's facade in column after column, replenishing its brilliance in strips, and round again.

Then there was the next level of service people who came and went, these with less frequency but still in regular intervals: an art restorationist to check on the paintings, the sommelier, the pool man.

Finally, there was Bruce, Mr. Stone's forever-drunk younger brother. He would show up unannounced every few days with his Saint Bernard, Chloe, and create chaos until, inevitably, Mr. Stone himself drove them both the six blocks home. Mr. Stone wouldn't allow Sam, his driver, or even Mickey to do it, figuring that his brother would make an inappropriate demand of them and that they would feel obliged to comply: a ride to a bar, a strip club, a casino. Palm Beach residents tended to stick to their side of town, on the island proper, but not Bruce. He'd cross the bridge for any promise of a good time.

According to Paul, Mrs. Stone was the one you needed to keep happy in order to keep your job at the Stone estate; according to Bruce, Paul was the one you needed to keep happy.

"Last two guys? Gone because Paul complained about them to Astrid," Bruce slurred to Mickey his third week as Chloe ran laps around a Grecian Madonna and child in Mrs. Stone's personal sitting room, making Mickey exceedingly nervous.

Mickey had decided that both Paul and Bruce were probably right. Paul possessed the same distaste for certain types of workers that Mickey held—those who made sloppy errors and didn't foresee problems, i.e., people who made his job harder. And as her sparring buddy, Paul had Mrs. Stone's ear.

Mrs. Stone's preferences and peeves were harder for him to read, but he was pretty sure she'd been the impetus behind butler school. More often than not she seemed irritated or displeased with a member of the staff, and rumor held that every few months, on a whim, she would fire someone without warning or cause, simply because she didn't like their socks or the fact that they'd chosen to wear an accessory in their hair. Her vitamins were to be lined up by Mickey in ascending size with one inch in between, another opportunity for failure. Her pillow before bed was to be fluffed and slightly askew.

Mr. Stone wasn't lacking in specific requirements—his shoes were to be polished but not so shiny that they looked freshly buffed, and his pillow was to be flattened in a fresh case (of course). But when they interacted, Mickey found him generally easygoing.

At night, after he and Rebecca ate a late dinner and followed it up with cocktails on their balcony, Mickey would log into butler school. Every now and then she would pluck out one of his headphones and put it in her ear, and he'd brace himself, hoping Simon, the instructor, didn't say anything preposterous. Simon was an old-school butler and prone to spouting outdated advice (at least Mickey hoped it was outdated) like: "If you have to use the bathroom during a dinner party, don't; hold it until you're off, even if that's in four hours." (Mickey was especially relieved the night that she handed back the headphone just before Simon said that, even if you get a call that your child is sick, you don't leave. You stay, and mention nothing of it to "the principals"—the official term for your bosses.)

"We need friends," she said one evening as Simon lectured him on the dangers of starch when creasing napkins. It had been only a few weeks, but already she missed being able to call someone up to grab a drink, or meet for a coffee. Now that she had warm weather to enjoy, she didn't have anyone to spend time with. "How do we make friends?"

"Want me to see if Paul wants to get a drink with us Friday?" Mickey said. "He's off." The Stones had a dinner elsewhere.

"Sure," she said. "Is he married? Can his wife or husband come?"

"He has a girlfriend," Mickey said. "I'll ask."

At E.R. Bradley's Saloon in downtown West Palm, twentysome-things played bocce ball on a sandy, outdoor court while families ate at picnic tables under a palm thatched roof. The floor was sticky, the utensils plastic, and the servers were all ponytailed teenagers who were definitely sneaking cigarettes in the alley on their breaks.

It took Rebecca no time to identify it as a tourist trap. The price of the drinks alone—fifteen dollars for a syrupy, slushy cocktail with an ombré fade—gave it away. That Paul, a professional chef and longtime city resident, had chosen to come here baffled her until she got a better look at the women on the bocce court: shorts that crawled up past the butt crease, bikini tops of nominal triangles hidden by long, swingy hair.

As she did her best to wipe grime off the wobbly high chair that a sulky server had brought over for Bash, Paul launched into a story about his latest Tinder date with a woman from Miami.

"I thought Mickey said you had a girlfriend," Rebecca said.

"She broke up with me Friday," he said.

"They'll be back together by tomorrow," Mickey said, grinning. She could tell he was happy to be here with his friend.

"So she takes the train up here because it's nice and all," Paul continued, ignoring Mickey's comment. "You should check out the train by the way. It's fucking pristine. No traffic to deal with, you got fifty-five minutes to Miami, door to door. I'm never driving again. Anyway, so she gets here and is like, are you going to pick me up from the station? But I'm in the kitchen doing prep for tomorrow's breakfast and need another half hour at least. So I'm like, no, listen, it's a really short walk to the restaurant. I'll meet you there in forty-five."

"I put my phone down and fucking hurry so I can meet her, right? I'm chopping the fruit and all that, and finishing off the soup because the soup has to sit overnight, and, I don't know, twenty-five minutes later I'm done and ready to head out, and, dude, I see that I have like *fifteen texts* from her."

He waits for a reaction but Mickey and Rebecca just keep listening.

"Get this—she's *gone back to Miami*."

"Huh?" Mickey said. "Why?" Their drinks arrived—highlighter yellow margaritas for Mickey and Rebecca that screamed *grocery store mix*, and a Bulleit on the rocks for Paul. Great. They'd just dropped at least forty dollars on undrinkable cocktails, more if Mickey planned to cover Paul's.

A month earlier, the price would have stressed her out enough that she'd not have been able to think about anything else—she'd have sat, irritated, fantasizing about returning her drink and asking for something else instead. But she'd never have done it.

Now, she realized, forty dollars was a drop in the bucket. It was strange how easy it was, suddenly, to shrug off that sum.

"She was pissed I didn't come get her! She didn't want to walk the hundred feet to the sushi place. Have you guys checked it out by the way? It's next door. It's not bad for this side of the lake. Dude, bullet dodged. I mean."

"Where's the station?" Rebecca asked.

"Like a mile west of here," he said.

"A mile?" she said, grinning. "That's not a hundred feet."

"I meant, like, half a mile," he said, then cocked his head toward the young women tossing balls in the sandy section of the outdoor restaurant. "Dude, those girls are hot."

Rebecca didn't bother hiding her disbelief as she looked at Mickey, and while he caught her glance, Paul didn't.

"Those girls look about sixteen," she said, pushing her margarita in front of Mickey to indicate that he could have it. "I'll just get a water," she said to him.

"Should have mentioned," Paul said. "You got to get beer or liquor here. Only way to go." He had already finished his whiskey and was scanning the restaurant for their server to order another. The server appeared, still slumped, still hating life. "I'll have another," Paul said. "And she'll have . . ."

"I'll just take an iced water," said Rebecca, opening the tiny box of crayons they'd handed her for Bash even though he was too young to color. She dumped them on the table and grabbed the green.

For the next hour, she filled in the farm animals on the paper place mat they'd placed in front of her son while he looked on. The guys talked about work, about Mrs. Stone's impossible demands, and about Paul's Tinder conquests and his ex-girlfriend's erratic moods.

Finally, Mickey said, "Well, Bash is going to need to eat soon, so we should head out."

"Does he eat food yet?" Paul asked.

"A little," Rebecca said, "but he's still nursing."

"Ah," Paul said. Was she imagining it, or did he look a little uncomfortable?

"I don't mind if you need to . . . you know. Do your thing," he said. "Doesn't bother me."

Her stomach seized with rage.

"It's his bedtime soon anyway," Mickey said quickly. "I'll grab the check." He stood, leaving Paul and Rebecca alone at the table with the baby.

"How old is he?" he asked.

"Almost ten months," she said.

"Talking yet?" he asked.

"No," she said. "Children don't talk until one or so."

"Walking?"

"No," she said. "Same. Like, one or so."

"So it's all going to get harder from here, in other words," he said with a chuckle.

She smiled without showing her teeth. "I guess so!" she said, looking around for her husband and spotting him standing at the register, handing his card to the woman there who was not their server.

On the drive home, Mickey said, "Sorry."

"For what?" she asked.

"You did not enjoy that," he said, with a small laugh. "That was pretty evident."

"Just like it's pretty clear he hates women?" she asked. Mickey shrugged.

"Was I rude?" she asked.

"Eh," he said. "I'd just say it was clear you weren't enjoying your-self."

"Well, he's a misogynist, so."

They rode in silence until he turned into their building's garage.

"Just don't make him your best friend here, please," she said. "I mean, pick anyone else."

They slid into their assigned spacious spot next to the elevator and the car purred to a stop.

"We have to return the car next week," Mickey said. Rebecca grunted. Buying a car was a bigger undertaking than she was in the mood to think about.

"We can extend," she muttered, opening her door before he'd turned off the engine.

CHAPTER 7

Rebecca sat in the Nissan as the rain pounded the windshield, obscuring her view of the house between swipes of the wipers.

The Stones' spread was in some ways smaller than she expected, or at least more discreet. She'd anticipated something ostentatious and grand, but this place was largely hidden behind foliage. In fact, from the road, it appeared to be one of the less showy homes on Coconut Row.

As he had at the Wamplers', Mickey had continued to ride his bike to and from the Stones' house each day, leaving Rebecca with the car, but on this night it was storming, a Florida thunderstorm, with vicious winds and warnings to stay indoors. He couldn't ride his bike home in this weather.

He'd worked late, and Rebecca hadn't wanted to wake Bash, who was deep in sleep in his crib, so she'd asked the night front desk attendant Samantha, who loved Bash and said, "When do I get to babysit?" every time they passed by, to watch him on the monitor.

She'd assured Samantha that she'd be gone no longer than twenty minutes.

Despite her anxiety over leaving Bash under the supervision of a near-stranger on a different floor of the building, she was not going to let Mickey bike home in a storm. She was also curious to see this place, and when it turned out to be hardly visible from the driveway, she was a little disappointed.

She looked down at her phone—four minutes since she'd texted Mickey that she'd arrived. It had been twelve since she left the condo.

Coming?? she texted again and waited. One minute passed. Two.

Maybe his phone wasn't on him. She knew that, in the past, some clients had a thing about phones—they insisted Mickey leave his in the kitchen. (One employer, he'd told her, would spontaneously ask him the time as a test to see if he'd reach for his phone.)

She turned off the engine, grabbed the umbrella, and stepped out.

The gate was unlocked, and she hurried to close it behind her then charged up the walkway to the front door, holding the umbrella out before her against the slanted rain. Even in the dark, she was vaguely aware of how expensive the property truly was to both her left and right now that she was behind the gate.

Before she could knock, the door flew open. Mickey stood in the doorway, alarmed.

He roughly grabbed her wrist and pulled her inside, snatching the umbrella with the other hand and tossing it back out onto the porch before shutting the door.

"I didn't know if you knew I was here," she said, unsure if his alarm was on her behalf—she was soaked—or because of her audacity in daring to approach the house.

"I'm coming," he said, sounding irritated. So it was the latter. "I just have to get my bag."

At that moment, Cecil Stone appeared, wearing what Rebecca hadn't realized was exactly what she'd expect a billionaire to wear to bed: silk pajamas and suede slippers.

She suppressed a smile. He reminded her of the terrible, rich boss in the Chevy Chase movie *National Lampoon's Christmas Vacation* that her family had watched every year when she was growing up: a cartoonish stereotype of a wealthy older guy.

As he rounded the corner, he said, "Mickey, did Diego bring in the cushions from the east patio? Oh," he said, noticing Rebecca. "Hello."

"Mr. Stone, this is my wife, Rebecca. She's just here to pick me up," Mickey said apologetically.

What was with his tone? She wasn't allowed to come in to pick up her husband? She'd have to talk to him about this. Every household had its quirks, but this seemed draconian.

"Ah, well, it's nice to meet you. Are you getting settled?"

"We are, it's lovely down here," she said.

"Have you had a chance to explore much yet?"

"A little. I'm home with our son, and I'm a journalist, so not much."

"My, busy woman!" he said as his wife appeared from behind a sweeping staircase. Astrid Martin (Stone, but Rebecca still thought of her as Martin), in the flesh.

Unlike her husband, Mrs. Stone was still dressed in daytime clothes, an ensemble much like the one she'd been in the last time their paths had crossed: black pants and a crisp white top.

Rebecca smiled. "Hello, Mrs. Stone," she said. "Sorry to bother you all. I just came in to let Mickey know I was here."

"Rebecca is Mickey's wife," Mr. Stone said. "She's a journalist. Who do you write for?" he asked.

"*New York* magazine," she said. "I'm not a staff reporter. I just have an online column." *Just.* Women and that word. She scolded herself for using it.

"Oh? On?"

"Inequality in America."

"Ha!" Mr. Stone said, not unkindly. Mickey looked like he might wet his pants. His wife was studying Rebecca, her head tilted.

"Have I met you before?" she asked.

"I was also at that luncheon in December benefiting the dog shelter," she said. "If I look familiar, that may be why."

"You're a writer?" She spoke before Rebecca had closed her mouth.

"Yes," Rebecca said. Why had she fought the urge to say "ma'am"? Why on earth would she ever say "ma'am"? Growing up in Tennessee, children were taught to "ma'am" and "sir" their elders, but she hadn't used either term in twenty-plus years.

"But not full-time, I presume?" Mrs. Stone said.

Rebecca shook her head. "It's biweekly." Why were they so interested in her? Mr. Stone was being courteous, but Mrs. Stone's questions were pointed.

"Do you ever ghostwrite?" she asked. Rebecca didn't answer, caught off guard. Did she? She was certain that she *could*. She *would*, if the right opportunity presented itself.

"I've been wanting to hire a ghostwriter," Mrs. Stone continued, "to work with me on my memoirs before I croak."

Rebecca laughed. Mickey chuckled politely; he still looked like a hostage plotting his escape.

"I'm going to bed," Mr. Stone announced. "Good night, all." He turned and disappeared into the dark house.

"Can you come over tomorrow morning? How is ten?" Mrs. Stone said.

Rebecca looked at Mickey. He was trying to maintain a supportive, neutral expression, but his eyes were full of panic.

"I'd love to," she said, "but since we're new to town, we don't have a sitter yet. Right now, actually, the front desk person for our building is just standing by . . ." As soon as she said it, she felt frantic to get home—she had definitely been gone longer than twenty minutes by now.

"Bring the baby," Mrs. Stone said. "The staff can help if necessary, but I don't mind babies."

And like that, Rebecca was hired—or, rather, enlisted—as Astrid Martin/Stone's ghostwriter.

"It has nothing to do with being embarrassed by you or Bash," Mickey was saying.

"Then what's the problem?" Rebecca asked, shaking her wet shoes in the carpeted hallway before setting them inside the door.

They'd sped home, sliding on the slick roads, to find Samantha watching a documentary on whales on her iPad, which sat beside their monitor. On it played a fuzzy, black-and-white image of Bash, sleeping soundly.

"Sorry we're late," Rebecca had said, breathless from jogging in from the garage.

"You are?" Samantha had said hopefully and checked her watch. It was 11:17. "Aw, damn, I hoped it was later. Only seven hours and thirteen minutes to go."

She'd groaned as she'd handed Rebecca the monitor.

"But next time, it needs to be in person so I can get my baby cuddles."

Heading upstairs, they'd resumed their discussion. Mickey thought it was a horrible idea. Rebecca didn't understand why.

"You don't understand rich people," he said, pouring whiskey into his favorite glass, a gift from his mother that read DAD ROCKS.

"I don't?" she said, feigning surprise. "I literally write about them for a living."

"That's different than working for them," he said. "They're worse than picky. They're particular in a way that you—and I mean this in the most flattering way, *you*—are not the personality to take on."

"You mean, like, they have you in butler school, and my personality is not a butler school personality," she said, acquiescing.

"Exactly."

"That's true," she agreed.

He slid open the balcony door. The winds had already subsided and the rain had stopped. Florida storms swept out as quickly as they swept in. She followed him out, went back in for a hand towel, and returned to wipe down the chairs.

They each took their regular seat facing the pool. This was her favorite part of living in Florida—these salty nights under the moon with Mickey.

"If it were just you coming to the house, I'd feel differently," he said. "But billionaires and babies . . . they don't mix."

"That can be the name of your autobiography," she said.

"Only if you'll ghostwrite it for me," he said, and they both laughed.

"Is your concern that you're going to get fired?" she said. "If Bash, say, drools on a plate of caviar?"

He paused for a moment, thinking.

"My concern is that . . ."

"I'm going to get you fired," she said.

"No," he said. "I don't think that will happen."

"Then what? Bash isn't going to break anything. He can't even crawl."

"It's going to stress me out. That's all. Having any baby in a billionaire's home would stress me out. When his brother comes over, hammered, with his dog, I'm a wreck. But the fact that it's *my* baby . . . I'm going to give myself an aneurysm. Do you want to be a single mother?"

"Okay, how about this," she said. "Let's see how much she wants to pay me, and how much I'd actually have to be there. I mean, it's ghostwriting. That doesn't necessarily require a lot of face-to-face time. Besides, my guess it that an eighty-year-old woman may not be as thrilled to have a baby around as she thinks."

"You're not making me feel better," he said.

For a moment they sat in quiet, both gazing into the night. The storm had cooled the air. It was almost chilly.

"It will be fine," he said, his voice high, like he was trying to convince himself of it. "I'm just hyperaware when it comes to rich people and their sensitivities."

"I know," she said. "That's why they like you."

So the plan was made. The next morning, Rebecca and Bash would drive to the Stones, and Rebecca would meet with Astrid to discuss her memoirs (plural, in Mrs. Stone's parlance), stationing Bash on the floor where, God willing, he would play quietly.

Mickey would attempt to do his job without obsessing over what was happening upstairs, and he would fail.

The crying was inevitable; Bash was a baby. Mickey just hoped the whole terrible idea would pass over quickly—either that Rebecca would realize how little she wanted to do it, or that Mrs. Stone would lose interest. Then they could all move on in their own separate spheres, the way things were meant to be.

At 9:55 a.m., Rebecca showed up at the door holding Bash in one arm and the bouncer in the other. *Shit.* Mickey cursed under his breath when he spotted it. He understood why Rebecca had brought the contraption along; Bash was more likely to remain pleasant longer with a seating option other than just the floor. (Even the youngest humans, those not yet capable of anything but sitting, craved variety, turned out.)

And yet, bringing a cheap piece of baby furniture into the Stone's home?

He knew what butler school would have to say about it: under no circumstances.

Rebecca could tell he was annoyed, which in turn annoyed her.

"What?" she said, in lieu of a greeting.

"Maybe leave this in the car, and if you need it, I can come out and get it?" he said.

She rolled her eyes. "You really think we won't need it?"

But he didn't care. He blinked, saying nothing.

"Fine," she said. He placed it outside the front door and gestured for her to follow.

Rebecca was no stranger to sharing spaces with the very wealthy. In college, she'd dined multiple times at the Northwestern president's residence, traveled to Paris for a journalism and government conference where she'd mingled with diplomats, and of course, she'd now been to a Palm Beach charity event, brushing elbows with America's blondest elites. She'd been to Dubai for Pete's sake.

But as she followed Mickey through vast room after vast room, she understood his anxiety a bit more: nothing about this space was child-friendly. It was the most museum-like residence she'd ever seen, more MOMA than household. There were no signs that humans even dwelled here, no mail lying out, no shoes, cardigans, or keys sitting absently in proximity of a door.

They reached the back of the house, the side overlooking Lake Worth (of *course* it was called Lake Worth, Rebecca thought suddenly—how had she missed that before?) and ascended a tall staircase.

As she climbed, Rebecca instinctively shushed Bash, though he wasn't making any noise. Man, she hoped her plan worked. She'd fed him later than usual that morning, timing nursing to give herself a couple of hours before Bash got hungry. She figured she had a good hour to ninety minutes before he started fussing and her chest swelled, though she'd stuck a couple of cotton rounds in her bra in case of leaking. Whether he got fussy for another reason, like being in an unfamiliar and, frankly, kind of terrifying place, was a different question.

They found Astrid Stone in her study, sitting erect before a desktop computer with her hands on the keyboard in a way that looked like she hadn't spent much time there.

"Good morning," Rebecca said, immediately pulling a muslin quilt covered in tangerines from her tote and laying it out on the rug in front a Victorian armchair that seemed like the most logical spot in which to station herself.

Mrs. Stone smiled stiffly and finished whatever she was typing before offering, "Do you want me to have Anna take the baby?"

Rebecca looked nervously at Mickey. She had no idea who Anna was, but no, she did not want to hand off her baby to a stranger. More importantly, she knew it wouldn't go over well with Bash. He'd lose it.

"I think it's probably smoothest for him to stay with me for now," she said. "He should be fine playing with his toys."

She pulled several colorful rings from her bag and set them on the floor before Bash, feeling Mickey cringe behind her. More plastic! In primary colors!

"I'll leave you all unless there's anything else, Mrs. Stone," Mickey said. "I'll send Anna with some tea." Her name suddenly rang a bell—Mickey had said Anna was the house cleaner. Why would Anna bring the tea and not Mickey? Rebecca wondered if this was how it was always done, or if serving her—his wife—made him uncomfortable.

All that was happening—Mickey's practiced tone; Anna's baby-sitting services being offered without her knowing, presumably—felt like material she should be capturing. Rebecca opened her bag and pulled out her laptop.

"I've been wanting to get my life down on paper for some time now," Mrs. Stone said as she swiveled to face Rebecca and crossed her legs. She wore the same Belgian loafers and straight pants, to-day with a light peach sweater. Her hands were slender, her nails painted with clear nail polish. In her ears were gold studs. Other than that, the only jewelry she wore was her wedding set—a gold band and yellow diamond that wasn't the biggest Rebecca had ever seen.

"How does this work? I tell you my story and you write it all down and type it up?"

The house was extremely quiet. Outside, birds chirped in the distance and a leaf blower kicked on, but the silence of the home overpowered these, muting it all like heavy velvet.

"To be honest, I haven't ghostwritten before," Rebecca said, "but I was thinking that—"

"But you're a journalist and you're smart," Mrs. Stone interrupted, "so you can figure it out. Listen, dear, don't start a project by an-nouncing your inexperience. As a woman, you can't afford to do that. You're more than qualified to indulge my silly idea of an au-tobiography, which I know is what you're thinking—that it's silly. But you don't know me yet. So shall I just start talking?"

"Why don't we just start from the beginning?" Rebecca suggested.

Mrs. Stone nodded. "Dear," she said, "you must understand. I went from rags to riches to actual rags to actual riches."

Mrs. Stone launched into a story she'd clearly told many times, or at least rehearsed many times. Born in 1942, she'd grown up on a Mississippi farm, which shut down when she was still young, right after the war, when farms were becoming specialized and farmers had to become scientists. *A fellow farmer's kid*, Rebecca thought, but she didn't want to interrupt to note their shared history.

"My daddy"–it was strange to hear regal Mrs. Stone still call her father "daddy"–"was no scientist. He became a salesman. He was terrible at it. So my mother became a Tupperware lady. *She* was very good at it.

"We got by on my mother's income from Tupperware parties. It was the fifties, and she was the primary breadwinner, although my father kept up his sales work to save face."

After Wellesley, which Mrs. Stone had attended on a scholarship, she'd married her boss at the financial firm where she worked, D. L. Harmann, partly because that was what she was supposed to do at that age, and partly because she was in love. They had a child two years into marriage–but before his second birthday he drowned in a friend's pool.

"It was the most traumatic experience of my life," she said with no emotion. Rebecca wondered how many times she'd had practice relaying that information without unearthing shattering grief.

"I can imagine," Rebecca said, her heart racing. She resisted the urge to reach out and grab Bash's small foot.

"The marriage did not survive Sherman's death."

Hearing the baby's name seared Rebecca.

"Did you leave him?" Rebecca asked, returning to the marriage.

"I did," she said. "I got nothing; I asked for nothing. I walked away and started over from nothing."

"What did you do for work?" Rebecca asked.

"I did what I knew." She smiled. "Sold Tupperware."

Downstairs, Mickey, Mr. Stone, and Paul gathered around the kitchen table, where Mr. Stone sat before a small pile of condiment packets.

When Mrs. Stone was out of the house or, in this case, occupied upstairs with Rebecca, Mr. Stone would appear out of nowhere, usually in the beige compression socks he put on after soaking his legs, armed with tiny ketchups and mustards. The condiment packets indicated that it was time for his secret splurge—frozen nuggets—which he didn't want his wife to know about. (This, though never spoken aloud, was understood.)

Paul had explained to Mickey that the nuggets themselves weren't the issue. Mr. Stone couldn't keep ketchup in the house because Mrs. Stone didn't believe in it.

"Believe *in* it?" Mickey had asked.

"Believe in it," Paul said. "Like it's Satan. Or God."

Paul said he'd offered to keep the ketchup in his own fridge in the chef's cottage, but Mr. Stone liked collecting and hoarding the little packets of ketchup and yellow mustard in his bottom desk drawer, saying they reminded him of his childhood.

Paul would heat the nuggets for him in the oven, and Mr. Stone would sit in the kitchen at the modest wooden table where the staff dined, tearing open the packets and squeezing them onto his plate. It hadn't taken Mickey long to learn that his boss expected him to join the conversation during these snack sessions. He'd pepper his employees with questions about the world outside of his mansion.

"What do you fellas make of smartphones?" he asked the morning of Rebecca's first day. "How do people feel about them?"

"They're not going anywhere, sir," Paul said.

"Do you try to curb your use?" Mr. Stone asked.

"Nah. On mine all the time," Paul said.

"I think a lot of people are trying to cut back, though," Mickey said as Mr. Stone grunted and dropped a dollop of ketchup onto a nugget.

Earlier in the week, Mr. Stone had asked, "What's the deal with young people and Twitter?"

"Paul and I might not be your best sources on this one," Mickey had said. "We're both pushing middle age."

Mr. Stone, carefully applying a strip of yellow mustard, had said, "Let me give you a lesson in business, Mickey. You don't have to have perfect data to make a decent business decision. You just have to be able to read faces."

It hadn't escaped Mickey that this was the same compliment Mr. Stone had given him when offering him the job.

The morning passed and Mickey, ears alert, didn't hear a peep—no crying, no whining. He made excuses to make trips upstairs, walking by Mrs. Stone's door, straining to glean what was going on inside. But all he could pick up were muffled voices.

On one level, he wasn't surprised by Rebecca's immediate interest in Mrs. Stone's proposition. She'd always had a curious fascination with his clients. Over the years, he'd return home from catering gigs and share with her the juiciest tidbits of gossip, which she gobbled up: the custom toilet with a seat designed to suit their unique physiques (a His and Hers); the piece of fine art that one of his guys thought was a trash can and filled with garbage until Mickey spotted it, thank God, before the client did; the woman who flew her full staff home from Zurich so that their stools could be tested for a parasite she'd read about and was paranoid about acquiring. Six women and one man boarded their employer's Gulfstream and were met at JFK by an infectious disease specialist. They'd pooped in vials right there at the airport then flown back to Europe. (The housekeeper, who had been among them, had later told Mickey the story.)

Rebecca's favorite story, the one she made him repeat whenever they met new people and the subject of his catering war stories came up: a million-dollar wedding in a converted Brooklyn warehouse—four hundred guests, black tie, Chinese-Greek Orthodox, Harvard grads blending family traditions and demands in an eight-hour ceremony and reception. At four thirty a.m., two hours into the cleanup, and in his seventeenth hour of work (having arrived at noon the previous day), he'd realized that there was no room in the last crate for the remaining twenty-three bowl-sized burgundy glasses before him. All that was left were narrow slots for champagne flutes. As it dawned on him that someone had put champagne flutes in a crate intended for goblets, one of the dozens of crates already stacked by the door, Mickey had known what to do. There was nowhere, physically, to pack them. He'd have to unpack a box to find the space, and he did not have the energy—or willingness—to take that on.

"So I just . . ." He'd mimicked smashing a wineglass by holding it by the stem and slamming it against a table. Then another. Then another.

"No!" Rebecca had squealed. "How much were they worth?"

He'd shrugged. "Twenty bucks each, retail? They were insured. Everyone knows glassware will break, especially at a wedding for four hundred . . ." She'd howled, loving any tale in which rich people were the butt of a joke.

On the other hand, hadn't she said *she'd* never work for the Stones?

At eleven thirty that morning, half an hour before the Stones' lunch guest was to arrive and ninety-three minutes after he'd left her upstairs, Rebecca emerged carrying Bash in one arm and the bouncer, which Mickey had taken up, feeling bad about it, in the other. She smiled calmly at him.

"See you at home later," she said flatly, revealing nothing.

Today's guest was a Silicon Valley venture capitalist. He showed up twenty minutes early—unheard of at the Stones'—with his girlfriend, a quiet woman more elegantly dressed than him. He wore a wrinkled T-shirt and emitted a hostile amount of positivity. She seemed unfazed by his manic reverberations but unnerved by her opulent surroundings.

When Mickey overheard that the man who could use an ironing lesson was there to make a pitch for his pet project, the anti-smartphone—a return to the flip!—the morning's earlier conversation made sense.

Nothing with Cecil Stone was frivolous.

"How was it?" Mickey asked the moment he entered the condo to find Rebecca on the floor painting her toenails and watching *Queer Eye*, while Bash, his face smeared with applesauce, cooed in his high chair. "And why is he awake?"

In response to his first question, she told him that she'd met with Mrs. Stone for an hour and a half, and it had gone "great"; to his second, she said "he couldn't sleep," as if babies operated like adults. "I couldn't take the wailing anymore." But the good news, she said, was that Bash hadn't fussed once that morning during the meeting. He'd been so perfect that Rebecca knew it would never happen again, and she hoped it hadn't set a precedent.

"From now on?" he asked, quoting her.

"We're going to meet every morning to work," she said casually.

"*Every morning?*" Mickey didn't bother hiding his horror. "This is really snowballing into a thing, huh?" He picked up Bash and gave him a big kiss on his left cheek, then his right. He wiped the applesauce off his own lips.

"She wants to tell me her whole life story," she said. "Is she sick or something?"

"I don't think so. Why?"

"She just seems to have this sense of urgency about her 'memoirs.' Why do rich people make memoir plural?" She finished painting her left foot and moved to her right.

"I've never heard another person say memoirs, period. So I guess we both work for the Stones now, huh?" he said, needling her.

She stopped, holding the nail brush in midair.

"I think it's different," she said, furrowing her brow. "It's research. I would be foolish to turn it down."

"That line sounds familiar," he said, grinning.

"Yeah, yeah," she said, resuming her careful strokes, hunched over like she was performing surgery.

But Mickey was confused. If Mrs. Stone hired Rebecca to ghostwrite, that couldn't be research for her own writing, could it?

"Are you going to write about her?" he asked. "Apart from writing *for* her?" His tone implied what he was thinking, that it didn't seem ethical to pretend to be doing one thing while actually doing another. In his line of work, discretion was a hallmark of employability. If you ever violated the privacy of a client, you'd be blackballed forever—not to mention in violation of your nondisclosure agreement, if you'd signed one. He'd been given the standard contract vowing him to secrecy on his first day and signed it as a condition of employment without thinking twice.

Even when he hadn't worked under NDAs, Mickey was so discreet that there were times he hadn't even told Rebecca something if he feared she might find it *too* interesting not to pursue. Like the coworker a few years earlier who was maybe groped by a guest, and how she'd not been seen again until Hugh Bogle ran into her on Twenty-Third Street, and she'd told him Wampler had cut her a check for fifteen grand. Mickey also hadn't told Rebecca about the boy he sent home one night—a young kid, new to the city, incompetent—after the kid dropped a case of wine on his toe and kept insisting it was broken. Freddie Wampler hadn't needed some twenty-two-year-old musical theater major who couldn't sing above the staff suing him. (Of course he was aware that the story didn't reflect so well on him either.)

As for Rebecca, she'd expected her husband's question. She'd asked it herself. The way she saw it, while she had no intention of abusing her access to Mrs. Stone, she was also a journalist, which Mrs. Stone knew. Neither of them had mentioned a nondisclosure agreement—or an agreement of any sort, for that matter. Until then, Rebecca was free to write whatever she pleased and, professionally speaking, there was nothing unethical about it. (A reporter didn't need to say "this is on the record" when speaking with an interview subject—this was one of the first things she'd learned studying journalism. It was the responsibility of the interviewee to state prior to speaking that a given comment was "off the record.")

There was one twist to this, however—payment. They hadn't yet discussed compensation, and Rebecca preferred it that way. She had more freedom without being financially obliged to Mrs. Stone, and she didn't know the law, but she guessed that once she was officially employed as a writer-for-hire, even without a contract, there could be limitations around what she was permitted to write.

This was why—and she was proud of this idea—she'd suggested to Mrs. Stone that they reserve discussion of payment until she'd gathered all of the information and understood the scope of the project. Up until that point, their meetings and discussions would be a part of the "information gathering" stage, and neither was under any obligation to the other.

"It's not that black-and-white," Rebecca said. "It's not like I'm either a writer for her and thus essentially a propaganda copywriter, or I'm out to take her down in some undercover, backhanded way."

He grunted.

To Mickey, the not getting paid "yet" seemed like a ruse, a deception masked as a technicality, and he wondered if it was a sort of superficial attempt by his wife to escape her cognitive dissonance around the whole thing.

But Rebecca was clearly excited about it. In a city where they knew no one, she had a project that played to her skills, and somewhere to be other than alone with Bash inside their apartment or wandering the streets of West Palm by herself.

His progressive, activist partner and his billionaire boss's seventysomething wife made strange bedfellows, but what was the saying—don't look a gift horse in the mouth?

CHAPTER 8

The next morning, Rebecca sat at a small handsome writing desk that had appeared in Mrs. Stone's study overnight. She alternated between typing and reaching down to let Bash hold her finger. His whining was like a soundtrack to their meeting—when Rebecca wrote, he whined. When she didn't, he was quiet. She did her best to ignore it, but she was sure it was bothering Mrs. Stone, because it was annoying her, and she was his mother.

As for the desk, Mrs. Stone had wanted Rebecca to be able to take notes comfortably, and so, before her arrival, she'd had Mickey bring up a "little" writing desk from the storage closet next to the garage, which he was also charged with removing once his wife departed (no reason for it to clutter). Despite its size, it was solid wood and at least eighty pounds—not the kind of furniture he was used to lifting on a regular basis—and he had to haul it across the property and up the stairs, then back. He'd suppressed his irritation as he'd carefully sidestepped up the staircase with it, thinking of how sore he'd be the next day.

"So there I was, selling Tupperware," Mrs. Stone said, "but really I just wanted to be around art. I applied to gallery positions and didn't get interviews. Eventually I landed a job as a receptionist at the Museum of Modern Art. That's where I was working when I met Wink—you know, we could have Anna watch him."

Bash was whimpering again. If only Mrs. Stone would let Rebecca record, Rebecca could play with him and just listen. But she'd declined that idea, saying that "recorders make people like me nervous."

"He's really not great with strangers," Rebecca said apologetically, a lie. They'd never actually tried to leave him with anyone. "One second . . ."

She got out her phone to text Mickey.

Hey—can you watch Bash for a few minutes?

"I'll see if Mickey can take him for a bit. Who is . . . did you say 'Wink'?"

"Wink Martindale. He was host of the game show *Tic-Tac-Dough* and the one who introduced me to Elvis."

Rebecca's eyes widened.

"I didn't mention that I dated Elvis?"

Her phone lit up. Um, not really, Mickey had texted back.

"What did he say?" Mrs. Stone demanded.

"That he's busy," Rebecca said, lifting Bash onto her lap. "It's fine. I can listen now and take notes later."

Without pause, Mrs. Stone launched into the story.

Wink Martindale, host of *Tic-Tac-Dough*, was how Astrid wound up on the show. (That piece of her history, which had seemed so random, now made sense.)

"I knew the moment I found out I was going to be on the show that I would win it," she said. "I've always been remarkably good at trivia; that's part of my charm. Or, at least, it was before Google."

She remembered every question she was asked on the show, and the correct answers, as well as the names of her competitors and the questions that lost them their games.

"Once I set the record, I lost interest. I had enough to buy my vineyard, an adorable rescue property on the Oregon coast."

It was funny to hear a vineyard described as a "rescue." Stray animals were rescues for most; for Mrs. Stone, it was a vineyard. (Rebecca had learned that Mrs. Stone's attendance at the doggy luncheon had been at the insistence of a friend who'd bought a table—the Stones had no pets themselves and never had.)

Had the vineyard turned out to be a good investment? Rebecca asked.

"Heavens, no. It was a money pit, but a labor of love. I bought it a year too late, just after the eruption of Mount St. Helens fertilized the vineyards and the Oregon wines won all the awards. But my little burgundy enterprise came along and couldn't get off the ground. I had no volcanos on my side. Goodness, I was nearly bankrupt when Cecil came along."

Cecil, she explained, had fallen in love with her immediately after meeting her at a horse race (Wellington), and he'd vowed to rescue her vineyard once again by purchasing it from her and paying her a salary to run it.

There was a problem, though. "I was engaged to someone else at the time," she said. "A very high-profile individual who lived in Oregon as well and whom I loved deeply, but whose lifestyle was going to put me in the spotlight, which my flash of fame on *Tic-Tac-Dough* had shown me wasn't what I wanted."

"Who was it?" Rebecca asked.

Mrs. Stone smiled, ignoring her question. "You know when you have a terrible idea, and it's just so terrible that the only thing to do is act on it immediately before your better judgment kicks in?"

Rebecca nodded, though she didn't, not really. The most impulsive thing she'd ever done was buy a $400 sweater, and the memory still gave her a wild tingle.

"As I was entertaining Cecil's offer to buy the vineyard and reconsidering my engagement to this public figure—it would be his second marriage as well—my fiancé convinced me that my hesitation was cold feet and that we should elope. So that's what we did."

"Vegas?" Rebecca said, smiling.

"Actually, yes," she said. "I mean, it was silly. He insisted we do it out of state because he was recognizable in state, and we weren't ready to come out as a couple yet. At least that's what we told ourselves. In reality, we weren't ready to be married yet."

Mrs. Stone was practically insisting that Rebecca beg her to divulge the man's identity, and Rebecca was happy to comply.

"I'm dying to know who it was," she said.

"Holden Hayes," Mrs. Stone said brightly. His name sounded familiar, but Rebecca struggled to place it. "At the time a congressman poised for a Senate run. By the next year he was the fourth Black senator in the U.S. Senate, and one of only eleven, to date."

It took a moment to sink in.

". . . you were married to one of the first Black senators?"

"Oh, barely," Mrs. Stone said, pawing the air, visibly pleased by Rebecca's reaction. "For less than a week. We had it annulled when we realized it was a bad idea. I'm far too direct to be a first lady. And a seventy-two-hour second marriage doesn't bode well for one's political career, especially when you're a *first* like that. We kept it under wraps."

Rebecca was speechless. If it was a secret, why was Mrs. Stone telling *her* these things?

"Why Vegas?" she asked. Mrs. Stone did not seem like a Vegas person, to say the least.

She sighed.

"The Court had struck down miscegenation laws by then, but let's just say it took a while for many judges to comply. Holden felt that in Vegas, well, we were sure to be the least interesting couple to marry that day."

Rebecca had returned Bash to his bouncer and was typing as quickly as she could.

With her marriage to Holden Hayes annulled, Mrs. Stone explained, she began to date Cecil Stone. Although she did not, in the end, let him buy the vineyard, she did accept a loan, which she paid back in full as soon as she was able.

The Oregon Wine Marketing Coalition—a wine lobby—was formed

in the '90s. The group won favorable legislation for state wine-makers that helped her vineyard to survive.

"I also added a tasting room," she said. "The wine-tasting tours were a hit, since, by then, Oregon wine country had become a destination."

Her vineyard was closed on Sundays—she grew up Protestant—but every other day of the week it was open, and within three years, she was able to pay Cecil back in full.

She dated him for nine years before marrying him in 1992. ("I'd been married twice, dear. I wasn't going to make a third mistake.") He proposed at least four times over that decade—she eventually lost count.

He was a billionaire by that point—but she insisted on a prenuptial agreement all the same, considering their finances to be completely separate.

"I didn't need his money, dear," she said. "I want to be clear about that."

"Why didn't you?" Rebecca asked, hoping the question didn't come across as gauche. Had the vineyard really done that well, after the addition of the tasting room and a few lobbyists?

No, it was something else.

In 1984, Astrid had purchased $250,000 worth of M&T Bank stock for $1.60. By 1998, it was worth $51 a share, and by 2004, it was worth $106—having grown over $16 million in twenty years. By making "a few good investments," she'd grown her personal wealth to $2.1 billion.

While journalists over the years had interviewed Astrid Stone numerous times ("They've said it all, and half of it missed the mark"), she'd never before told anyone about Holden Hayes . . . or Elvis. ("It was only a few evenings out dancing. He was already quite bloated by then.") She dropped this bit of information as Rebecca gathered her things to leave.

"Why are you comfortable telling *me*?" Rebecca asked.

"I'm seventy-six, dear, and I still have all my faculties," she said. "If not now, when?"

Every day over the coming days, Rebecca typed up the woman's one-liners, word for word.

Like: "When I buy or sell art, there's typically a horse in the wings."

And: "Lists are tacky, *Forbes* especially. Thank heavens we can pay to be excluded." To pay to be left out of the Forbes wealthiest Americans list was a level of irony that delighted Rebecca as a writer.

Late one morning in their second week, when they'd veered back to Mrs. Stone's college days, she said, "I've always gotten along better with men than with women."

"Why'd you choose Wellesley, then?" Rebecca asked. "As an all-girls school."

"Because Yale wouldn't start accepting women for nine more years, dear."

Of course, Rebecca thought.

"So did you have male friends? Were men allowed in the dorms?" she asked.

"As long as the door was cracked and there were three feet on the floor," she smiled, a glint in her eye.

"She's fantastic," Rebecca said over takeout sushi lunch by the pool. On the ground between their lounge chairs, Bash was a fuzzy lima bean, still and silent, napping on the monitor.

After spending ten days with Mrs. Stone, an idea had begun to form in Rebecca's mind—still vague, it had something to do with turning this into a bigger project, a calling card for herself. She didn't know what yet—profile multiple billionaire women? Write about the intersection of feminism and wealth? The more she learned about Mrs. Stone, the more she felt drawn to spin it into something larger. She had much more to discover before she'd know what was there, but one fantasy that had flashed through her mind: a book that would propel her writing career to the next level, freeing Mickey from having to cater anymore.

"It makes no sense that she married Cecil Stone," she said. "After dating Elvis. And a Democratic senator. How does bug-faced Cecil Stone follow those acts?"

From the small plastic tray in his lap, Mickey popped a piece of spicy salmon roll into his mouth then reached over to nab a piece of a dragon roll from Rebecca's tray.

"She doesn't make you nervous?" he asked. "She fucking terrifies me."

"You make me more nervous than she does," Rebecca said.

"What do you mean?" he asked, though he knew what she meant.

That morning, Rebecca had once again tried to time nursing so as not to have to deal with the stress of a fussy, hungry baby during her session with Mrs. Stone. But Bash had been on a schedule of his own, refusing to eat before they'd left, so that by the time they'd pulled into the smooth driveway on Coconut Row, he was already starting to whimper.

Thinking fast, she'd unbuckled him and nursed him in the back seat of the Nissan before going inside. Just a few feet away, a lawns man had clipped hedges and averted his eyes. The windows weren't tinted.

"I realized today when I was breastfeeding Bash in the driveway of a house with a hundred rooms that it was because I thought it would freak you out."

He chewed slowly. "Correct," he said, knowing it wasn't the right answer.

"Because . . ." she said.

"Because *anytime* you're in the house it freaks me out."

She shook her head. "I'm an adult, you realize. Like a fully grown, functioning adult, who has been inside the homes of many, many people and managed not to destroy their art or shit on their carpet," she said.

"No, no, no," he said. "I'm not scared of you breaking something."

He paused. "Okay, I'm a little scared of you breaking something. But mostly I'm scared you're going to do something that pisses off Missus, and she's going to unleash on you, and then I'm going to feel the need to intervene, and it's going to get bad."

It was weird how he called them "Missus" and "Mister," like he was a character in *Downton Abbey*. He hadn't done that before he worked for the Stones. She blamed Paul.

"Unleash, how?" she asked. Astrid Stone wasn't an especially warm presence, but she seemed more distant than volatile.

"What it sounds like," Mickey said. "Lay into you. Fire you. Tell you off in a real dickish way."

"*Really*?"

"Apparently, she fires someone every few months out of nowhere, just to keep everyone on their toes."

Rebecca laughed.

"That's funny?" Mickey said, doing the one eyebrow thing.

"It just does not sound like the woman I've been talking to," she said. "But I guess I've only known her for a couple of weeks."

Mickey took the last piece of sushi from Rebecca's tray and held it up. She nodded to indicate that he could have it.

"I wouldn't bust out a boob in her presence if I were you," he said. "Last week she threw a tantrum because a radish rolled off the table and no one caught it."

"Where did the radish roll off to?" she asked, giggling.

"Just the floor. Henry Kissinger noticed it when he accidentally kicked it across the room."

Rebecca spit out her seltzer.

"Henry Kissinger?" she asked. "Kicked a radish? Their pal, Henry?"

"Everyone knows Henry Kissinger," he said. "He'll show up anywhere there's shrimp."

She covered her face with her hands. "Why in God's name do you not tell me these things?" she asked, her voice muffled.

"I just did," he said.

CHAPTER 9

Her column on Wine and WOOF! came out on a Tuesday in late January. To her relief, Henrik, her editor, loved it so much that he asked what five-hundred-dollar ticket she wanted him to pay for next. Several other outlets listed it as a "must read" of the week, leading it to garner more views, shares, and comments than any column she'd written.

Still, she did not expect the Stones to have read it.

But when she showed up on Wednesday morning with Bash, Mr. Stone intercepted her on her way in the foyer.

"Nice article," he said. "I've never understood why Astrid goes to that thing."

Had she not told him what she'd told Rebecca—that Carolyn from her book club got a table at the doggy fashion show every year for twenty-five thousand dollars and implored them all to come?

"Thank you," Rebecca said, surprised not just that he'd bothered to read it, but that he spent any time online at all; she knew that Mickey printed out his emails.

"The one on the stomach is just a bit ridiculous though, no?"

The gut biome.

. . . he'd read *all* of her columns?

"I guess that depends on your perspective," she said. "People lacking essential bacteria in their gut biomes would probably disagree." She tried to keep her tone friendly.

"You really think that economic status is linked to the bacteria in your stomach?" he said, a slight but unmistakable sneer in his voice.

"I would say," she said, thinking *as I wrote, and as you read*, "that being poor affects your diet, which affects the microorganisms in your gut, and that these aren't fully understood yet. But a lot of evidence suggests they influence all kinds of health metrics mentally and physically. And when you aren't healthy, it's harder to break out of poverty. So, yes."

She shifted Bash to her other hip and wondered if Mickey was somewhere within earshot having an anxiety attack.

"I've had cancer four times," Mr. Stone said. "And it hasn't stopped me from steadily increasing my net worth since the seventies."

What was she supposed to say to that? You're very fortunate to have recovered? You're very *unfortunate* to have had so many recurrences (four times!)?

"I'm sorry to hear that," she said. "You must have excellent doctors."

"Indeed," he said. "Well, thank you for the thought-provoking material. I always appreciate a new take."

"Thanks for reading," she said, with a genuine smile.

Upstairs, she found Mrs. Stone's study empty.

Rebecca set up the bouncer and placed Bash in it, then handed him his new favorite teething toy, a giraffe that made a soft and tolerable squeak.

Her phone rattled—a text. She looked down, expecting it to be from Mickey (few other people texted her these days), freaking out about the conversation he must have just overheard, but it was from an unknown number. She didn't even recognize the area code.

Loved the article.

She didn't want to ask who it was. Clearly she was supposed to know.

Thanks. How are you? she wrote back.

Good, still in Austin.

Who did she know in Austin?

Are you still in New York? the texter asked.

No, she wrote, Florida.

Florida???

My husband got a job down here. We moved in December.

Interesting.

Where are you working these days? she wrote.

I'm at the Statesman. For a minute I tried to start my own alternative weekly but that didn't work out.

Someone in journalism. That narrowed it down to about a hundred people.

Remind me—where were you before Austin?

After Paris, I was in Pittsburgh (long story) (for a girl) (didn't work out) (don't move to Pittsburgh for a girl). Got squeezed out of there after only seven months though. One of those Starr travesties.

Jason Pirozzi.

It was Jason Pirozzi.

They'd had a brief thing at the very end of college—it had begun and screeched to a halt all during the last two months before graduation. It had been a whirl of pleasure arriving at the precise moment when they both had only promise ahead of them. She was twenty-two and blinded by her own future, about to start at *GMA*. He was moving to Paris for an internship. They'd never once discussed the possibility of staying together once he headed overseas. Why would they? They'd each had the whole world to discover.

Oh, right. Well, good to hear from you! she wrote, and slid her phone into her bag before Mrs. Stone came in.

Her thoughts returned to her conversation with Mr. Stone moments earlier. Surely a man like him—a man who had, alone, accumulated the wealth of several small nations—understood the difference between a personal anecdote of surviving cancer and actual health data based on real sample sizes. He was posturing. Pretending. What was it with rich people and the refusal to acknowledge that demographic factors largely determined wealth? It was as if, by accepting that perhaps, *perhaps*, poor people were poor due at least in part to circumstances beyond their control, his own status was threatened.

But no one could touch Mr. Stone and his fortune. He wasn't even traceable online, for God's sake.

This is what she was thinking when Mrs. Stone entered, slightly winded.

"Apologies, I was on the phone with my daughter. She never calls, so I didn't want to rush her."

"I didn't know you had a daughter," Rebecca said, suddenly recalling the image of the girl of nine or ten in their wedding photo she'd found online and realizing she'd assumed the child had belonged to Cecil.

Mrs. Stone sighed and sat. "Where to begin . . ."

Bash, who was now teething, had inched his way to the coffee table, pulled himself up, and was trying to gnaw on the edge.

"Good, Bash!" Rebecca said instinctively—he'd only recently started pulling up. "Oh, but no, no, baby," she said, handing him the giraffe. "Chew on this."

Bash didn't find the toy an acceptable alternative. He began to wail.

Mrs. Stone swiveled in her chair and pressed a small yellow button on a black box in the corner of her desk that Rebecca had noticed before but never asked about. Moments later, Mickey entered.

"We need you to take the baby for a bit," Mrs. Stone said. "So that your wife can concentrate."

Mickey, with no choice, quietly gathered up the quilt, bouncing seat, and toys, and left with Bash, cooing happily to be reunited with his father.

Over the next hour, Rebecca learned more about Elle Stone,

daughter of Astrid and Cecil Stone. Born seven years before they were married, in 1984, Elle was Rebecca's age. She quickly did the math—that meant that Mrs. Stone had been forty-one when she gave birth.

"An unexpected but welcome conception," she called it.

Out of wedlock! Rebecca thought, certain that had been somewhat scandalous. Or maybe, once you were that wealthy, nothing was that scandalous.

With her characteristic flippancy, Mrs. Stone explained: their daughter had grown up attending the best schools, of course. She'd accompanied her parents on extravagant vacations, tutored by the priciest tutors available. She'd gone to Brown, graduated and joined the Peace Corps, and then Teach for America. She'd been a teacher in rural Alabama ever since, going on nine years.

"Who knows," Mrs. Stone said. "She could be a lesbian by now. I have no idea what her life is like."

"How often do you speak?" Rebecca asked.

"She calls when she needs money, and on Christmas," Mrs. Stone said, then paused. "Actually, I think she missed this Christmas."

"So today's call . . ." Rebecca said.

"It's not Christmas today, is it?" Mrs. Stone said quietly, the corners of her mouth just barely lifting. "She's been calling a little more often to check in. Only recently. Don't tell Cecil."

Mickey had no idea how he was supposed to get any work done while watching Bash. He supposed he could bring him around with him in the stroller, but that just seemed ridiculous. Plus, Bash fussed if the stroller wasn't in constant motion.

He could wear him, but the baby carrier was at home.

He placed him on the quilt in the kitchen and tried to knock out tasks that he could do from his phone, but Bash was in a fussy mood and started to cry whenever he wasn't being given Mickey's full attention.

"Um, there's a baby here," Paul said, entering with a bag of fresh baguettes.

"Mrs. Stone ordered me to take him so that my wife could 'concentrate,'" Mickey said.

Paul cackled. "You're screwed, man. She's setting you up to fail."

As Mickey trimmed the morning's delivery of white lilies and Mrs. Stone's customized green-gray hydrangeas (grown for her by a florist in North Carolina and shipped weekly) and Paul prepared lunch, Bash made himself known, bored, on the hard kitchen floor.

Finally, after an hour, Anna, who as always had been in and out of the kitchen all morning, passing through on her way to do something else (unlike Mickey and Paul, Anna never stopped—Mickey had never once seen her sitting), muttering something under her breath, reached down and scooped up the baby and blanket.

"What are you doing?" Mickey asked.

"I'm tired of hearing you two complain about this baby," she said. "I'll take him upstairs with me while I fold."

Mickey knew that Anna had three kids. She was probably used to working while surrounded by little people, he thought, and let her go, relieved.

When Rebecca and Mrs. Stone wrapped up for the day, Rebecca headed downstairs where she was surprised to find Mickey sitting at the kitchen table eating a sandwich and reading the newspaper. Bash was nowhere to be seen.

"He's upstairs with Anna," he said, and could tell by her expression how it looked—him having a leisurely lunch while someone else on the clock watched their kid. "It's at the end of the hall."

She paused to glare at him before heading back upstairs, past Mrs. Stone's study, until she reached a room in which she heard a woman's voice.

Inside, she found Anna folding towels while talking to Bash about the ocean. He was happily sitting in a laundry basket on a folded bath sheet.

"I had to go back and forth to the closet and didn't want him to get too far, so I stuck him in there," she said. "He doesn't seem to mind."

"I'm sorry," Rebecca said, mortified. "I can't believe Mickey asked you to watch him."

"Oh, he didn't," she said. "I offered."

Rebecca lifted Bash from the basket and said, "Thank you."

"I have three," Anna said. "They're four, nine, and twelve. All boys."

"Sounds like a handful," Rebecca said.

"My husband got the snip after number three, that's for sure!" Anna said. She eyed Bash, who was in a pair of cotton pants and a T-shirt that were clearly too small—just what had been on top in the drawer that morning.

While most of his clothes weren't *this* tight, they were all borderline too small. Rebecca had put off buying yet more clothes for him, horrified by the environmental waste of baby clothes—items they grew out of in four weeks, or three, all being dumped into trash heaps. Not to mention, the cost of replacing even $7.99 items so frequently seemed ridiculous, even if you could afford it.

She'd planned to research used and recycled options but hadn't gotten around to it yet.

"You know, after three boys, I have a lot of toddler clothes I need to get rid of. I was going to take them to church to put in the donation bin, but do you want me to bring them for you to look through first?"

"Oh, wow," Rebecca said, suddenly in a hurry to leave, brimming with guilt. "That's so nice of you. Sure."

"I'll bring them," she said, waving her hand as if shooing Rebecca off.

"Sounds great. Thanks again," Rebecca said, grabbing Bash. She stepped into the hallway and nearly collided with Mickey.

"Sorry," he whispered. "I know how it looks."

"We'll talk about it at home," she said, shouldering past him.

"Rebecca," he said, "you're overreacting."

"I'm not reacting at all," she said, pressing her hands firmly against the stack she'd just assembled: towel, tofu slices, towel. She had to wick out all the moisture or the tofu steaks wouldn't be crispy. "I'm pointing out the facts. You, a male, handed off our baby to a woman to watch him because you had to work. But you ignored that she *also* had to work. So the woman ended up both working her job while taking care of *our* baby so you could eat lunch and read the paper."

"That's not . . ."

"What about that isn't true?"

Mickey sighed.

"She's not a victim, okay? Anna is a busybody. She likes being needed."

Rebecca closed her eyes and opened them.

"Did you ask her if she *wanted* to watch Bash?"

"I didn't have to! She offered!"

"That woman is working there to support three kids—"

Mickey laughed.

"What?" she said.

"Anna's husband manages the W Hotel in Miami. Anna is doing just fine, okay? She works for the Stones because she hated being a stay-at-home mom. She gets bored."

"How do you know that?"

"She told me!" he said. "And those poor kids you're talking about? One of them is, like, a fucking piano prodigy. He goes to some conservatory. She wants him to go to this school downtown— the one we pass, the school of the arts. It's apparently one of the best arts high schools in the country."

"Hmm. Well, that's cool," Rebecca said, wringing out a dish towel and grabbing a chef's knife to slice the tofu. "Okay, I'm glad Anna's doing fine. But my point is the same," she said.

"I mean, I didn't say she's rich. I don't think Daniel's piano lessons are cheap."

"Do you see my point?" she asked, still exasperated, but trying to sound calm.

"I do," he said. "I get it. She shouldn't have to watch him. But also, I can't either. We need to figure something else out."

"I get it, too" she said. If she couldn't watch Bash and do an interview, he certainly couldn't watch Bash and run a whole estate. "We will."

But they didn't figure something else out. Over the following days, if Bash started to cry, Mrs. Stone would buzz for Mickey, and he'd be expected to fetch his son and somehow be responsible for him while running a massive home.

There were maintenance issues and endless landscaping questions, along with a steady stream of entertainment matters to be dealt with: guest lists, dietary requirements, menu sourcing. By February, the social calendar at the house had picked up steam. Even in warm South Florida, rich people tended to hibernate the first few weeks of the year, but as spring drew closer, the Stones resumed hosting five or six nights a week, plus three or four lunches. The extra leaves stayed in the table. There were place settings to count, crystal to polish, and linens to deal with, an endless cycle of linens.

And Mickey was trying to do all of it while entertaining his eleven-month-old.

"Dude, this is fucking crazy," Paul said one day as Mickey bounced Bash on one knee while issuing orders to a contractor in the front yard of the house—only a few hundred feet away—over FaceTime because the sound of the Weed Eater outside frightened Bash to tears.

But what was he to do? Mrs. Stone had issued an instruction. Rebecca had forbidden him from asking for Anna's help. And Mr.

Stone had no idea. He golfed during Mrs. Stone's and Rebecca's sessions, and even if he wasn't on the course, he wasn't going to stand up to his wife.

"Your wife has got you doing it all, man," Paul said.

Shared disbelief over the situation accelerated Mickey and Paul's budding friendship, which by then had slid into an easy camaraderie. Whenever Mrs. Stone snapped at someone, they'd whisper "drink." They created stories about the guests to keep themselves entertained in the kitchen—who was an opiate addict, who was the mistress of a senator, who was new money. (New money ordered a second cocktail with their entrée instead of just accepting the wine pairing. New money said "thank you" to every little thing. New money gushed about the food.)

For Mickey, shooting the shit with colleagues had always been the best—as in, the most tolerable—part of catering. Back when he'd first moved to New York, he'd spent forty hours a week making cappuccinos for Singaporean businessmen at the luxury men's store Ermenegildo Zegna on Fifth Avenue. For some reason, Zegna always employed at least four guys at a time to serve cappuccinos, even though one, at most, was needed, so they lounged all day in the back kitchen behaving like idiots. Reagan Ronald from Wisconsin, who was constantly the butt of their jokes not only because of his name (he claimed his parents had a weird sense of humor) but also because he continued to call himself an actor even though he hadn't worked in a decade, would take bets on how many feet of the six-foot Blimpie sub—the staff meal provided daily—he could eat come end of shift.

Back in Manhattan, it was his catering buddies who were also actors: Reagan, Hugh, the others. Here, it was Paul.

With Bash around, Mickey was less and less able to get his work done in the mornings, and started having to stay later. Gradually, Mickey and Paul adopted a new routine. Post-dinner cleanup, after Mr. and Mrs. Stone had retired for the night and Mickey had knocked out the tasks he hadn't been able to do with Bash in his lap, the two of them would sit in back of the house overlooking the lake and drink wine. Mr. Stone never minded if they finished whatever bottle had been opened for the evening—and there was always some left over. Whether it was a seventeen-thousand-dollar 1996 Clos de la Roche or a twenty-thousand-dollar 1990 Conti, they'd knock it off on the long wooden deck before calling it a night, Mickey heading across the bridge on his bike and Paul walking the few yards to his cottage behind the tennis courts.

One night, Paul shared that Anna—who'd been there longer than anyone, preceding him by four years—had once gotten drunk and told him about the great wine scandal of 2005.

"Turns out the cellar had a bunch of fake wines, all bought from the same auction house," Paul said. "Mister had no idea until one of the Koch brothers told him. Mister hired an investigator who found that he had over a million dollars in fake wine down there. Shit like a 1922 Ponsot magnum when there was no Ponsot magnum that year."

"Damn," Mickey said. "Did he sue the auction house?"

He shook his head. "Auction house said it was on him, and he shrugged it off."

To shrug off a million dollars.

"I think he was embarrassed. Mister doesn't like to be duped," Paul said. After a moment, he added, "It's kind of a brilliant scheme when you think about it."

Not really, Mickey didn't say. It seemed like the kind in which you were guaranteed, at some point, to get caught.

"You haven't spent any time with him. If you got to know him, you'd realize he's a pretty good guy. He's just rough around the edges," Mickey said. He and Rebecca sat in their usual seats on the balcony. It was almost midnight.

Once he started sticking around in the evenings to chill with Paul, Mickey would arrive home too late for dinner. He'd eat leftovers at the Stones' or snack during cleanup. She ate alone.

"I'm pretty sure if I spent more time with him I'd feel the same way I do now," she said.

While Mickey had always had a greater tolerance than Rebecca for vulgarity, casual sexism, and other stereotypically bro-y indulgences, it worried her that Mickey spent his days with a soulless billionaire and a forty-five-year-old frat boy. You become who you're surrounded by, she believed. "I mean, to be fair, I've only met him once. Although that one time, he did use the word 'tits' and talk about hitting on adolescents."

"Let's all hang out again," Mickey suggested.

And so three nights later, the three of them sat on the balcony overlooking the pool and sipped frozen mango margaritas Rebecca had whipped up in the blender. The night was breezy, and the moon was just shy of full, illuminating the planes that passed overhead.

"So I told Missus I was going to take two weeks' vacation in May when we go back up north . . ." Paul traveled with the Stones wherever they went, which meant he was in the Hamptons during the warm months and in Palm Beach during the colder months.

"But she said no," Paul said. "She blamed Carla. Said that I don't need someone with kids. I already have my own to deal with. I don't know how you stomach her, man. She drives me fucking nuts." He was looking at Rebecca. She took a sip.

How to explain her fascination with Mrs. Stone?

The woman had built her own wealth, and not in the predatory way that her husband had. Her ascent wasn't nefarious like that. Mrs. Stone hadn't wanted to be reliant on a man. She'd seen a role model in her mother and followed suit.

In some ways, Mrs. Stone was less hypocritical than the über-rich liberals Rebecca had written about, the ones in tech who fancied themselves world-changers, social do-gooders, when they were as capitalistic and cutthroat as anyone. Astrid Stone wasn't pretending not to care about money. She also didn't pretend to be guilt-free about it (she had, several times, in discussing her charitable giving, seemed almost embarrassed by it–like it should be much greater, even when she was giving hundreds of thousands). She didn't seem to be pretending, period. That was why Paul and Mickey didn't like her, Rebecca suspected. Men tended to be unnerved by women that direct, she'd found.

"How many kids do you have again?" Rebecca asked, avoiding his question.

"One," he said. "In Jersey. He lives with my ex-wife in Morristown."

"How old is he?" she asked.

"Fourteen," Paul said.

"How often do you see him?"

"As much as I can," Paul said. "Summers he comes out to East Hampton." He took a sip, his eyes darting about, like he felt judged. "He's got a great three-point shot."

At that moment a plane burst into the sky overhead, drowning out the conversation. Rebecca watched the inky pool below. The pool light had been turned off for the night, but in the moonlight Rebecca could make out a shadowy figure wading in the darkness.

It wasn't until the plane passed that they heard the sound of Bash's cries coming through the monitor.

"He probably took a shit. I'll check him," Mickey said, sliding open the door and going inside. Rebecca cringed. Babies pooped. They didn't "shit," unless you were playing it cool in front of your bro-y colleague.

"Do you miss your son?" Rebecca asked. She couldn't imagine living so far away from Bash.

"Of course," Paul said. "But I know one day he'll appreciate me. What I do."

They were silent for a few moments, alone.

"He made the right call coming to work for Mister," he said.

"Mister's a good guy. And there are, you know, perks." He was looking at her out of the side of his eye.

"What do you mean?" she asked.

He leaned forward. "You think I own a boat and a condo in Miami and one on Long Island, and send my kid to private school on my salary alone?"

Rebecca didn't follow. ". . . yes?" she said.

"Talk to your husband," he said. "Ask him about the paperwork he sees."

"What?"

"That's all I'm going to say. Just ask him." He took a long inhale on his vape pen and leaned back in his chair.

"Why did Paul tell me to ask you about paperwork you see?" Rebecca said the moment the door shut behind their guest, well after midnight.

"Shh," Mickey said, gesturing for her to move farther into the apartment.

She followed him into the kitchen. "He was talking about paperwork. At the Stones'."

"Huh?" Mickey asked, turning on the faucet and handing her a kitchen towel. He squeezed a dollop of dish soap into the three dirty glasses.

"He implied that it makes you—or him—money."

"I have no idea," he said, yawning as he handed her a clean glass to dry. "That's weird."

"I don't like it, whatever it is," she said, giving the glass a quick once-over. "It doesn't sound aboveboard. Do you see Cecil Stone's financial documents or something?"

Mickey frowned. "I see Mr. Stone's correspondence," he said.

"Email and mail?" she said.

He nodded. "But that's it. And I don't read them, not really. I just sort of make sure it's, you know, not spam."

"I don't like him," Rebecca said, putting away the glasses.

"I know you don't," he said as he expertly rinsed out the interior of the stainless steel sink and wiped it down until it gleamed. "Don't worry. I won't invite him over again."

"It's more than not wanting to hang out with him. I think he's shady," she said. "You should make sure not to be associated with anything he's up to over there."

"If I get fired," he said, poking her collarbone, "it's not going to be because of him. It's going to be because I can't do my job while I'm babysitting."

She deflected. "I thought it wasn't called 'babysitting' when you're the father?"

He snapped her with the kitchen towel then folded it neatly and hung it on the cabinet hook beneath the counter.

"You know what I mean," he said, flipping off the kitchen light.

CHAPTER 10

Mrs. Stone and Rebecca stood watching as a woman from Sotheby's carefully wrapped an Andrew Wyeth painting the size of a standard sheet of paper around a tube.

"That one I could bear to part with," she said to Rebecca. It was a muted portrait—all tans and grays—of a young woman with a mischievous smile wearing a very flat hat. "She used to remind me of me. I've had it almost thirty years."

Mrs. Stone owned some of the most iconic art of the twentieth century, most of which she kept in "her" wing of the house, and she would spontaneously put pieces up for sale to fund causes she deemed important to her.

"Thank you, Mrs. Stone," the woman said. "I'll be in touch."

"Mickey will show you out," Mrs. Stone said to the woman as Mickey appeared on cue, never missing a beat.

"Why not just give money?" Rebecca asked as she followed Mrs. Stone down the hallway and into the study.

"I do prefer to keep a low profile, dear. But I'm also not an idiot. It's only twenty percent about the money, and eighty percent about the headline." She understood the importance of PR for nonprofits, and she played the game well.

In 2008 she sold Norman Rockwell's *Rosie the Riveter* to fellow billionaire Patti Heart Howell—of cereal manufacturing fortune—for six million.

"Patti is a collector as well," she said. "We used to take art trips together before she lost her mind."

"How did she lose her mind?" Rebecca had learned to play Mrs. Stone's game. Teasing remark? Ask a question. More teasing? Probe further. She liked to be teed up.

"Oh, she has a long-standing friendship with the Clintons," she said, "and ever since Hillary lost, she's got a chip on her shoulder. She won't shut up about that election. I can't stomach incessant political ranting."

This was the mystery of Mrs. Stone. She had contributed—generously and more consistently over the years than to any other cause—to criminal justice reform efforts, even though she was a registered Republican according to public records, and married to Cecil Stone, who himself had contributed to every Republican presidential candidate since the '80s.

"You give to the ACLU to support criminal justice reform but you're a Republican? How does that add up?"

Mrs. Stone, ever unflappable, answered quickly.

"I don't trust the government to make good with my money, and I don't trust the government to get criminal justice right, either. That's how."

"So you're libertarian?"

"I don't like labels," she said.

So what did she vote based on?

"Taxes, of course," Mrs. Stone said. Ah. Right. Then she added, "And air traffic."

"Pardon?" Rebecca asked.

"It's going to sound petty," Mrs. Stone said. "But have you noticed how loud the planes are when they fly directly overhead after taking off from PBI?"

Rebecca nodded. In fact, she had. At night, sitting on their balcony, the engines would be so loud she'd stop talking until they passed.

"Well, they're now rerouted so that they don't fly over Mar-a-Lago whenever the president is in town. It's how you know he's here, which of course is basically all the time. I swear, people think I'm crazy, but I suspect that's why he ran. He's been fighting the airport for years."

"You think he ran for president so planes wouldn't fly over his house?"

She shrugged.

"Sure," she said. "Anyway, it's not just him. Whenever someone is elected to office, air traffic control changes the takeoff protocol based on the location of the politician's home on the island, as well as the homes of his most important people. Diplomats and secretaries. It's a security issue—we can't have planes flying over their properties at such a low altitude when they're on site. And everyone is always here because of course they are."

Rebecca wasn't following. She understood that many of the kind of people who ran for office—particularly high offices, like president and senator—had houses in the area. But that many of them?

"And that influences your voting . . ."

"If I vote for someone with a house on the south end of the island, it means four years of noise. If I vote for someone with people on the north end, it buys us some peace."

Rebecca realized her mouth was hanging open and closed it, dumbfounded.

"I see," she said.

"But only in the primaries, of course," Mrs. Stone said. "I'm not *that* ridiculous."

Rebecca's wrist buzzed with a text from Mickey. Against her wishes, Rebecca now owned an Apple Watch. Mickey had driven to the Apple Store the weekend prior and bought her one for this purpose—so he could access her even when her phone was away, since Mrs. Stone didn't like phones sitting out.

Can you take him? I can't do this.

"You'll be glad to have it once we start letting people babysit," Mickey had said. But Rebecca didn't anticipate that being anytime soon. Rebecca didn't think of herself as superstitious, but the mere idea of leaving Bash for too long with someone other than Mickey surfaced a foreboding feeling, an overwhelming fear that something would go wrong. Feminism was embracing all kinds of approaches to motherhood, she told herself, and hers was: their baby couldn't leave their sides.

After fetching Bash from Mickey in the kitchen—he gave her dagger eyes—she hurried toward the front door to get out of his way, but as she entered the foyer, Anna stopped her.

"I left the clothes for you by the door," she said.

"Oh, right, thank you!" Rebecca said.

"Need help carrying them out?" Anna asked.

"Um . . ." Rebecca said.

"Yes, you do," Anna said. "There are four. I'll help you."

Anna led the way to the front entrance, where four packed and tied garbage bags stuffed full sat, Grinch-style, on the marble floor. Anna grabbed two in each hand and heaved them up.

"Open," she commanded. Rebecca opened the door and followed the woman out, thinking about how there was no way Mickey had passed by the entryway with those sitting there. If he'd seen where Anna had left those black garbage bags full of kids' clothes, he would have had a meltdown and moved them.

"Did you know they have a daughter?" Rebecca sat in the passenger seat of their new car—a silver Honda Pilot. (Rebecca had never imagined she'd own a gas-guzzling SUV, but man, she loved this one—the seats were roomy (and warmed! Not that they needed that feature here), and the vehicle's size made her feel like they were safer on the road, whether it was true or not).

She was tearing through a paper roll of SweeTarts, skipping over the greens, yellows, and oranges in favor of the pinks, blues, and purples. The discarded pieces formed a little pile in her lap, pooled on her mustard linen T-shirt dress.

They were headed a few miles north of the city to a sea turtle hospital—endangered loggerhead turtles rescued from the ocean for one reason or another, on view while they recovered.

In the back, they'd packed a picnic to take to the beach after the turtle visit.

"They do?" Mickey said. He was waiting for the right moment to tell her that she had to stop bringing Bash to the house. He couldn't do it anymore. On Friday, he'd had him out on the deck in the hot sun while supervising the shipwright, who was there to examine the damage to the teak. The damage had been inflicted by a day laborer who, not knowing teak protocol, power washed it; the deck's surface was now bumpy and pitted—unacceptable. As the shipwright explained that it would need a full sanding to be restored, Mickey hadn't been paying close attention to the man's recommendations, frantic to get Bash back into the shade, and later had struggled to remember what he'd said.

"She's semi-estranged," Rebecca said around a mouthful of sugar. "I don't know why."

Rebecca tried to remember when she herself had last spoken to her parents. A month earlier? Christmas? They got together about once a year, and it always felt like work. She couldn't really remember a time that things had felt easy between them. Age seven? It was before she'd turned eight.

She had been eight when she first accompanied her father to the feedlot. It had been so horrendous that she'd hyperventilated and had to wait in the truck.

Her parents had seemed to view her vehemence about animal rights as childhood rebellion of a predictable variety: cattle dealer's daughter announces that she's a vegetarian, then vegan. Rebecca's mother, a child of farmers herself, felt that farming in twenty-first-century America was, if not a noble calling, at least a decent one. They tolerated Rebecca's principles like a phase. She could hear the eye roll in their tone whenever the issue came up.

When Rebecca finally left for college, a part of them—all three of them—was relieved. There would be less tension, they all hoped, now that there was distance.

Just out of college, when her parents came to New York to visit, their differences buoyed up, in the way no matter how hard they tried not to bump into them.

To her, New York was heaven, the place she belonged. To them, it was a filthy, polluted metropolis where they had to squeeze themselves onto a small love seat in the living room of her tiny Harlem apartment, dinner plates on their laps, and listen while her roommates brazenly discussed the stupidity of anyone in the world who didn't think exactly like them, which seemed to be anyone who didn't vote for John Kerry.

To Rebecca, her parents, sitting there silent while her classmates attempted to connect with them, came across as stubborn and proud. To them, she knew, she came across as self-righteous.

By then she understood that most people didn't want information that would demand they change their habits. They wanted to eat their bacon without knowing that baby pigs are castrated without anesthetic, that adult pigs are slaughtered in front of one another, screeching. As they consumed their first, second, or third burger of the week (the average American's number) slathered in cheese, they didn't want to know that even on the "good" farms, the free-range ones, dairy cows were separated from their calves so that their bodies would continue to produce milk, and that for days they wept, crying out for their offspring. That they repeatedly, year after year, were put through this emotional torture until they stood skeletal and sucked dry, the trauma as apparent in their mammalian eyes as it would be in any human mother.

There were chickens who never once, in their lives, saw sunlight.

But it was easier for Rebecca to forgive strangers for eating ham, dairy, and eggs than to forgive her own parents for producing it.

Their chickens saw sunlight, but not enough, and not the male chicks, who couldn't produce eggs. Like on every other farm in the country, they were macerated right after birth.

"It's just politics!" her mother would say. "We can agree to disagree."

"It's not just politics," Rebecca would say. "It's my values. It's what I believe. How is that a small thing?"

It was understood on both sides that she judged them, and neither loved the feeling of that weight bobbing between them like a thick cloud, obscuring their view of each other. They liked Mickey, of course—but his easygoing nature did only so much to lighten their dynamic. They'd had a tense visit not long after Bash was born, and though they were thrilled to receive pictures of their grandson, keeping them at arm's length had proved the simplest way to keep the peace.

"Have you talked to your mom lately?" she asked Mickey, shifting her thoughts to her mother-in-law. Both of them loved Fran. Fran was easygoing, delighted by everything, happy just to be around her grandson. That she'd been not only a single mother but a professional tap dancer elevated her in Rebecca's mind to heroine status. She was more than happy to eat vegan on her visits and made no snide comments about whatever she was served.

"Yesterday," he said. "She wants to come in March. For his birthday."

"Cool," Rebecca said. "We should do something outside. Picnic in the park or something."

"I wonder if he'll be walking by then," Mickey thought aloud. "At one."

"In his own time," she said, in a snappier tone than she'd intended.

Whenever Mickey brought up the fact that Bash still wasn't crawling or walking, it irked her. In these moments, he seemed to be suggesting something was wrong with their baby, like he was ashamed or embarrassed that his son was slow to hit certain milestones. Her protective instinct would spring up, this time against her own husband: *Make me choose, and I swear I'll choose him over you.*

She didn't want to have to remind him again that their pediatrician back in New York had said it was normal. Bash was only eleven months old. Most didn't walk until one year. Sure, he wasn't crawling, which happened by ten months typically, but some kids, he'd said, didn't crawl at all. Rebecca knew someone (well, knew someone who knew someone) whose daughter went from sitting to walking at sixteen months. "She *never* crawled or walked," her friend had said, "and then suddenly, she stood up one day and sauntered across the room."

Was Rebecca anxious about it herself? Of course, a little. It didn't help that Bash was frustrated with himself, too, trying to inch forward but not moving, a helpless creature squirming on his belly, unable to make himself mobile. She let him try everywhere: at home, in the park, by the pool. It broke her heart to watch, and yet she knew she had to keep allowing him to struggle, that she had to encourage it.

When she'd placed him facedown in the grass of a large, dewy meadow one afternoon the week before, a man walking by with his dog said, "That's what I'm talking about! Let him explore!"

I'm trying, she'd thought, eyeing the man's Doberman, which wasn't leashed.

If Fran came in March and stayed for a couple of weeks, she could watch Bash while Rebecca was at the Stones. But if he was walking by then, it could be an issue, because Fran herself was nearly seventy and had fibromyalgia and arthritis (even years of dancing hadn't counteracted those propensities in her genes), and they lived in Florida, the land of water around every corner, and alligators.

Motherhood. She could be absolutely fine, and in a millisecond, her mind would concoct the worst possible scenario imaginable, a fantasy that left her heart fleeing.

The giant turtles floated in shallow tubs of water labeled with their "names" and the injuries that had brought them there.

Rebecca pointed to each and said its name aloud to Bash.

Lucifer—Caught in boat propeller

Juan—Shark bite

Geppetto—Buoyancy disorder

"Buoyancy disorder?" Mickey asked the young man stationed behind the tubs, who looked bored roasting under his sun hat.

"He has gas," he mumbled. "So he couldn't swim down. Once it passes he'll be fine."

After viewing the fifteen or so turtles, they carted their peanut butter and honey sandwiches and watermelon slices to the beach, where they set up a large umbrella and a beach blanket and cracked open grapefruit seltzers.

Rebecca looked over at Mickey with Bash in his lap, feeding him melon, pink juice dripping over them both. She reached for her phone to take a picture just as it began to vibrate.

Henrik, her editor, was calling. She stood and took a few steps away.

"Hi, Henrik," she answered, wiping the sand off her hands and holding the phone to her ear with her shoulder.

"Hi, Rebecca, how are you?" he said.

"Fine, what's up?"

"Sorry to call on a Saturday, but I wanted to run an idea by you."

"No problem," she said, approaching the surf. The water rushed up over her feet, cooling them.

"Your dog fashion show thing was killer. I think there's a real appetite right now for content in that area."

"Like, more doggy fundraisers?" she asked, laughing.

He laughed.

"I mean in Palm Beach. Have you seen *America the Beautiful* with . . . what's his name . . . Sujit Dhar? It's on Netflix."

"No . . ."

"It's one of those satirical talk shows. Anyway, he recently did a segment on this guy down there who apparently is gutting the local news industry. What do they call him . . . it's some kind of capitalist? A hawk? Raptor? It's a bird of prey."

"Vulture," Rebecca said.

"Vulture capitalist! Right. He didn't actually get access to the guy, and I thought, if anyone can . . ."

"I haven't seen it," Rebecca said, keeping her voice even. He meant Cecil Stone, surely. Certainly there weren't multiple people doing what Stone was doing. Newspapers weren't that big an industry. "What's the idea?"

"I don't know if you can get access to that guy. Stone. Cecil D. Stone."

"I think I can," she said, eyeing Mickey, who was wiping watermelon juice and sand off Bash's fingers with a wet wipe. "I can try."

"Seriously? Awesome," he said. "Okay, have a great weekend. I'll call next week to check in. Talk soon."

She trekked back over to her family.

"What'd Henrik want?" Mickey asked.

"He asked me to write about Mr. Stone," she said.

Mickey's eyes grew big.

"You're not going to, though . . . ." he said. "Not without telling him at least."

"Not without telling him, no," she said. "But do you care if I ask him for an interview?"

Mickey turned and squinted into the horizon.

"I won't if you're not cool with it," she said. "But I would be courteous and professional, of course."

"I'll think on it," he said as Bash took a lump of peanut butter and wiped it down the front of Mickey's T-shirt. "But speaking of work, we need to talk about . . . I can't keep watching Bash. It isn't working."

He told her the story of the shipwright. Bash in the blazing sun, sans sunscreen.

What if he'd chosen that moment to start crawling? Rebecca thought. It was going to happen any minute. What if he rolled? What if a bird of prey, a *real* vulture, saw him as a target? What if, what if, what if?

"I hope you were keeping an eye on him," Rebecca said.

"Of course," he said. "But that's the point. I can't keep a good enough eye on him and do my job, even in a half-assed way. He's going to be mobile any second. It isn't a risk we should be taking."

"I agree," she said. "I'll figure something out."

CHAPTER 11

"It'll be boring," Mr. Stone insisted in an unconvincing voice—he was no actor—to his swaying, bloodshot-eyed brother in the foyer while Mickey chased Chloe the dog through the first floor. "No one fun or interesting is coming."

It was after three p.m., and the crowned prince of a small Middle Eastern country was the evening's dinner guest—major even for the Stones. To Mickey's horror, Bruce had shown up drunk and unannounced less than two hours before His Majesty was due to arrive. Mr. Stone had a great deal of business in the region, and he wasn't going to allow his gregarious younger brother, reeking of stale booze, to ruin the meeting.

As Mickey monitored Chloe to make sure she didn't pee on a carpet, Mister continued trying to convince Bruce to leave. Mickey could never tell if Bruce picked up on his brother's less-than-subtle attempts to get rid of him. Sometimes he seemed oblivious, and other times he seemed to be trolling Cecil, daring him to come out and just ask him to leave.

Paul sidled up to Mickey and whispered, with a wink, "Who makes your job harder, your wife or Bruce?"

"Today? Bruce," he said.

Serving actual royalty wasn't a situation Mickey had ever been in before. After "graduating" from butler school in February–he'd gotten a certificate in the mail and everything–he'd called in his included "one-on-one" with his butler school instructor to ask how he was to refer to the prince.

"His Royal Highness," Simon had said, and Mickey–not for the first time–felt an overlap between his old life and his new one. In how many shows over the years had he addressed a performer playing a royal with those exact words?

He'd googled the prince to try to figure out how large his entourage would be. He didn't know what they'd expect–to be fed? To be seated? He needed to be prepared for anything.

But Paul eased his mind.

"Last year he came with two guys," he said.

"Oh, he's been here before?" Mickey asked.

"A few times, yeah."

Eventually Bruce left, and Mickey hurriedly surveyed the house for signs of Chloe, sniffing maniacally, touching his palm to the rugs in shadowy spots.

A single black Mercedes pulled into the drive just before five o'clock.

"Right this way," Mickey said, leading the prince and four men in his wake into the parlor. There was no cocktail hour–His Royal Highness didn't drink–but they'd meet their hosts in the parlor anyway.

The prince, who was younger than Mickey by a few years, had a youthful energy. His white robe billowed behind him as he walked, his men nearly jogging to keep up with his brisk clip.

He greeted Mr. Stone by gripping his host's right hand while covering it with his left and giving it three pumps, a gesture that surprised Mickey not only for its intimacy but because it struck him as so very American, something a football coach might do.

As the group migrated to the dining room and began to take their seats, a commotion erupted in the front of the house.

Barking.

Both Mr. and Mrs. Stone's heads whipped toward Mickey in panic. It was Chloe.

"Pardon," Mickey said, hurrying to the front door to find it standing open. In the doorway, holding the knob for balance, stood Bruce. He was yelling at Chloe, who held a bunched drape in her large jaws.

"Can I help you, Bruce?" Mickey said.

"What's for dinner?" Bruce said. He'd been gone for only half an hour and had already forgotten that he'd come by.

"Mr. Stone has guests this evening," Mickey said. He had to think fast. How could he get rid of Bruce without spending more time stalling? He needed to get back and start service. "Warren, and a few others. Will you be joining for dinner?" Chloe leaped on Mickey's front, leaving white fur on his black pants.

Mr. Stone's associate Warren was not actually joining them, but Mickey knew Bruce couldn't stand him—it was the first idea that came to mind.

Bruce groaned. "Sounds like a barrel of laughs. But in that case, see you tomorrow." He turned and whistled for Chloe, who barreled after him.

After watching Bruce disappear from sight, Mickey exhaled and headed back through the dining room into the kitchen to fetch the first course. Hearing him enter, Paul spun around.

"Mickey," he said, in a voice Mickey had never heard him use before. "You set the table backwards!"

Mickey groaned. *Dammit.* He'd never been formally diagnosed as dyslexic. He hadn't ever realized he was dyslexic until a few years before he met Rebecca, and only then because a girl he'd met on Tinder had suggested that he might be.

"I've wondered since our first date," she'd said. "When you insisted you'd swiped left on me instead of right. You showed me the motion and everything. I thought you just didn't know your right from your left."

She'd emailed him a free, online diagnostic test—a fifty-question survey that had ranked him so assuredly as dyslexic that he had taken three more tests, all of which came back with the same result.

It had been stunning to realize something so fundamental about himself in his thirties. How had no one ever noticed—not his mother, not any teachers, not himself? He wasn't angry that it had gone unnoticed for so long, but it just seemed odd—impossible even.

The pieces fell into place: he'd dreaded reading aloud as a kid; faked his way through reading assignments—getting summaries from friends, copying off of Wayne Sorenson's quizzes, pretending to have a headache. He'd gone into the performing arts because he was talented; that's what he'd always assumed. But had there also been another reason? On some level, had he run, not *toward* one profession but away from the many of them in which he would be expected to read well?

At first the idea that he was maybe, probably, definitely dyslexic unearthed a sadness in Mickey that he recognized as shame. He knew, intellectually, that dyslexia was nothing to be ashamed of, and he knew that it didn't mean he wasn't capable or smart. He'd clearly learned to compensate for it. He could battle his way through cold reads and first-day read-throughs and still be cast. (He did so, usually, by pulling all-nighters to memorize scripts.) But eventually he'd accepted that the unofficial diagnosis was true, and by the time he was working for the Stones, it was just a part of everyday life.

It slowly dawned on Mickey . . . in his preoccupation with Chloe earlier, and his absentmindedness as he'd set the table, he'd forgotten to check his screenshot of a formal place setting first. (Another red flag he'd missed during his catering days but that now made sense—he could never remember the proper placement of cutlery and always had to check his work against a stock photo on his phone.)

"Fuck," Paul said, shaking his head. "Sayonara, dude."

As Mr. Stone and the prince discussed oil prices, whether a free press was compatible with a monarchy (Rebecca would have died), and a beachfront property of Mr. Stone's that the prince was interested in acquiring, Mickey fixed the utensil placements as subtly as possible and proceeded with dinner service, mortified. Neither man said anything, but Mr. Stone had absolutely noticed. It was a bald, glowering error, beyond rookie. Fireable, like Paul said.

Mickey was just glad that Mrs. Stone wasn't in attendance.

Early the following morning, Mrs. Stone was out on a walk and Mickey and Paul were in the kitchen when Mr. Stone entered wearing his golf clothes and clutching a handful of ketchup packets. As if on autopilot, even though it was barely nine a.m., Paul turned on the oven, fetched a bag of frozen nuggets from the freezer, and dumped them onto a baking sheet.

Mr. Stone took a seat at the table, and Mickey poured him a glass of room-temperature seltzer with one lime wedge.

He had come to anticipate his boss's needs, just as a good butler does: having the driver text him as Mr. Stone left the golf course so that he could fill the sink basin minutes before Mister arrived, purchasing a cushion for the countertop to make him more comfortable, setting up a sound system via Bluetooth so he could listen to Bach while soaking.

"I'm sorry about last night, sir," Mickey said. "I'm dyslexic, and I have to look at a place setting before I set the table, or I flip it."

Mr. Stone's face was blank as he considered this. "Let me see the picture," he said.

Mickey fetched his phone from the counter where he stored it during the day, found the illustration saved in his photos among the dozens of Bash's toothless smile, and held it out.

"Huh," Mr. Stone said. "I'll be damned." He sipped his seltzer. "Next week Astrid's book club meets."

Mickey knew this. Mrs. Stone's book club met monthly over lunch. He'd now catered two of their gatherings, enough to know that it could hardly be called a book club. First, it didn't seem like anyone actually read the book. They came in carrying pristine copies, bindings unbent, and talked about everything except it.

Second, as often as not, the book was chosen because it was by a local author, someone who showed up to "lead a discussion" (tell people who hadn't read it what it was about). The women all half listened while sliding into tipsiness on very, very good wine.

"Can you imagine," Mr. Stone said, "if you did that at her book club?"

Yes, he could, and picturing Astrid's rage made his stomach twist. But Mr. Stone found the idea of it happening again hilarious. A giggle bubbled out of the old man, and then another, until he was cackling, high-pitched and wild. He threw his head back, tears in his eyes.

After a few seconds, Paul and Mickey couldn't help but join in. For a minute, the three men laughed from their bellies in the morning light.

Thank God it was last night and not any other, Mickey thought.

Rebecca had brought up the idea of asking Mr. Stone for an interview several times, and Mickey had put her off, saying it wasn't a great time. But finally he relented, with the caveat that she ask only when her and Mr. Stone's paths crossed naturally. He wasn't going to bring her in to interrupt his boss's routine to ask a favor.

As luck would have it, when she arrived the morning after Mickey's place-setting mishap, she found Mr. Stone examining his golf clubs on the porch.

"Good morning, Mr. Stone," Rebecca said.

"Morning," he said. "She's upstairs."

"Great," she said, balancing Bash on her right hip. "I actually wanted to ask—I'd like to interview you for my column if you can spare a half hour. Not now, of course. At a convenient time."

"I don't do media," he said without pause.

"May I ask why?" she asked. She'd expected this to be his initial response.

"Because it doesn't matter what I say," he said. "You'll spin it to suit your purposes. And that's fine. There's nothing wrong with that. You have your purposes, and I have mine. But our purposes are not aligned."

"My purpose in interviewing you would be to understand your perspective," she said.

He laughed, a big, hearty laugh.

"You don't believe that?" she asked.

"I believe that would be your purpose in interviewing me, yes," he conceded. "I do not believe you would give a damn about my perspective as you were writing about me."

That was technically true. As a journalist, it was her job to strive for objectivity. If journalists wrote in an attempt to please their interview subjects, journalism couldn't serve the public, its highest goal.

She opened her mouth to say this, and he stopped her.

"It's nothing personal," he said, holding up a hand. "But I don't do it, so don't ask again."

"I understand," Rebecca said. "Thanks, anyway."

Upstairs, Mrs. Stone was waiting.

"Sorry to keep you," Rebecca said, setting up. "I ran into your husband downstairs and asked to interview him."

"And?"

"He said no."

"He shies away from public attention," Mrs. Stone said, pressing the yellow button. Seconds later, Mickey appeared.

"Apple slices, please, Mickey?" she said before noticing that he was already carrying a plate of them. He smiled and set them down on the coffee table.

The week before, Rebecca had arrived to find a fruit plate on the coffee table and, ravished, devoured the apple slices. (Of course the Stones had the most delicious Pink Ladies she'd ever tasted.)

Ever since, Mrs. Stone had had Mickey bring up apple slices. It was a small gesture, a thoughtful act that Rebecca appreciated—even if it was really her husband who was doing the work.

"Thanks, Mickey," she said, setting down the baby. Just after Mickey disappeared, Bash began to cry, and Rebecca suppressed a curse.

For the entire weekend he hadn't stopped nursing. She'd googled possible causes for his voracity, and they'd ranged from low milk supply to a growth spurt. She planned to schedule a doctor's appointment—he would need his one-year checkup soon, anyway—but hadn't had a chance yet. In the meantime, Mickey wasn't going to take him because he couldn't. And, anyway, that wasn't going to help. Rebecca was going to have to feed him.

She'd never nursed in front of Mrs. Stone.

"I think he's hungry," she said. "Is there somewhere I can take him to nurse . . ."

"It's fine," Mrs. Stone said quickly. "But can you take notes? Or should we wait until you're finished?"

"I can write," Rebecca said. It was half true. She couldn't take notes with her left hand when he nursed on the right (even on her phone she struggled to type quickly enough with her left hand), but she could pull off the reverse. She lifted Bash under her loose, tuniclike top. He latched and grew quiet. In her right hand, she held her pen over a fresh pad of paper.

"Where did we leave off?" Mrs. Stone asked.

"Something I was wondering," Rebecca said, "is why your daughter and husband don't exactly speak?"

That was the phrase Mrs. Stone had used: "don't exactly speak."

Mrs. Stone sighed.

"Ten or so years ago, Elle came home from college convinced by some class about the labor movement that her father was evil. Of course, capitalism is to blame for everything. She confronted him about his investments, and they argued.

"She threw a tantrum—crying, screaming—and said she couldn't stay here. Of course, she kept accepting our tuition money . . ." Mrs. Stone, making her almost-eye-roll face. "But she's refused to have a relationship with him since, and she won't take money from him. She'll only take it from me."

"You mean she won't ask him for it?" Rebecca asked, confused.

"No, I mean she'll only take it from me. We still keep finances separate, dear," she said. "Haven't I mentioned that?"

Rebecca's left breast was dry. Bash wasn't slowing, and she needed to switch to the right—she'd just have to listen without taking notes.

Mrs. Stone noticed her attention shift.

"Is something the matter?"

Rebecca flipped the baby.

"I can't take notes with my left hand, but it's fine," she said. "I'll just listen."

"What happened to your recorder?" Mrs. Stone asked.

"It's in my bag," she said—she took it everywhere—"but I thought you didn't like—"

"Oh, I don't care," Mrs. Stone said, waving the air. "I didn't know you before. Now I trust you."

Rebecca nodded, feeling a tinge of guilt as she reached into her bag with her left hand to pull it out and press Record. Mrs. Stone saw her as an ally. She wasn't sure how she felt about that.

As they were wrapping up, Mrs. Stone said, "We're having a dinner tomorrow night with the CEO of Cecil's company and several employees. They're all nice young people, your age. We'd love you to attend."

"That's so generous," Rebecca said, prepared to decline. But—his company? The one that owned the papers, Starr Capital? It wasn't an interview with Mr. Stone; it was, possibly, even better.

Mickey, of course, would have to work the dinner, leaving them in a bind for childcare.

"Let me talk to Mickey," she said. "Can I let you know by tonight?"

CHAPTER 12

"And if he cries for longer than ten minutes, it's probably his diaper. But you could always wait fifteen if you think it probably isn't. Like if he has pooped within the last two hours, it probably isn't."

"Got it," Samantha said, making a goofy face at Bash.

Rebecca consulted her handwritten list—was there anything she'd failed to mention? The only hard part would be bedtime. After that, Bash would be asleep and it wouldn't matter. But no one else had ever put him to bed.

"Maybe I should tell them I won't be able to make it until seven," Rebecca had suggested the night before. "So I can do bedtime."

Mickey's sudden foot tapping had belied his panic over her suggestion.

"People don't do that to the Stones," he said. Dinner started at six o'clock sharp. Guests understood this; they were invited for a particular time. It wasn't negotiable.

"It'll be fine," he'd said, and she'd agreed, still nervous.

"Is it going to be awkward for you?" Rebecca had asked before accepting the invitation.

"No," he'd said quickly. "Why would it be?"

"Because I'll be eating dinner with your employer while you

wait on us?" she'd said, stressing with her tone that the awkward-
ness was obvious.

"You realize I've done this hundreds—or thousands—of times?
Including to people I know from shows or whatever? God, that's
depressing." He looked off, lost in thought.

But not people you're married to, Rebecca had thought.

Rebecca had brushed up on Starr Capital, Mr. Stone's privately
held hedge fund, which, like its founder, was largely hidden from
public view.

The company's website consisted solely of a simple landing page:
no links, no menu, no "About Us" page. Just a title, a copyright notice, and a generic banner photograph of a beach at sunset.

From other sites, she learned that the company had netted $780
million the previous year, and since most of its holdings were newspapers circling the drain, one could infer that most of this profit
came from sucking them dry.

What "sucking them dry" meant varied, but there was no short-
age of personal accounts from reporters at these papers describing
everything from massive layoffs, to forfeiture of office space (just
work from home!), to refusal to fix basic equipment when it broke.
A copier that was never replaced (just don't print). A watercooler
that stayed empty and grew mold. One person had said he stopped
going into the office once the company had cut off the supply of
hot water for the coffee machine.

It hadn't always been clear that this gutting strategy was Mr.
Stone's aim. He'd started the fund in 2005, buying up newspapers
along with other digital media properties. At first it saw big re-
turns, and pundits speculated that Stone was interested in trans-
forming the newspaper industry into something more modern
and sustainable in the digital age. Surely he had the well-being of
his asset publications in mind, many thought; it was only through

their success that he would be successful. So the traditional view went among those who didn't know about, or weren't paying attention to, his '90s shopping mall conquest–anyway, shopping malls aren't exactly a public good.

Instead the gutting began in year three, though before the market crash . . . so that was no excuse. In recent years, leading the charge was a man Rebecca's age: London Fry, a young, New York-based venture capitalist, Wharton-grad-turned-CEO after being hired by Stone in 2014 to oversee the fund.

"His name sounds like a fish-and-chips joint," Rebecca had said when she learned of it.

"He's a nice guy," Mickey said.

"Nuh-ice guh-uy, you mean," Rebecca, attempting a British accent. "Get it? Fish and chips?"

"Your British accent is terrible," Mickey said.

"Nuh-ice guh-uy," she said again.

"He looks you in the eye, which can't be said for every guest of theirs," Mickey said.

"Huh," she said.

Well, Rebecca would get to see this phenomenon for herself, because London Fry would be at dinner.

When she arrived and Mickey showed her into the parlor for cocktails, the three men from Starr Capital joining them for dinner were already there–London, and two others also dressed in pastel button-downs and Tom Ford slacks. London wore sneakers–Stan Smith, clearly custom-made, with an LF on the side–but the others were in loafers.

"Rebecca is a writer. She's working with me on my memoirs," Mrs. Stone introduced her.

"Nice to meet you," said London, reaching out a hand and smiling widely. He had Joel Osteen teeth, too white, crowding his mouth.

He was at least six foot three with a full head of wavy hair gelled back. It was obvious he was the most magnetic of the three men, the others trailing behind him in all ways.

In the dining room, Mrs. Stone sat at one end of the table and Mr. Stone at the other, which struck Rebecca as a little funny, a caricature of wealthy people dining. On one long side of the table sat the other two associates, and across from them, Rebecca and London.

As they took their seats, London resumed telling a story he must have been telling before she'd arrived. It involved a business meeting in which someone had requested strawberry-flavored Fanta, the soft drink, and made clear that no agenda items could be discussed until it was found.

"So I have Christy walking in and out of every Midtown deli looking for strawberry Fanta," he said, "while we all make small talk about the heat wave."

Polite chuckles peppered the space while Mickey served a chartreuse pea soup in shot glasses, a sprig of fresh mint popping out of each one. Rebecca tried not to make eye contact with him as she took hers and thanked him, unsure if the avoidance was for her sake or his.

Watching him cater was as strange as watching him act.

Days after meeting Mickey, she'd gone to his first play, an off-Broadway debut that ran for only two weeks. It was the worst theatrical performance she'd ever seen, but Mickey was spectacular in it: adorable, acting his heart out. God, she'd had no idea how precious acting could be—so vulnerable, so human. After the show they'd convened outside on the sidewalk. It was cold, and he'd been wearing a charcoal overcoat and a black cashmere scarf speckled in pills after a decade of New York winters.

"So what'd you think?" he'd asked.

"*You* were fantastic," she'd told him.

He'd laughed and kissed her.

Now, she watched and thought about how good he was at

pretending—it was how he succeeded at acting, and at this job. He wasn't Mickey, right now. He was playing a butler.

Suddenly, she felt deeply sad. He should be onstage, not on duty. He should be invisible because he was in character, not invisible because he was carrying a platter of tiny soups. Even without a voice, he could be doing so much more, so much better. If only her writing would lead to something so he could quit this nonsense.

"So Astrid, you're writing a memoir?" one of the associates asked. "That sounds like fun."

"I'm writing nothing. Rebecca is doing it for me," she said. "I just talk, which I'm very good at."

They all turned to Rebecca, who smiled but wasn't sure what to say.

"What other biographies have you ghostwritten?" London asked. "Anyone we'd know?"

"None," she said. "This is my first."

"Rebecca is a reporter," Mrs. Stone said.

"Oh. For us?" London asked as Mickey delivered his Arnold Palmer. She wondered if he didn't drink. He struck her as the type to refrain so he could hit the gym at five a.m. and follow it up with green juice.

"I actually write an online column for *New York* magazine."

London finished off his soup shot in a quick sip and dabbed his lips with his napkin as Paul, in chef's whites, peeked out from the kitchen, surveying the diners' progress.

It hadn't escaped Rebecca that of the myriad house staff she encountered every day—at least a dozen people, from the gardener to the cleaning crew—everyone was Hispanic except for the two men in the positions of authority, Mickey and Paul. And Mickey had had no experience coming in.

"Rebecca's beat is wealth inequality," Mr. Stone said.

"Oh," London said, openly surprised. So her presence at the table was as odd to him as it was to her—and equally surprising to her was that Mr. Stone had so readily outed her. She wondered if Mickey had heard this exchange from the kitchen.

For the rest of the meal, London dominated the conversation, changing the subject back to their mutual business acquaintances and focusing his attention on Mr. Stone, whom he called Cecil. The next few courses came out, all tiny servings accompanied by individual glasses of wine.

Rebecca noticed that while all of the pours were light, Mrs. Stone's was lighter. When Mickey filled her glass, her eyes cut to the level, both of them so laser focused on precisely how much he poured that the intensity of their gazes seemed it could burst the glass.

Still, she hadn't witnessed her snap at anyone, yet.

Mickey brought out the food and others bussed the table. The entire team was robotic, working in perfect synchrony and so efficiently that no one ever sat behind an empty dish, dirty utensil, or spattering of crumbs for more than a few seconds.

The conversation proceeded through innocuous topics—the arts gala Mrs. Stone was chairing, and the works that would be featured in the auction; the trip abroad that London was planning for his family over the summer; the book written by Mr. Stone's friend about China's rise as a global threat that everyone must read, because it was brilliant. (Once, Rebecca had asked Mickey what billionaires talk about, and he'd answered, "Art and China." It had seemed hyperbolic to her at the time. Now, here they were, discussing art and China.)

Then the chitchat drifted to a flyer that had been placed in all of the mailboxes in the neighborhood.

"What flyer?" she asked.

"Zealotry," Mr. Stone said. "A lunatic's doing."

"She hasn't seen it? She should see it. It's great," London said, flagging Mickey by lifting his finger into the air. Rebecca cringed.

"Do you have that flyer for her to see?" he asked. Mickey disappeared and, moments later, reentered. He handed her a xeroxed sheet that stated in large, bold print: DO YOU KNOW WHO YOUR NEIGHBOR IS? In lengthy paragraphs of tiny, unpunctuated print that did, indeed, scream *wacko*, it went on to assert that Cecil Stone—"American demon"—was evil, citing the papers he'd closed and the malls he'd turned into suburban wastelands. Rebecca skimmed; there was too much to read in the moment, but although the tone and style reflected someone unhinged, there was some truth to the allegations.

"Absolutely ridiculous," Mr. Stone said. "It was in everyone's mailbox. The funny part is, they say I used newspaper money to buy my houses. I didn't use a dime of that money."

London and his associates laughed like this was hilarious.

Rebecca had read about people protesting not only outside of Mr. Stone's home in the Hamptons but also outside London's Hamptons home. She knew that many of the thousands employed and thousands laid off by them—not just journalists but printers, carriers—were vocally upset about their business operations.

Before she realized what was happening, Mickey had taken the flyer from her hands and was interrupting to offer drink refills. This was how he was so good at his job! His subtle control of the room!

"People don't like that other people have more than they do," London said, nodding at Mickey's offer for a refill without pausing. "It's rudimentary human psychology. It pisses them off for anyone to accumulate wealth, and they can't see past that basic fact to understand that wealth creation is a boon to the economy and that they benefit from it in endless ways, from employment opportunities to a strong market."

Even though he was looking at his colleagues as he spoke, Rebecca sensed that he was speaking to her. She kept her eyes lowered—she felt like she was in a first-year political science seminar, and London was the overconfident private school kid.

"I imagine the wealth inequality reporter has thoughts on that," Mr. Stone said, a hint of amusement in his voice.

Rebecca smiled tightly. She was certain Mickey did not want her to take this on.

"I think it will surprise no one that I have views on wealth accumulation and its impact on society," she said, trying to sound lighthearted.

"What about wealth accumulation in order to preserve democracy?" London said, suddenly defensive.

"What do you mean?" Rebecca asked, filling with dread.

"Starr Capital invests in dying news organizations. If not for us, the local news industry would be dead by now."

Unable to stifle a laugh, Rebecca attempted to mask it as a cough. But she saw London's wounded expression and realized she hadn't succeeded.

"Are you kidding?" she asked, taking advantage of the fact that Mickey had just stepped out of the room. London raised his eyebrows, a look meant to convey cluelessness.

Either he actually believed what he was saying, or he was testing her to see just how gullible she was. Mickey entered, and she could tell that he was trying to catch her eye. She avoided his gaze.

"There is one reporter in Vallejo, California, right now," she said. "One. That's a city of one hundred twenty thousand people."

Now London laughed.

"If we hadn't bought Vallejo? Guess what? Vallejo wouldn't have one reporter. It would have zero."

She said nothing, focusing on her breath.

"We saved newspapers," London pressed. "Nearly every paper we own is one we bought out of bankruptcy. If we hadn't made those cuts, they'd be history."

"You're turning off the lights to sell the lightbulbs. And firing all the staffs," Rebecca said. The seal had been broken. Her anger was rising, her pulse, gaining speed. "How is that saving anything?"

He snickered. "That's cute. No one is working in the dark."

"That's not what the people working in the dark say," she said.

She sensed Mickey hovering behind her, almost as if he was about to reach out and clap a hand over her mouth.

"Maybe they were working in the dark for a few days before we relocated—we do seek out more economical office space for our holdings. I'll give you that," said London.

"Weeks," she said. "They haven't had lights for weeks."

"Aren't reporters supposed to have thick skin?" London smiled and looked around the table. His colleagues chuckled. The Stones didn't. They looked interested, but not alarmed. It was enough to encourage her to continue.

Rebecca cleared her throat. "My point is that the cuts appear to be unnecessary and extreme, and for short-term gain, which ultimately leads to the demise of the papers. So it's not actually saving them. You must know this."

"Is that a quote from Bob Waterfield? Easy for him to say." Bob Waterfield was the publisher of the *Boulder Sun* before it shuttered, and the most outspoken critic of Starr.

"An alternative model would be, say, the *Omaha Daily*," Rebecca continued, ignoring his remark. "Stuart Perkins bought it out of bankruptcy and now it's doing better than it has in years. Or Gannett."

"Ha! Gannett owns, like, a hundred dailies and thousands of weeklies. You don't think Gannett is a threat to local journalism?"

"Well, yes, of course. But in a different way," she said.

Mickey had left and returned with the final course, a cheese plate. He loudly announced each of the cheeses, swiftly glaring at her as he carefully pronounced their French names.

"I'm not sure it's so different," London mumbled as he sliced himself a triangle of Provençal Comté.

"What about the reporters who have tried to talk to you?" Rebecca asked.

"I've done interviews," London said, now openly annoyed. "Google it."

"I mean your employees who want to talk to you about their

future with the company. They say they've written you letters asking for a meeting and haven't heard back," she said as Mickey reached her with the plate of cheese and jabbed his knee into her thigh below the table. She shoved his leg away with her hand.

"I haven't gotten any letters like that," he said. "I don't know what you're talking about."

As they all picked at the cheese and sipped the sweet, violet wine in silence, Rebecca glanced at Cecil and Astrid Stone. Neither appeared at all fazed, their faces blank and easy.

After dinner, Rebecca left to relieve Samantha, and Mickey stayed on to clean up and shut down the house for the night.

Waiting up for him, she'd wondered if she'd gone too far. But no self-respecting journalist would have sat there and not taken the opportunity to talk to London Fry (since Mr. Stone himself wouldn't answer any questions) about his determination to orchestrate the demise of journalism.

As it sunk in that she might have lost both of their jobs, however, she started to second-guess her doggedness at the table. One person she hadn't been thinking about during that conversation had been Mickey. She had a fun little side project going with Mrs. Stone, but he was the one who had to work there sixteen hours a day.

The saying was "don't shit where you eat," but she'd shat where *he* ate.

Just before eleven, he came in, dropping his keys on the counter without looking at her on their new sofa—a plush, creamy sectional from Restoration Hardware with enormous, dream cushions. It had cost three months' rent.

"Sorry," she said. "I got carried away."

He sighed and opened the fridge. "Do we have anything to eat?"

"Frozen pizza?" she said. Usually, these days, he ate leftovers at work with Paul. "You didn't eat at work?"

He shook his head. "I just needed to get out of there."

"Here," she said, going to the kitchen and opening the freezer to pull out the pizza. I'll throw this in. Sit down. You've been on your feet all night."

He reached for her, pulling her into a hug, which surprised her, but then he groaned and pulled back, squeezing her shoulders with his hands.

"Why did you do that?" he said through clenched teeth.

"I got carried away," she said again, setting the oven to 425 degrees. "Do you think I'm fired?"

"Oh, you're definitely fired," Mickey said. At least he was laughing. "The only question is whether I am, too."

"No way. You aren't going to be let go just because I got a little real."

"You accused my boss of destroying American journalism. In front of his employees. And his wife."

"Yeah. I could have said so much worse, though," Rebecca said. "That's the irony. I didn't even mention how loss of local reporting undermines democracy. And how because of them, fake news from Russian bots polarizes the country and so he's the reason America is dying. See? I held back."

"Rebecca, you were their dinner guest."

"I'm still me. They knew what they were getting. I'm not going to turn myself off just because someone has nineteen more zeros in his bank account than I do."

"They were serving you wine that cost thirty-five thousand dollars a bottle."

"I didn't ask for that. I didn't really like any of those wines. I wouldn't have paid more than fourteen dollars for any of them. Except maybe the first."

He shook his head.

"I'm going to bed and hope I have a job tomorrow," he said, heading to the bedroom and shutting the door behind him.

"You don't want the pizza?" she called after him.

"No," he said from the other side of the door.

She turned off the oven and went to the bathroom to brush her teeth.

Moments later, lying next to him, she whispered, "Are you mad?"

"I don't know, Rebecca," he mumbled. "I'm tired."

"Do you think, if you're mad, part of it is because you don't feel like you can speak your mind around them? But I can?"

He opened his eyes.

"I don't have anything I'm secretly thinking that I'm not saying. I don't care that he's a billionaire. I don't care that he owns newspapers and doesn't run them like you want him to. You don't get that, but I don't care."

He rolled over, and she lay there in the dark, staring up at the ceiling.

Maybe he was upset about having to serve her. After weeks of hauling the writing desk to and from the study every day, slicing up apples, and watching Bash while he tried to work, he'd had to serve her at the table with his clients—even if it was subconscious, she could imagine him resenting her.

"I'm sorry," she whispered again. "From now on, when I'm at the Stones', I'll try to refrain from speaking truth to power." She said "truth to power" in a self-deprecating tone to make him laugh. At first she thought it had worked; he laughed for the first time that night.

But then she realized he was laughing at her.

"Don't worry," he said. "I'm pretty sure you aren't going to be invited back."

When Mickey had awoken the morning after the 2016 election and found the apartment empty, he'd wondered if Rebecca had gone to get a coffee (decaf—she was five months pregnant) from their local bakery. It had taken him a moment to remember the events of the night before, and when he had, he'd groaned, knowing how upset his wife was going to be about the outcome.

He didn't like Trump, of course, but the day before—the day of the election—he'd barely thought about it. With a free day, he'd stationed himself in the Barnes & Noble café, having collected all of the books he could find on fatherhood (there weren't many) and, for three hours, made his way through the unpurchased stack. He'd learned that he should wake up in the night to help with feedings. *Do not offer and wait for an answer*, the book had counseled. *Just do it.*

He'd jotted down notes in a small Moleskine, studied the diagrams of changing a diaper, of safely installing a car seat, of correctly positioning a newborn in a body carrier across the chest. Suffocation, hip dysplasia, SIDS—the dangers were terrifying.

Back at the apartment, he'd found her napping and gotten started on the vegetarian chili they'd serve at their election party that night. After slicing onions, peeling red peppers, and draining kidney beans, he'd realized it was nearly five, and he still hadn't voted. Did he care enough to trek all the way over to his polling place, Frank Sinatra School of the Arts?

No, he didn't.

It wasn't that Mickey didn't care about politics. He'd like to pay fewer taxes. He'd like universal health care. Gun control—of course he supported it; he wasn't a monster. But the NRA was so powerful that whoever was elected didn't seem all that consequential. Racism, and all the phobias—those were bad, bad, bad, but elections didn't make or break those. Culture did.

To Mickey, politics felt more like a lightning rod than anything, drawing out people's grievances in a blaze of noise and spark, then nullifying them. They got nothing done, year after year, election after election. It was more a fireworks show than a working system of change. Righteous anger over inequality was projected onto elections because those felt simpler, easier to wrap one's mind around, than how to change people.

To change people was gritty and complicated. Maybe impossible.

He hadn't voted in the end. He lived in New York; it didn't matter anyway.

And then the bad guy had won.

Hungover the next morning, he'd forced himself out of bed and into the shower. He'd stayed under the hot water until it began to turn lukewarm, and had just stepped out from the bathroom wrapped in a towel when Rebecca had returned, yoga mat in hand.

"How was yoga?" he'd asked.

"I'm glad I went," she said. "The teacher asked who was afraid now that if you're not white you have to go back into hiding. This guy raised his hand. It was so sad."

"I doubt anyone could be that afraid in a New York yoga studio," he said.

"That's not what she was talking about," she'd said with a look of disgust, peeling off her top.

Over the coming days, it had become clear that her reaction to the outcome of the election was personal, like by voting in the wrong guy, America had done something to her. She stopped coming to bed with him, staying up into the early hours of the morning reading think pieces on American discontent on the Internet. All she wanted to talk about was how disappointed she was in people.

"I now understand that history happened because of people like us," she said one evening.

Or at least like me, he thought. *I didn't vote*. He considered saying it as a joke, then thought better of it. He'd never told her.

CHAPTER 13

Mickey was relieved that their first meeting after the dinner, Mrs. Stone acted like nothing out of the ordinary had happened. Meanwhile, there was something more important that he had to worry about.

It was a silver Incan alpaca worth $1.2 million (he'd consulted the books). It was small—only about four inches tall and five inches long—a modest piece in the Stones' art collection. The alpaca lived on a table in the library alongside a Jeff Koons metal kangaroo and a Chagall painting of an emerald-colored donkey worth more than most houses in Palm Beach. The pocket-sized alpaca was the cutest of the animals, adorable even, especially next to the reflective kangaroo and mystical donkey.

The Monday after the dinner party, Mrs. Stone noticed that it was missing.

All of the regular staff knew that while the Stone home was armed with exterior security cameras on every facet, inside there were none. Mr. Stone was more paranoid about hacking and government overreach than he was about theft (everything was insured, after all). Nothing of this magnitude had ever happened in the home before. They'd had bottles of brandy or wine go missing, perhaps a towel or sheet set or two—and each time, someone had been fired as a result.

But the disappearance of the alpaca was monumental, a breach that led Mrs. Stone to promptly assemble the full staff to discuss where it might have gone—the full staff minus Anna.

"Where is Anna?" she asked.

"She's home sick today," said Bernice, also on the cleaning crew.

When no one reported knowing or seeing anyone touch the alpaca, Mrs. Stone dismissed them all and pulled Mickey aside.

"Someone here knows what happened," she said. "I want you to get to the bottom of this. Today."

But as Mickey asked around, feeling sheepish that he had to press his coworkers on this, he learned nothing. Either everyone was being loyal to the thief, or (more likely, he thought) it was true that nobody had any clue what had happened to the sculpture.

At dusk, just before dinner, he stood in the doorway of Mrs. Stone's office to report on his findings.

"No one saw anything," he said.

"Precious items don't just go missing, Mickey," she said.

"I know," he agreed. "I'm as baffled as you are."

"Well, someone is going to have to pay. If we don't figure out who is responsible, we'll have to decide who was responsible."

"Yes, ma'am," he said, understanding her not-so-veiled threat.

Over the coming days, a rumor emerged among the staff that Bruce had taken the alpaca. It wasn't out of the question—he'd come by for a couple of hours the afternoon before it had been discovered missing. The problem was that there was no way for Mickey to suggest this or inquire further without offending the Stones.

"I can't say, 'I think your brother stole your statue,'" he said to Anna when she brought him the latest intel.

"Why not?" she asked. "Everyone knows how Bruce is."

But Mickey couldn't find the words or the opportunity, and as the days passed and neither Mr. nor Mrs. Stone mentioned the alpaca, he hoped they'd decided to file the insurance claim and move on, though he knew it was unlikely.

Sure enough, the next Saturday morning, Mrs. Stone showed up in the kitchen after breakfast while they were starting the dishes. It startled both Paul and Mickey to hear her voice behind them.

"Anna's no longer with us," Mrs. Stone said as she entered. "After interviewing select members of the staff, I concluded that she was most likely the one responsible. I gave her the opportunity to return it, and she didn't. She's now been terminated. Grace will be promoted into her position."

She exited without awaiting their reaction.

"Damn," Mickey muttered.

"Savage," Paul whispered, handing him a silver serving spoon to dry.

"You know the saying that something has to be in your life for three months before you dream about it?" Paul asked.

He and Mickey stood at the counter plating an endive salad with sheep's cheese.

"I haven't heard that," Mickey said.

Paul was learning French on Duolingo in order to speak it when the Stones went to their private island in the French Caribbean, which they did several times a year. It was just off the French-speaking side of St. Maarten, and so that was where he went to gather supplies and local ingredients, any foods they hadn't flown in with them. He'd struggled to communicate during every previous trip, and he figured it was time to learn French and save himself the hassle.

"I finally dreamed in French last night. It took four months."

"No way," Mickey said.

"This woman—beautiful, hair down to her waist, big eyes, killer body, told me that it wasn't important," Paul said.

"What wasn't important?"

"Whatever we were talking about. I don't remember. She said *n'importe quoi*. I woke up so excited, dude. You have no idea."

"So we're doing nothing to acknowledge his birthday," Mickey confirmed, ignoring Paul's dream review.

"Nothing," Paul said. "He doesn't want it mentioned."

Other than a champagne toast and Mr. Stone's favorite dessert, poppy-seed ice cream with a forty-year aged balsamic vinegar, nothing about the meal being served was to be out of the ordinary: five small courses, all paired with the appropriate wines.

Mickey entered with the first course, a puffed cauliflower with green orange gelée and wild sorrel.

In the dining room, Rebecca was seated with the group.

They'd been wrong about her not being invited back. On the fourth day after the dinner, Mrs. Stone had said, "We're having some friends to dinner for Cecil's birthday on Sunday. Would you like to join us?"

Both Mickey and Rebecca had been baffled, but she'd accepted, seeing no other choice.

The evening's other guests included an older couple—the Webers, from down the street—and a fiftysomething woman Mickey hadn't met before, also there solo. She wore a blazer that suited her but didn't quite look sleekly fitted enough to be custom-made, a refreshing change for a guest in the Stone home.

"Catherine," Mr. Stone said, "how is the beauty industry faring in these times?"

"Beauty is thriving, Cecil," she said. "Beauty is always in." She winked at Mrs. Stone, who smiled back politely as she flagged Mickey to refill her water glass. The woman had a warm smile, a thick midwestern accent, and a no-nonsense demeanor that left Rebecca feeling almost like she was with a family friend.

"It's been down for the last year, no?" he said.

"I mean, listen, consumer behavior is always changing," she said. "But makeup is still a thing. Trust me, makeup isn't going anywhere."

Mr. Stone turned to Rebecca. "Do you wear makeup?"

"Me?" she said. "Um, yes. Some."

"All women wear makeup, Cecil," Mrs. Stone said.

"I know that, but I didn't know if the young people do."

"Gen Z is very into makeup," Catherine said. "They like the more natural look, but they wear it."

"Well, I'm not that young," Rebecca said with a chuckle. "What do you do?" she asked, realizing as soon as she spoke how ridiculous the question sounded. "Do" was for someone who had a job. The people who came to dinner at the Stones didn't have jobs; they had empires.

"I'm CEO of Aura," she said. Rebecca would later google her: Catherine Priest.

"Catherine has had a career in food, pharma, mobile technology..."

"Not pharma," she said. "But the others, yes."

"Oh, great," Rebecca said, lifting her fork. *Oh, great?* Somehow, at the last dinner she had not realized that she had no idea how to speak to these people if she wasn't debating with them. "I love Aura."

"Do you?"

"I like that you carry vegan brands, and I like that the store feels happy."

Catherine beamed at her. "It does feel happy, doesn't it? Teens love us. We're the number one beauty destination for them."

"What's vegan makeup?" Mrs. Weber asked.

"A product that contains no animal or animal-derived ingredients," Catherine said.

"Like cows?"

Catherine and Rebecca both laughed then stopped when they saw that Mrs. Weber wasn't laughing.

"Sure," Catherine said. "Anything animal or animal-derived. So nothing they produce, either. No dairy, no animal-based oils. It's all plant-based."

"How do you explain last year?" Cecil asked between bites.

"I'm not concerned about it," she said. He must be an investor, Rebecca thought, to keep bringing the conversation back to the company's performance. "Business in every industry is cyclical, Cecil; you know that as well as I do. Younger consumers have gotten very into skin care lately, and that's why we've made a quick pivot in that direction."

"Skin care, like moisturizer?" Mrs. Weber asked. Mr. Weber hadn't spoken a word.

"Exactly," Catherine said. "Serums, CC creams, eye creams, physical sunscreen. It's all big right now."

"I never used sunscreen," Mrs. Weber said. "My whole life, I never used it."

"Cecil has had skin cancer and still doesn't wear it," Mrs. Stone said.

Mr. Stone grunted then said, looking at Catherine, "You don't think it's because everything has gone digital?"

She shook her head. "Beauty is about human connection, and our guests love to come into our stores. They want to test out colors."

"I could never order a lipstick online," Mrs. Weber said, turning to Mrs. Stone and then Rebecca. "Can you imagine?"

Rebecca shook her head, obliging.

"That's why we're going global, Cecil. This isn't public yet, but we'll be opening thirty new U.S. stores in the fall," she said. "And one in Canada soon. After a very good first quarter this year."

"When is your announcement?" Mr. Stone asked.

"May," she said.

He motioned to Mickey that he was ready for the next course.

"And you know, makeup is becoming more democratic, more egalitarian. We finally have shades in mainstream brands for skin colors that aren't white!"

"Do Black people wear makeup?" Mrs. Weber said.

"Of course," Catherine said. This time, Rebecca managed to hold in her laugh. "Their options have just been more limited in mainstream beauty. Until now."

"That reminds me," Mrs. Weber said, turning to Rebecca, "maybe you can explain something to me. What's the deal with all this political correctness?"

Rebecca opened her mouth but no sound came out.

"What's the deal, meaning . . ." she said.

"I don't understand the goal of it," Mrs. Weber said.

Oh boy. Rebecca was glad that Mickey was in the kitchen.

"I would say it's a reaction to the fact that, for a long time, only white men were valued in this country," she said.

"I see, thank you," Mrs. Weber said, satisfied, as if Rebecca had, in one sentence, clarified everything she'd ever wondered or needed to know about her question.

As the meal progressed, Mrs. Weber continued to interrupt the flow of conversation with random questions for Rebecca, ones that were sweeping and impossible to answer, or overly personal.

What was the appeal of email?

Did people actually enjoy rap music?

Was the silver streak in Rebecca's hair real?

It was as if she'd never been around a person under forty.

Rebecca would do her best to respond, and Mrs. Weber would nod, seemingly satisfied, and move on. Not once did she ask a follow-up.

When Mickey entered with champagne for a toast to Mr. Stone—poured from a bottle that she knew probably cost thirty grand, as much as his student loan balance—he grinned at her, and she sipped her tea to hide her face.

"Mickey," Mrs. Stone said. "Would you do us the pleasure of singing 'Happy Birthday' to my husband?"

Mickey's face flattened. Rebecca could tell he was trying to determine if she was kidding. She wasn't.

"I know, dear, you don't like us to acknowledge your birthday," she said to her husband, "but we have a professional in our midst."

He doesn't have a voice, Rebecca thought. He hadn't told them.

Paul, the professional he was, must have overheard the request and appeared to take the tray of champagne glasses from Mickey, passing them around as Mickey took a few steps back, cleared his throat, and raised his chin.

Her husband, once he committed, was not going to let anyone down.

"Happy birthday," he sang, arm raised, looking directly at his boss. His voice was definitely raspy, but they probably thought he just had allergies or something. It sounded kind of cool, if you didn't understand that this was how he would always sound now, forever. After drawing out the last note, he playfully bowed, grinning, to their light applause.

"That was excellent," Mrs. Stone said. "Bravo."

"Thank you, Mickey," Mr. Stone said.

"He used to work at a restaurant like Macaroni Grill in high school, so he's used to this," Rebecca said, before realizing that no one at the table was likely to have heard of the Italian chain restaurant where the waiters serenaded the diners.

"To Cecil," Mrs. Stone said, raising her glass. They all followed suit. "May your next forty years be as good as the last."

They all laughed and sipped, and Rebecca had a vision of a snapshot being taken of her in this moment—one of those paparazzi photos that surfaces to expose the hypocrisy of a public figure. *See? She's a fraud.*

"Thirty-five?" Rebecca guessed, three hours later. Just after eleven, they sat on the balcony watching a dark storm gather in the distance.

"Higher."

"Forty-five?"

"Lower. Thirty-six."

The cost of the champagne had become a game. Whenever Mickey told her the price of their wine, sometimes it was an estimate (it was easy enough to google the bottle and year) and other times it was because he'd seen the books, or Paul had been present for the purchase.

"I didn't realize," she said, changing the subject back to Mrs. Weber, "that anyone could be that removed from the world. I mean, I knew people could live in bubbles, but that was like speaking to a six-year-old for three hours. Is she always like that?"

"I've never noticed anything out of the ordinary with her until tonight," he said.

"I wondered if she had dementia or something," she said.

"I don't think so," he said. "But it was like a Google search bar come to life."

"Huh? How so?" she asked.

"You know how Google recommends searches based on what you've just asked, but they have nothing to do with what you've just asked?" He picked up his phone. "Like if I type, 'how to,' I get"—he typed—"how to make French toast, how to get rid of ants, and how to lose my belly."

"Yes," she said, laughing. "Exactly like that."

Lightning, far away, flashed across the orange sky.

"Why do you think they're friends with the Google search bar?" she asked.

He shrugged. "We're all friends with the people in our orbit. These are the people in their orbit."

She considered this.

"But they must feel like they have enough in common to want to spend time together," she said. "Otherwise, wouldn't you find a different orbit?"

"Sure," he said. "They have plenty in common. Money, art, money, money . . ."

"Like, I didn't like my orbit when I was in Tennessee. So I found a new orbit," she said. "I moved to New York."

"It seems like billionaires have all the choices in the world," he said after a moment. "But it's a pretty narrow life, I think."

"How so?" she said.

"I look at them, and I see people who have about a thousand fewer options than we do."

She gave him her most skeptical eyes.

"They will never pick up and fly to a random city in Costa Rica with no plan for where they're going to stay or what they're going to do there. Or try a new hole-in-the-wall to grab a bite just because it happened to open nearby and they want to see if it's any good. Or roam into a bookstore and pick a book off the shelf randomly, then read it."

"Right, because they'll fly to their private island on their private jet, and eat food prepared by their gourmet chef, and read whatever shows up on their bedside table because it was hand-selected for them. That doesn't strike me as a lack of choices. It strikes me as extreme privilege."

"See, not me," he said. "I think it's something different."

She thought for a few seconds. "What, being spoiled rotten?" she said.

"The saddest thing in the world," he said.

They sat in the quiet, a soft thunder echoing in the distance.

"You know, I agreed to the first dinner because I felt like I couldn't say no. I didn't want to put you in a weird position."

"Mmm," he said.

"But now I'm glad I went. If I'm just educating them even the slightest bit, that's something, you know?"

Mickey grunted, keeping to himself what he was thinking: that there was no way anything she said was changing how they thought.

CHAPTER 14

"What did people learn about Flagler that struck you as especially interesting?" Rebecca asked a room of seventy-something women. They sat primly, perched on plush furniture, ankles crossed, books resting neatly and unread in their laps.

She was met with blank stares.

When Mrs. Stone had invited Rebecca to her book club, set to discuss a new biography out about Henry Flagler, the railroad baron credited with creating modern Florida, Rebecca accepted, hoping she could skim and show up. But then Mrs. Stone had said, "Perhaps you could lead the discussion."

Upon arriving in Florida, all Rebecca had known about this guy was that his name was all over the place. The street that ran along the west bank of Lake Worth: Flagler Drive. There was Flagler College, Flagler County, Flagler Memorial Bridge. But after picking up a couple of books on the history of the region, she'd learned that as the lesser-known cofounder of Standard Oil with J. D. Rockefeller, Flagler took South Florida and, from sand, developed an empire. Building a railroad that ran from top to bottom of the state's coastline, he also erected the hotels and resorts along its path that would make tourist destinations out of Palm Beach and Miami.

Compared to those books, this one was atrocious. Hailing Flagler, Rockefeller, and their compatriots, it erased everyone else from the story. Plus, it was unjustifiably dense at five hundred pages, including every detail of every decision Flagler ever made, down to his breakfast preferences. Rebecca was certain that few, if any, women in the group would make it past the first chapter.

Indeed, over tea cakes and sandwiches that Tuesday late morning, it seemed that they were set on discussing anything else until Mrs. Stone had said, "Rebecca has agreed to lead us in a discussion of this month's book. Rebecca."

"I had no idea he died by falling down a flight of stairs!" a woman said.

"Yes, that was quite a tragic way to go," Rebecca said. The startled expressions on the other women's faces confirmed that they hadn't made it to the end.

"Anything else?" Rebecca asked.

More blank stares.

If no one was going to participate, she was going to talk about what she wanted to talk about.

"Did anyone notice that it doesn't really talk about the people who actually built the railroads and hotels?" Rebecca asked. As she expected, no one had an answer. "This isn't in the book, but after the Civil War, Flagler leased convicts—mostly Black men—from the state. It was after the Civil War, but some people say they were treated worse than slaves because they were rented, not owned. It's like how you treat an apartment when you rent it versus when you own it."

She realized as soon as the words left her mouth that the women had probably never lived in apartments.

"It was basically slavery," Rebecca said, "by another name."

"At least he didn't have slaves," the Gucci woman said. "Right? It's better than that?"

"He wasn't allowed to have slaves, Lillian," Mrs. Stone said.

"I know, but I'm just saying . . ." Lillian sank back, embarrassed.

"All of America's Founding Fathers were both good and bad," a soft-spoken woman said. "We can still acknowledge the incredible feats he accomplished."

"Right," Lillian chimed in, her confidence renewed. "We can't fault him for being human at the time." (Later, when Rebecca would tell Mickey about the meeting, they would crack up at the phrase "human at the time," and whenever one of them made a mistake, the other would say, "Can you fault me for being human at the time?")

"How do we know," a quiet woman asked, "that any of this happened? None of us were there."

"That part is interesting," Rebecca said. "In 1907, he was exposed by a journalist in a publication that you definitely know about today. Want to guess what it is?"

"The *New York Times*," Mrs. Stone said.

"The Shiny Sheet?" Lillian said.

"*Cosmo*," Rebecca said happily.

"The magazine?" the quiet woman said.

Rebecca grabbed her phone. "Here's an excerpt. *'In a new and sinister guise, slavery has again reared its hideous head, a monster suddenly emerging from the slimy sordid depths of an inferno peopled by brutes and taskmaskers in human semblance,'*" she read, "*'Whites and blacks are to-day being indiscriminately held as chattel slaves, and the manacle, lash, bloodhound, and bullet are teaching them submission without partiality to color.'*"

"Wait, white people were also enslaved?" Gucci said, noting what Rebecca had been about to point out, that the focus of the article hadn't actually been on the atrocity of ongoing Black slavery, but on the horror of *white* people's inclusion.

Rebecca nodded. "Some historians think that's the only reason why Flagler stopped getting away with it."

A long pause passed. The women exchanged uneasy glances.

"Anyway," Rebecca said, reading her crowd. "Has anyone heard the rumor that his third wife was murdered?" It wasn't in the book, but who cared at this point?

"Good grief," Mrs. Stone said. *This* the women wanted to hear. Rebecca told them about the suspicious circumstances of Flagler's wife's death not long after his own.

"You have to wonder about his death, too," Lillian said. "A fall down the stairs . . . or . . ."

And suddenly it had become a murder mystery.

Finally, it was time to wrap up, which Mrs. Stone signaled with a sharp clap.

"It's been lovely, ladies," she said, standing.

"I think we can all agree that Henry Flagler is remarkable," said a woman who appeared to be pushing ninety from the corner, her voice shaky with age.

"If not for him, Palm Beach wouldn't be here," Lillian agreed.

"We're all a product of our time," Mrs. Stone said decisively. "Every one of us here has something in our past that could make us seem terrible."

"Well said, Astrid," Lillian said. "Well said."

Back in the kitchen, Mickey and Paul were killing time until the women were through. Paul had told Mickey all about his latest trip to Vegas on his weekend off, and Mickey was half listening, half drifting, through yet another drinking and gambling story.

"Why do you think they invite Rebecca?" he asked abruptly. Paul had been around for, what was it, seven years? Eight? He flew with the Stones everywhere they went and knew them far better than anyone else on staff. "It doesn't make sense."

"Sure it does," Paul said.

Mickey raised his eyebrows.

"She's a pony," he said.

"A pony?" Mickey said, afraid he understood.

"Yeah, like a show pony. She's here for entertainment."

"It's entertainment to hear someone criticize your business and lifestyle?"

"Sure," Paul said. "Because it's not a real threat. Nothing is. It's like . . . watching a little Chihuahua yap at a German shepherd. You're like, that's cute. It's something to do. It's why they don't mind Bruce coming around, either, not really. They pretend to be annoyed. And, yeah, Bruce is a pain in the ass, but at least he offers some variety. Everybody would rather have some action than the same nothing day after day."

Mickey frowned. Now that he thought about it, Rebecca and Bruce had never been invited to dinner at the same time.

"I guess I can see that," he said, "but seems like they'd rather just be entertained by people who are like them."

"Nah. It's less interesting that way," Paul said. "Plus, she's kind of like, you know . . . uh, intel. You know, 'What are the Little People thinking'?"

"Like a spy?" Mickey said, skeptical.

"Spy is a bit much. But trust me. Rich people don't like surprises."

"Dude, we have seventeen people coming," Paul said the next Monday. "You're going to need another guy."

The lunch would be far bigger than any Mickey had served at the Stones', and for the first time since starting, he would need to bring in another guy—the small team that bussed the table didn't include anyone whom he knew well enough to feel comfortable making a server, which required a solid handle on protocol like serving from the left, among other things he didn't have time to teach anyone. The problem was, he still didn't know anybody in Palm Beach, and he didn't want to take a risk on a stranger; he'd made that mistake enough times in New York to know it was sure to backfire.

He called his closest friend, Jake, back in New York, a fellow actor in between jobs. What better excuse for a winter trip to Palm Beach, paid for with frequent-flier miles, than a cool hundred and fifty dollars for two hours of easy work with your buddy?

Jake arrived the night before the lunch, and Rebecca stayed home with Bash, who was asleep, while Mickey headed to the airport to pick up his friend.

The Arrivals area at Palm Beach International wasn't like Arrivals at any of the New York airports—no one rushed you or honked. Mickey waited by the curb with the motor running until Jake appeared, rolling his carry-on, coat in hand. He didn't need it here.

"Hey, man, Florida looks good on you," Jake said as they embraced.

Mickey's day-to-day included just enough outdoor time—supervising activity around the exterior of the house, checking on things across the property—that he'd acquired a sun-kissed glow.

"You're just not used to seeing what a person normally looks like. You've been in the tundra for months. Everyone in New York still has tundra face and will until May."

"What's tundra face?" Jake asked as he climbed in. "Never mind. I know. Pale and sad."

"Exactly."

"By Sunday I better look like I've been here or I'm staying. I'm not going back without a tan."

In under ten minutes they were seated in the apartment, drinks in hand, while Rebecca made dinner.

"Smells great," Jake said.

"Curry lentils," she said. "And naan." She'd been as excited as Mickey if not more so about Jake's visit, and she'd always liked cooking for him, a fellow vegan. He gushed about her cooking in a way most people didn't.

They stayed up well past midnight, drinking outside on the balcony. The moon was a sliver, barely there. The blue light of the pool shone up like an iridescent seabed, the kind with the glowing coral, fluorescence framing the palm trees from below, the new moon overhead unable to compete. Mickey sat on the ground at Rebecca's feet while he and Jake reminisced.

"Remember in *Cats* when . . ." Jake couldn't finish the sentence. His head dropped between his knees, laughing, and Mickey did, too, his head thrown back.

"Oh my God," Mickey said. "Rebecca, you know this story, right?"

"I don't remember," she said, happy to see him so happy.

"We were both ensemble, but I was on as Rum Tum Tugger that night. Backstage you just grab body mics—Mickey was Exotica."

"That's another cat," Mickey said.

"I figured," Rebecca said.

"All the body mics are just on this wall . . . you just grab the one with your name on it. But the audio tech had mixed ours up. Mine was labeled with Mickey's name, and Mickey's was labeled with my name. By the time we realized it, it was too late."

"How can it be too late? Can't you just switch it on the switchboard?"

Both men looked baffled, as if she'd asked an impossible question.

"No, no." Jake was shaking his head. "That's a crazy ask on the fly. You can't ask the tech that."

"And you can't just trade mics?"

"Oh, God. Do you know what *Cats* costumes look like? Getting dressed takes four departments. The wigs are like living creatures. The wire goes through your unitard—"

"Okay, I get it," she said, laughing. "So what happened?"

"Mickey had to sing 'Rum Tum Tugger' for me!" Jake howled.

"And you . . . lip-synced it?"

"Yes!" He was crying.

"Wasn't that obvious to the audience?"

"Probably," Mickey said, wiping a tear from his eye.

They dove immediately into the next story—on the *Jersey Boys* tour, which they'd also been on together.

"The guy playing Frankie Valli was feeling under the weather and said he couldn't sing the high A in the closing number. You know it . . . *Who loves you, pretty baby? Who's gonna help you through the night?*"

Rebecca nodded, though she couldn't quite recall the tune.

"But he didn't want to call out, so he asked Jake to sing the high A from offstage." Remembering that Rebecca didn't speak the language of the scale, he added, "It's like a soprano A. That's really high."

"Oh, God," Rebecca said.

"So I was standing there mic'd up, ready to sing it, and he sang it anyway."

". . . wait, and so did you?"

"Yes. We *both* sang it."

"Did it sound like two people?"

"Yes, because his voice fucking cracked! It sounded insane is what it sounded."

"Plus it blew the tech guy's ears out," Mickey said between belly laughs, "because his mic wasn't set for the high A at that point. Jake was supposed to sing it."

They were both wiped out from laughter.

As the conversation turned slippery, meandering and tequila-soaked, Mickey cupped the top of Rebecca's foot.

If only Jake knew how much they needed this visit, she thought. To be reminded of who they were before they were Floridians.

"Why be cremated or buried when you can be frozen?" a sharp-edged man with a shock of white hair asked chirpily, red laser pointer in hand.

Rebecca, plus seventeen other guests—one gentleman had showed up with an uninvited date—sat around the fully expanded dining table while the peppy man stood at the end opposite Mr. Stone, clicking on a PowerPoint presentation for which Mickey had rented a portable screen.

"Cryogenics is your only hope, at this point, of immortality. I'm sorry to say it, but even stem-cell injections aren't there yet."

"Aren't we *supposed* to get stem-cell injections?" a woman asked.

"Yes, and you can, at my lab in Nassau." Murmurs. Anyone who didn't know about stem-cell injections before was now distracted. "But those are for longevity, not for immortality."

Across the table, Jake was refilling water glasses as Mickey poured wine. Jake lifted his eyes just barely in Mickey's direction, not enough to make eye contact but merely to signal: *I am also hearing this*. Rebecca, hyperaware of the expression on her face, kept her focus on the PowerPoint, knowing that if she looked at either Mickey or Jake, she'd reveal something she shouldn't.

The speaker, without pretending otherwise, was selling spots in his graveyard freezing lab. They cost two hundred thousand apiece, pocket change for these people. But the freezing and its cost weren't a sticking point. The issue under heated debate among the lunch guests was how you ensured you'd be properly restored to life once the technology allowed for it: in whose hands were you to leave your dead but preserved flesh, entrusted to others to revive? The stakes were enormous.

Over foie gras ice cream, a lively discussion erupted. Certainly you couldn't rely on cryogenicists of the future to rejuvenate your icy remains. Not unless they were accountable to other people—*living* people—who were personally invested enough to enforce any agreements made before your death. And even then, how could you be sure that it was done with adequate care and attention? What if you didn't have children and grandchildren? What if you did, but they were ingrates?

The unarticulated question at the heart of the debate was: How will the people of the future know how very special we are?

It was Mr. Stone, who had been relatively quiet throughout the afternoon, who finally put the debate to rest. Leave money to a foundation earmarked to oversee your revitalization, with a hitch: funds should be designated as unavailable until your successful return.

"Not a trivial amount," he added. "A motivating sum."

They nodded slowly, all pondering, presumably, what sum would be considered "motivating."

"Ah," said a British woman drenched in sapphires. "Brilliant."

Jake mixed Moscow mules in the copper mugs that he'd given them as a wedding present and that they never used unless Jake came over and made the drinks himself, while Rebecca and Mickey bathed Bash in the kitchen sink. He lay on a baby-shaped strip of teal foam and giggled when Rebecca pointed the faucet at his toes.

"They talked about immortality like they were debating which show to see on a Saturday night," Jake said, summarizing for them what they already knew. He looked at Rebecca. "You have to write about it."

Lifting Bash from the sink and wrapping him in a hooded lion towel, Rebecca said, "I don't want to get Mickey fired." Then, after a moment, she added, "But I want to write about it." She looked at Mickey. "Would they read it? Or if they did, would they care?"

"I don't think they'd read it . . . ?" Mickey said, ending on a question mark.

Paul calling her a "show pony" came to mind. He hadn't said anything about that conversation to Rebecca, but it nagged at him, this feeling that she was being exploited in some way.

On the other hand, he knew that his wife was, in her own way, also exploiting the Stones. Both parties were playing a game in which they thought they were calling the shots.

"Guys, I'm going to be honest. I don't think it's that crazy," Mickey said.

"What isn't?" Rebecca asked from the living room, as she diapered Bash on a towel on the floor.

"Not wanting to die," Mickey said, tapping his icy copper mug against Jake's. "Hope in technology. All of it. I think it's easy to make fun of because we don't have the option, but if we had the means, you never know. We might do it, too."

Rebecca threw him a *really?* expression.

"Fine, *I* might," he said.

"Speak for yourself," Rebecca said. "Do you know how bad that is for the planet?"

"Can you not see why someone might want to, though?"

Rebecca shrugged and disappeared into the bedroom with Bash to fetch his footie pajamas. When they returned, he wore a flannel onesie spotted with bananas.

"I thought more about it, and no, I'd never do it," she said.

"Wait, you wouldn't?" Mickey said. "I'm confused—would you, or wouldn't you?"

"Shut up," she said.

"So you're going to write about it?" Jake said. She turned to Mickey and waited.

Maybe it didn't matter, he thought. He was tired of caring. If she wrote about the dinner, maybe that would get their attention and they'd stop inviting her over so much.

"Write whatever you want. Fine by me," Mickey said.

"Done," Jake said. "Don't leave out the part about the price differential based on how much of your body you want included."

"I thought it was a two-hundred-thousand flat fee," Mickey said.

"That's for your whole body," Rebecca said. "You might have been in the kitchen during that part. For eighty, he'll do just your head."

On March 3, Bash's first birthday, Fran, Mickey, and Rebecca drove a mile over the bridge to the Society of the Four Arts sculpture garden for a picnic. In a cooler bag in the trunk, she'd packed the vanilla vegan cake she'd made as his Smash Cake. The idea was for the new one-year-old to cover himself in icing and crumbs by smashing it into bits.

"That looks delicious!" Fran had said upon entering the kitchen before they left. Her mother-in-law wore giant shades and a violet sundress with a yellow silk scarf tied around her head.

"I want everything you wear, Fran," Rebecca had said, fingering the scarf. "And I'm pretty sure the cake is not delicious." Rebecca loved cooking but wasn't a baker. Her baked goods never turned out quite right—they were too gooey, or fell apart, or just had lumps.

"Did you follow the recipe?" Mickey asked. "You know it's not like cooking. You have to be precise with baking."

"Mm-hmm," Rebecca said. "Is that why your baked goods always turn out so well?"

Mickey gave her butt a pat with his hand. He didn't bake.

"Please," Fran said. "I'm here. And your mother."

She'd packed the rest of the picnic basket, insisting on it after borrowing their car to buy supplies: a checkered picnic blanket, and two bags of fruits, crackers, and vegan cheeses.

The Society of the Four Arts garden didn't look like the kind of place one could enter without being a member, but it turned out that it was. Anyone could breeze in, spread out lunch, and make an afternoon of it.

The weather was mild—in the high seventies, cool for Florida in March. They found a spot under the shade of a large tree. The grass was wet and dewy.

"Don't worry, I got the waterproof one," she said, spreading out the blanket.

A few minutes later, they were singing "Happy Birthday" to Bash as Rebecca held the cake before him on a paper plate, and he regarded it with skepticism.

"Yummy!" Fran said over and over. "Yummy!" He poked it with one finger. They laughed.

"You need some milk," she said. "Does he drink milk yet?"

Rebecca shook her head, ignoring the *yet*. He still nursed, but she had no plan to feed him cow's milk. There were plenty of non-dairy milk options for toddlers, not that she expected Fran to understand this. People tended to freak out at the idea of a (mostly) vegan baby (he'd tried sausage once), as if it were abuse.

Finally, he plunged his face into it and, licking his lips, discovered sugar. They watched him discover it, his eyes lighting up. For the next hour he picked at it, grinning, while they took a thousand photos and almost as many videos.

Soon it was time for Bash to nap. Fran wanted to see the exhibit inside, and so Mickey took Bash to stroll him to sleep while Fran and Rebecca paid the ten dollars to venture into the small gallery featuring Rembrandt's line drawings.

The clerk, a kind-eyed older man with a VOLUNTEER pin, handed them each a magnifying glass.

"You'll want these," he said. Rebecca accepted, thinking, *there's no way.*

But inside, she saw why. The line drawings were tiny, many the size of postcards, and some closer to postage stamps. You had to get very close—inches—and peer through the thick, convex plastic in order to make out the details: a man pulling a rope; a bare-breasted woman clutching a snake; a tired-looking elephant.

"Do you think Mickey is okay?" Fran whispered. There were two others in the gallery, both serious and alone.

"What?" Rebecca said, confused.

"He's working so hard. It breaks my heart," Fran said at full volume. One of the fellow visitors in the gallery shushed her. Rebecca motioned for Fran to follow her back through the doorway and into the lobby.

"Wait, why?" she asked, once they'd passed the volunteer, who said, "Have a nice day," as if they were already leaving. "He seems fine to me," she said. "I mean, he works long hours, but he's always done that."

Fran's expression filled Rebecca with something like shame. It was a look of disbelief, as if her daughter-in-law was clueless.

"He should be performing," she said. "It's his soul's calling. He's a shell of himself."

Fran looked away.

"Anyway," she said, "let's finish looking." She headed back into the gallery, leaving unsaid what Rebecca suspected she was thinking: How little was Rebecca paying attention that she hadn't seen what Fran saw?

CHAPTER 15

"Bec, you nailed this one," Henrik said. "People are losing their shit. I love this part . . ." A pause. "*Longevity is not the goal. They don't want to extend their lives. They want to come back once life is eternal, once that final, nagging worry—mortality—has been eliminated. Death is an inconvenience, and they would prefer that you handle it—along with its environmental impact—while they rest.*'"

"This is the kind of billionaire stuff I was hoping you'd find down there. Fucking gold."

"Thanks, Henrik," Rebecca said. She'd already heard from a number of people about the article: friends she hadn't talked to in ages had texted her to say congrats, and acquaintances she hadn't heard from in years messaged her on Facebook and Instagram.

You have to be making this shit up.

Rich people are fucking cray.

How on earth do you get into these things??

The general sentiment was that the subjects of the piece were both unbelievably narcissistic *and* gullible. Their vulgar rapacity (to want to live forever—how greedy!) paired with foolishness filled her readers with self-satisfaction. People could gawk at the entitlement while feeling intellectually superior to the whole discussion. Who would actually believe that one day, someone would unfreeze you and give you all your money back? Maybe rich people were all idiots!

As the reactions trickled and then poured in, Rebecca was exhilarated at first, refreshing the page to see how many more times her column had been "Liked" or "Shared" in the previous few minutes, and cycling through her social media accounts to check for new comments.

But as the response snowballed—Buzzfeed picked it up, along with the *New York Post* and Mashable—she began to feel uneasy.

The truth was, an icky feeling was gathering in her gut. The reactions to the piece, the tweets about it—dozens, then hundreds—were biting. Some called for the Stones and their friends to die.

And she'd invited them. She'd catered to her readership, intentionally caricaturing the people at the dinner, including the Stones. Even though she'd kept them anonymous, she hadn't attempted to capture their humanity. She'd left out the desperation in their eyes, the gravity of their questions. She'd left out how old they all were—graying, wrinkled in all the places cosmetic surgery couldn't touch. No doubt some of those present were quietly cancer-ridden. From that vantage point, the one she *hadn't* taken, it had been a grasping assembly, not a greedy one. As Mickey might have put it, the saddest thing in the world.

Rebecca had left out all of this because she'd wanted her article to be punchy and, well, seen. She wanted people to read and share. Who wants to sympathize with someone who makes a thousand times what they make?

But while that part bothered her a little, it did so less than the part where she hadn't been upfront with Mrs. Stone about her intentions. She'd been invited into their home, then made them the butt of her joke.

I trust you, Mrs. Stone had said.

Yes, it was a little slimy of her.

She sighed, and logged in to her bank account to knock out some bills. She paid the electric and cell phone bills, then contributed to their retirement accounts. She dumped some money into the 529 college plan she'd opened for Bash.

Rebecca had always managed their finances. As the one who shopped for groceries, who'd set up their electric and Internet accounts, who filed their taxes and had opened both of their retirement accounts (did Mickey even know his password? She doubted it), it only made sense. She was the finance half of the marriage; he was the half who picked up heavy stuff.

She made Mickey's student loan payment, the minimum amount due. (It seemed silly to pay off his loans when they were accruing interest at such a low rate—2.4 percent. Besides, they wouldn't be rich forever, and he was still in an income-based repayment plan, meaning that his loans would be forgiven in a few years now that he'd been paying them down forever—unless the Republicans wiped out that policy.)

To finally have money coming in consistently—fourteen thousand dollars via direct deposit on the eighth of each month—felt good, and she let herself enjoy it. When she wandered into the Sephora a few blocks away, she'd find herself grabbing products by Hourglass, a high-end cruelty-free brand. One recent afternoon, she'd walked out with six hundred dollars' worth of new makeup and a cleansing system she didn't need. She'd picked up a two-hundred-ninety-dollar dress at Anthropologie because she could. And still, they had plenty left over.

Her phone buzzed.

Another one out of the park, read a text from Jason Pirozzi, his number now saved in her phone.

Thanks. Feel kind of weird about it.

Why?

Tone was off.

Distinct, not off. Intentional.

Eh.

Do it differently next time if you don't like it.

I think it's what Henrik expects of me now.

Who gives a fuck what Henrik expects of you?

I do? Because he's my editor? lol

Henrik's not going to fire you because you tweak your tone.

Henrik wouldn't fire me because I tweak my tone. He'd fire me because my columns stop being read because I tweaked my tone.

Rebecca, I say this with love. You're a good writer. You need to grow a pair. You'll be fine.

Ha-ha. Okay, thank you.

Let me know if you're coming to the New Media Summit in April, he wrote. It's here in TX! We can meet up for a drink.

The suggestion excited her more than she wanted it to.

"I'm ready to start writing," Rebecca said. She sat across from Mrs. Stone with Bash on her lap, bouncing him as he babbled happily. She didn't need her laptop today. "But I've been thinking about it, and I'd like to write it under my name. I'd also like full creative freedom—so we would work together, but I would make the final calls."

Rebecca had gotten tired of feeling like a quasi-double agent and had decided that this was the best scenario for several reasons. First, it was clear she couldn't keep coming every day—Mickey couldn't watch Bash at work anymore, and since Samantha worked nights, she couldn't watch him during the day, when she was sleeping.

But also, she didn't have to come every day anymore. She had hundreds of pages of notes, and it was time to start writing.

Driving to the Stones' that morning, she'd felt lighter, like she'd peeled off a layer of pretense.

Mrs. Stone didn't flinch, her hands folded neatly in her lap.

She opened her desk drawer and pulled out a leather billfold. She opened it and scrawled, then ripped a check from the checkbook and handed it to Rebecca. It was for seventy-five thousand dollars.

"I'm fine with you having authorship," Mrs. Stone said. "But I'd like more than just nominal influence over the content. I assume I'll self-publish, so we can avoid the hullaballoo of publishers and whatnot. That's no issue. I'll take out a full-page ad in the *New York Times* if I need to."

Rebecca, without hesitating, held the check out for Mrs. Stone to take back.

"I understand your desire for that," she said, "but I'm a journalist. It's a thing. I can't. I'm sorry."

Mrs. Stone studied her but didn't speak.

"I assure you, though, that I'll do my best to tell your story in a way that's honest," Rebecca continued. "I have no interest in doing anything else. And I think we should consider trying to publish traditionally. If it doesn't work out, you still have the option to publish yourself."

"I read your column," Mrs. Stone said thoughtfully. "Your piece on the cryo-lab dinner."

Rebecca cringed inside. If she'd known Mrs. Stone was going to read it, she'd have written it differently. The Stones could see through her article in a way that no one else could; they could see that for the sake of the punch line, she'd left out a layer: the layer of their knowing, of their self-awareness, their undeniable appreciation of irony. Not Brooklyn-level irony, but enough.

Suddenly, Rebecca was overcome with the sensation that she'd been wrong about everything. She'd thought she was being taken seriously, a person with a point of view who might exert some influence. Now, she felt like she'd been handed the equivalent of the jack-in-the-box toy Bash loved to wind and watch spring up, delighted every time by its magic, happy with himself for making it happen, again. Meanwhile, the grown-ups in the room knew: there was no magic, there was no surprise. There was only a toy to keep his attention so that he wouldn't notice they were busy doing something else.

She shook off the feeling.

"Not like that," she said slowly. "It won't be in that tone."

Mrs. Stone nodded, seeming to think it over.

"Well, I thought it was cute. Quite clever."

"Thank you," Rebecca said.

"But good, we have a deal then," Mrs. Stone said. "Let's move along."

With Bash in her arms, Rebecca quickly made her way down the hallway, heading out much earlier than usual. She'd been there under twenty minutes, and there was no reason to stay longer. She had her material and her charge and was ready to begin writing.

As she approached Mr. Stone's office on the left, she noticed the door was open—unusual for this time of day. Typically, it was closed, since he golfed in the mornings. Glancing inside reflexively as she passed, she startled.

Standing over Mr. Stone's desk was Paul, holding up a sheet of paper that he was intently examining. She froze. Backlit by the bay window, the sun shone through the sheet enough that Rebecca could make it out: a letter.

She turned away and hurried off, blinking hard as she rushed as carefully as possible down the stairs.

Driving home, Rebecca couldn't stop her mind from racing.

She knew he'd seen her. They'd made eye contact before she'd turned and run away.

There was no question that it was something he shouldn't have been doing; she'd seen it on his face.

The "paperwork" comment—which she'd not forgotten, although she'd tried to—now made sense.

Her first instinct was to call Mickey. But she hesitated. Perhaps she should say something to Mrs. Stone first. But she wasn't scheduled to see Mrs. Stone the next day, now, and didn't know when they'd next meet in person.

Or maybe it wasn't any of her business.

By the time she got home, she'd decided what to do. She was being more forthright now, and Mrs. Stone had shown nothing but respect for and honesty with Rebecca.

She knew the woman didn't text, and so she dialed her cell phone number.

CHAPTER 16

"Are you serious?" Mickey asked. It was a Saturday, the next morning, and they sat at the kitchen bar next to Bash in his high chair, trying to feed him avocado, which he kept spitting out, scrunching up his face like it was the grossest thing he'd ever tasted and making them laugh.

"Yes, I want to surf," Rebecca said.

She'd decided not to tell Mickey about the Paul situation, not right away. When she'd spoken to Mrs. Stone, she'd told her only what she'd seen and nothing more. There was no reason to involve Mickey right now; she figured it would stress him out, and he might be angry that she'd gone to Mrs. Stone. Paul was his buddy. A buddy by necessity, but still.

"Do you think you still know how?" he asked, teasing.

"Did I ever know how is the question," she said.

Three and a half years earlier, when they'd been together only a few months, they'd taken a last-minute trip to Costa Rica after finding a deal on CheapCaribbean.com. Neither had ever surfed, and they'd taught themselves. They'd shared a fifteen-dollar-a-day rental board to save money and took turns watching each other from the sand. They were both terrible, fighting the waves to get out past the break, then tumbling over, belly up, as soon as they paddled into one and attempted to scramble to their feet.

At night they lay head to toe in a net hammock outside of their hostel, eating takeout burritos for dinner and getting feasted upon by mosquitos. They sipped whiskey from plastic cups and listened to Stevie Wonder on Mickey's iPhone. Around midnight they'd fall asleep sticky, wiped out by the sun and salt, under a paper-thin sheet in their un-air-conditioned room, a rickety ceiling fan working hard above them.

In the mornings, they hiked to breakfast at an outdoor restaurant on a dusty, unpaved road many yards from the beach, where most of the diners were local, not tourists. When cars drove by, you could hardly tell their color behind the layer of dirt, and in their wake, you had to cover your mouth with a napkin or your shirt. Occasionally, a bony cow would saunter through the dining area, and no one seemed bothered by it.

The honeydew was cold and sweeter than ice cream at that restaurant. She still sometimes craved that honeydew.

By the end of that trip, she could do it—she could get up on the board. The next year, they'd gone back, and she'd gotten better.

Now, here they were, once again on a coast, but life had changed. Hearing from Jason Pirozzi had reminded her of how rarely they did the things they used to love.

After receiving his first text, their only correspondence in years, she'd looked him up on Facebook. He'd aged, of course; there were crinkles around his eyes, and he was thicker around the jaw than he had been in his twenties. But it was still him.

She'd found herself pulling up memories she hadn't thought about in a decade, small moments she was surprised she could recall: accompanying him to have keys made at the hardware store. Watching *Jersey Shore* together. Dressing up as snowmen for the J-school winter costume formal, then waking up the next morning to a pile of white fluff on the floor, fabric carrot noses and felt button eyes in disarray, like they'd melted right there next to the bed.

She'd pictured a ghost ship of her other life, the one she'd not wound up living, floating in a parallel universe.

This life she was in was the one she'd have chosen—there was no question about that. But she still wanted to surf.

"Where are we going to get a surfboard?" Mickey asked, glad for the change in routine. He, too, had had a twenty-four hours in which the past had reared its head in an unwelcome way.

The night before, Freddie Wampler had come to dinner and clapped him on the back like they were old buds. "Mickey! How's the kid?"

"Chubbier," Mickey had said. "Still drooling."

Seeing Freddie had been strange, like looking through a window at his younger self, a guy who'd seen Wampler as bigger than life, the pinnacle of success. Now Freddie seemed almost quaint. An old friend from a former life in New York.

It had brought back a memory: shortly after Rebecca had moved in with him years earlier, Mickey had found himself at the Wampler Foundation lugging Lexan tubs full of ice up the six wretched flights from the cellar (service staff wasn't permitted to use the elevator), followed by Hugh Bogle, the other strongest actor on the job.

It was before his vocal hemorrhage, but he was in a dry spell. Auditions weren't yielding results, which meant he'd been in his catering blacks more than usual. There had been some excruciating moments tending bar—the former castmate who'd ordered a merlot without recognizing him (or pretending not to); the casting director he'd worked with before who, brutally, had spoken encouraging, uplifting words to Mickey as he'd shaken her martini; the group of finance bros who'd drunkenly pestered him about how much he "charged" because they needed a bartender at some upcoming bachelor party, the line behind them thick and impatient. The most hopeful thing that had happened to him in months had been a *Seussical* callback for the role of Yertle the Turtle.

But then, climbing the stairs, Hugh had spoken words he'd been waiting, literally, years to hear: "You going in for the *Bridges* tour?"

Mickey had stopped and turned.

"What?" he'd said, resting the tub against a stair.

"You're perfect," Hugh had said. But Mickey had already known this. He'd been waiting a year and a half, ever since *Bridges of Madison County* premiered on Broadway to sold-out audiences. His dream was to play Robert, a handsome stranger from out of town with fantastic, haunting ballads in Mickey's range. How many times had he sung the songs for Rebecca, struggling through the chords on the dinky keyboard he stored in the closet with his shoes as she closed her eyes and listened?

He'd stood over the tub of ice in the stairwell and texted his agent that he needed to go in for Robert Kincaid. She'd booked him. He'd made it through the first audition and gotten a callback. He'd gone in, gotten a second callback.

And just before he went in for that one, he'd woken up with no voice.

Forty-five minutes later, they'd found a surf shop, rented a board, and managed to secure it on top of the Honda. They parked on the street across from the ocean, unloading everything with great effort—the umbrella, the tote of towels and snacks, the diaper bag, the surfboard—and ambled down the wooden stairs to the public beach, where they got Bash settled in his sunhat, sucking on a pouch of mashed-up fruit.

Rebecca took the board and waxed it with the fresh stick they'd purchased for two dollars, then pulled her hair into a ponytail and said, "Here goes nothing."

"Yay, Mom!" Mickey cheered, clapping while looking at Bash. Bash clapped along. Rebecca dropped the board to join them. "Yay!" she said.

He'd just started clapping, and it made them absurdly happy.

The day was still early, and not many people had gathered on the beach yet. The water wasn't terribly cold, she was glad to discover, and seaweed clung to her legs as she pushed out into the surf.

It didn't matter that she'd fall. She'd needed to do something physical, jolt her body out of its patterns. Fighting the current, pushing through the crashing waves, pulling the slimy plants off her goose-bumped legs—it all felt good, the antidote she'd hoped it would be to whatever she was feeling—stagnation, or maybe just parenthood.

They hadn't checked the surf report, having forgotten that was a thing. It turned out that the beach wasn't crowded not because it was early but because there were no waves. For twenty minutes she waited, and just as she was about to head back in, a wave arrived.

She climbed onto her stomach and began to paddle as hard as she could into it, her muscles remembering what to do, springing to life.

She caught the wave and stood, kept standing, was still standing—oops, wait, still standing—and then she was on sand, hopping off the board into two-inch water, grinning at her husband and son only a few feet away now. They were both clapping again, with big smiles.

Her ponytail had fallen out, and her hair was stuck in her mouth. She wiped it away.

It was a single moment, a flash: perfection.

And then, a dampening. A feeling of dread washed over her, as real as the slimy water stinging her skin. She couldn't name it, but it was unmistakable, like she'd entered the shadow of a cloud passing overhead.

She would look back on this moment months later and wonder... had she known what was coming? Or was she so blind to her own fortune that she failed to see how good she had it? In a way, they would seem like two versions of the same thing.

CHAPTER 17

On the following Tuesday morning, Rebecca stood at the kitchen counter chopping Brussels sprouts into domes when Bash awoke and began to whine. She hurried to finish slicing so the vegetables could roast while she nursed, chopping knobby cap after cap as Bash's whining escalated into a full-blown cry. She chopped faster.

"Coming, baby!" she called.

And then, the inevitable—the knife slid off the round top of a flaky sprout and into the pad of her thumb. Blood streamed onto the cutting board, pooling instantly. She reached for a roll of paper towels, smearing blood across the warped wood and countertop.

Dammit. She turned off the oven and ripped a paper towel with her good hand, cupping the pooling blood in the other. She wet the paper towel and pressed it against her palm. It turned instantly pink. She lifted it to examine the wound. It yawned, a ravine. Fuck. She was definitely going to need stitches.

Suddenly, she realized that Bash had stopped crying.

"Bash?" she called. Holding the darkening paper towel around her finger, she went to the living room, where she'd pulled his bassinet so that he could nap on his stomach in her immediate proximity. Newborns weren't supposed to be placed on their bellies to sleep, but Bash seemed more comfortable that way, and so after consulting her various mommy Facebook groups she'd begun to allow it as long as she could keep an eye on him. He wasn't a newborn anymore, but she kept it up; no harm in playing it safe.

Bash's eyes were wide open, and he'd rolled over onto his back. His body, stiff as a porcelain doll, was quaking.

"Sebastian!" She dropped the paper towel and scooped him up, oblivious to the blood gushing all over them both. His little body gave nothing, did not bend. Holding his rigid form to her chest, she frantically searched the apartment for her phone. Hands trembling, she dialed 9-1-1.

"My baby is having a seizure," she said to the woman who answered.

"Address?" the woman said. Rebecca squeezed her eyes shut. The only address that came to mind was their New York address. *Kill me and not Bash. Kill me and not Bash.* The prayer ran through her mind until his small body finally softened, and he began to cry a precious, normal cry, and when she lifted her shirt to calm him, he started to nurse like nothing had happened until the paramedics arrived.

Across town, Mickey and Paul were stocking the galley of the yacht when Paul said, "Dude, something happened last Friday, and I want to explain."

"Okay," Mickey said, sliding a bottle of Krug 1969 into the wine cooler.

"I was in Mr. Stone's office and your wife saw me."

"What?" Rebecca hadn't said anything. "Why?"

"I was looking at an NDA."

"Your own?" Mickey asked, hoping Paul would say he was just reviewing his own nondisclosure agreement, but knowing that was unlikely.

"It was between this company called Oxon that sells corporate services—software-to-run-your-company kind of thing—and this company P&T that makes uniforms. They just announced a merger yesterday."

"Okay . . ." Mickey said again. His gut told him he should halt the conversation before he heard something he shouldn't know, but he was curious.

"Last Thursday, I bought thirty-two hundred shares of P&T. Then I got seven hundred for my mom and three hundred and fifty for Carla. They were seventy-seven dollars a share."

Mickey could see where this was going. He resisted the impulse to check if anyone was behind him. They were alone inside the belly of the boat, and there were no security cameras that he knew of in place. Nonetheless, this didn't seem like a prudent location for this conversation.

"They announced yesterday that Oxon bought P&T for ninety-eight dollars a share, it closed at ninety-eight and change. That was a twenty-seven percent gain, my friend. Do you know how much I just made on that deal?"

Don't ask, Mickey.

"How much?"

"Do the math. An easy sixty-six thousand dollars. My mom made sixteen grand, and Carla made eight. And that was just one trade. We could have made a lot more, but you want to keep it pretty small to be safe."

"Dude," Mickey said, "this strikes me as very risky."

Paul smiled. "That's the beauty of it. The question isn't whether it's risky for *me*—the question is why that document was on Mister's desk in the first place."

Mickey's gaze settled on the glossy wood paneling in front of him. The boat, called *Intrepid*, had a cozy, warm feel—more so than the house. That he'd never once pondered any "whys" behind the documents he printed, transcribed, and attached for Mr. Stone now made him feel naive. It took all of his energy not to spell incorrectly, and he had to proof the emails by reading them aloud to himself.

It was clear that at least on the writing side of his communications, Mr. Stone didn't say anything private or proprietary; he saved that for phone calls. Besides, anything that Mickey did see was none of his business.

"When you're a little fish, no one's gonna come after you. But if you do, and you can say, 'Hey, I got info on this much, much bigger fish,' you're in a good spot."

"You're saying if law enforcement comes after you, you'll throw Mr. Stone under the bus?" Mickey asked.

"That's a crass way of putting it," Paul said, crossing his arms. "I'm just saying I have collateral."

Back at the house, Mrs. Stone and several friends had convened over egg salad sandwiches and ramekins of Greek quinoa salad. In the distant corner of the yard, a worker had begun blowing leaves despite clear instructions from Mickey to hold off until two p.m. when the women left, and so as he and Paul approached the house, Mickey stopped on the veranda to motion for the worker to stop. He stood waving frantically for several seconds to get the guy's attention—Mrs. Stone did not like yelling.

Paul, who'd already headed inside, reappeared holding Mickey's phone.

"Your wife just called three times in a row," he said, handing it to him and going back inside.

Mickey called back, his chest thudding.

When she answered, her voice was even—that's what he would remember, how calm she sounded.

"Bash had a seizure. We're on our way to the hospital. It's . . ." She paused. A muffled male voice gave her the name.

". . . Good Samaritan Medical Center."

His heart was now beating so fast that he was sure if he looked down, he would see it billowing in his chest.

"What do you mean? Is he okay?" His stomach turned in on itself like an umbrella closing. He squatted to steady himself.

Mickey crouched, dizzy and alone on the dusty veranda—dusty no matter how frequently it was swept, sandy forever—as Lake Worth winked a thousand winks. A yacht oozed by. The muscles in his legs gave way, and he fell back into a seat.

"He's okay. We're in the ambulance. He's awake and nursing."

Mickey exhaled. If he was nursing, he thought, he must be all right, at least for the time being.

"I'm on my way," he said. "Love you."

"Love you," Rebecca said back, her voice finally cracking.

Their perfectly healthy baby had shown no signs of any health issues since his birth a year earlier. Surely there would have been some indication if anything was truly amiss, right?

CHAPTER 18

There was no hospital on Palm Beach itself. Good Samaritan Medical Center on North Flagler Drive, just on the western side of Flagler Memorial Bridge connecting West Palm to Palm Beach, served the haves and have-nots alike. Rebecca and Bash were led to a curtained section of triage where, to their right, a rail-thin woman in a tennis skirt sat clutching her head while her husband paced in boat shoes, and, to their left, a woman with matted hair surrounded by grimy Publix grocery bags stuffed with clothing snored in a chair.

Bash had fallen asleep again. His eyelids fluttered when he breathed out, and his plump hand gripped her finger even as he slept. Rebecca thought suddenly of the pink and fluffy cherubs in European oil paintings. Of course all of art for all of time was derivative of this kind of beauty.

"Has he had any medical issues before?" The nurse stood at a wheeled computer cart.

"No."

"Allergies?"

"No."

"Surgeries?"

"No."

"Medical complications at birth?"

"Just a C-section."

After a moment, the nurse mumbled, "Crap. I'm going to need your health insurance card again. I must have put in the wrong number."

Rebecca carefully reached for her purse so not to disturb Bash, and the nurse intervened.

"Let me," she said, reaching into Rebecca's purse to get her wallet, and this small act of kindness caught in Rebecca's throat. She swallowed.

"I don't know if we're in network here," she said softly.

Rebecca tried not to think about the cost—the ambulance ride alone, she knew, would be exorbitant if the medical insurance they were on through the marketplace didn't cover it. She'd considered driving, but what if it had happened again? She couldn't fathom having him in the car seat in the back, out of reach. She shuddered just thinking about it.

And yet she knew it wouldn't be good. The plan they'd elected, that she'd chosen for them, was the least expensive, the high-deductible plan, the plan you get when you're young and confident and believe nothing will ever happen to you.

"Okay, you're right," the nurse said. "It's not showing we're in-network for you. Do you want to call your insurance company and ask? Or see where you can get in-network coverage?" The nurse leaned forward, her giant chest pressing against the edge of the cart. "I'd go somewhere in-network if you can. You'll save yourself a fortune."

Rebecca's face fell, and the nurse quickly stood upright.

"But don't let me stress you out. We're happy to take care of you here."

She put a bracelet on both of them and left, pulling the blue curtain shut behind her. Rebecca studied Bash in her lap. His reddish-brown hair covered a bulging blue vein (or were the blue ones arteries?) under the pale skin of his left temple. She'd noticed it before, but it had never seemed ominous until now. Was it throbbing? Had it darkened?

As she watched his tiny chest rise and fall, the feelings came, flooding her sinuses, burning and punitive. How entitled she'd been to take his health for granted. What were the lines of the Kahlil Gibran poem her labor and delivery nurse had shared with her back in New York, which felt like a lifetime ago?

In her tenth or eighteenth hour of labor—she had no idea—Mickey had left the room briefly to meet his mother in the hospital lobby, and Rebecca, in the throes of labor, hormones surging, sweat beading and scampering in all directions, had confided a secret fear to the nurse.

"I don't know if I can do it," she'd said. She'd meant a natural childbirth, finishing the process without pain meds, but the nurse had misunderstood. The nurse thought she'd meant motherhood.

"Of course you can," she'd said. "Remember what Kahlil Gibran wrote. Children are merely on loan to us."

Hours later, Rebecca would lie holding Bash, a person now, and, half awake, she'd remember the conversation with the nurse like a fever dream. What a weird thing to say to someone in labor, she'd think before sinking into sleep.

But later still, back home, she'd remembered the conversation again and looked up the Gibran reference.

The lines, which she couldn't recall word for word, said something like: your children are not your children. They belong to tomorrow.

Rebecca had always viewed herself as a piece of a web, a stretch of fiber in an interconnected universe. Now, she saw herself as having a singular purpose: to be there for this soul in the nook of her arm, to guard his tomorrows.

When Mickey finally pulled open the curtain where his wife and son had been stationed for half an hour, Rebecca sighed, relieved. They weren't alone. Mickey was here.

He knelt next to her, placing a hand on Bash's head and peering at him intently, like he could see inside his tiny brain to what was wrong, if only he focused hard enough.

"The doctor will be with you soon," said the nurse who'd escorted Mickey there, before leaving them alone.

Rebecca and Mickey shared a look of mutual terror. She didn't bother mentioning what the nurse had said about the hospital not being in-network. They would stay put.

"Sorry," Mickey said. "It took thirteen minutes for the Uber to get here. You'd think it'd be faster given that the island is, like, two fucking miles big."

In fact, what Rebecca was thinking was: *No one at that house could drive you? They couldn't spare a single person for ten minutes after your child was rushed to the ER?*

"Sebastian had what's called a tonic seizure. I want to run an EEG and draw blood," said the doctor, a skinny, bearded child in a white coat that swallowed him. They'd waited two hours before being shown to a private room. Bash had awoken and behaved completely normally—no seizing, just smiles and babbles. "Basically, I want to rule out the low-hanging fruit. Then we'll move on to other tests if necessary. How does that sound?"

"What's the low-hanging fruit?" Mickey asked, an edge in his voice that Rebecca understood—the term had annoyed her, as well. It wasn't fruit. It was their kid.

"Was just getting to that. HIE stands for hypoxic-ischemic encephalopathy—birth trauma. Rebecca, can you tell me about your childbirth? What was it like?"

"It was fine," Rebecca said with a shrug. "Normal."

"There was nothing that could have been traumatic to Sebastian?" The way that his eyes cut to Mickey as he said it ticked her off.

"Nope," she said.

"Well, except for . . ." Mickey looked at her, eyebrows raised, prompting her to say more.

"What, the cord thing?"

"The umbilical cord was wrapped around Sebastian's neck while she was in labor," Mickey said once he could tell Rebecca wasn't going to. "Sebastian was in distress, and that's why we ended up having an emergency C-section."

"But then it was fine," Rebecca said. "It was a near miss."

The doctor grunted. "Okay, well, glad to hear it was smooth from there. We'll still do the EEG to be safe, okay? Might as well."

"Whatever you think," Rebecca said, her throat tight.

Three hours later, they were discharged, the whole affair an anticlimactic question mark. The EEG had been inconclusive, and in the absence of any evidence other than the story about the umbilical cord and a single tonic seizure, the doctor had made a diagnosis of HIE—birth trauma. He'd also encouraged them to follow up with a neurologist to confirm the diagnosis, though he "felt pretty confident" in his assessment.

"It's the most common cause of seizures in infants," he'd said, "and can absolutely be caused by even a brief deprivation of oxygen."

It could also, he'd suggested, explain the developmental delays—that, at eleven months, he still wasn't crawling or walking.

As for treatment, there was none. It wasn't a reversible kind of damage. The only thing to be done were various therapies to treat the symptoms of the trauma rather than the trauma itself—occupational therapy, speech therapy, and so on—options listed casually on a bright turquoise brochure that Rebecca found insultingly cheerful.

As she waited for Mickey, who'd offered to Uber home and get the car and car seat, Rebecca wasn't sure at whom to direct her anger. If it had indeed been birth trauma, whose fault was it? Her OB's? Her own?

It had been only an hour since the doctor had made the diagnosis,

and already she had replayed those moments of the birth over and over dozens of times.

While in labor, she'd noticed on the heart-rate monitor that his—the baby's—was dipping and rising, dipping and rising, like a hawk. Clenching her teeth and sweating through the sheets, she'd pointed it out several times to anyone who would listen, but everyone—the nurses, Mickey—kept telling her it was okay. When she'd asked for her OB, she'd been told he was delivering another baby and would be in shortly. It was only when the OB did finally appear, followed by a flock of attendants gloved and masked under panicked eyes, that anyone other than Rebecca seemed concerned about the situation.

From there, it had been only a matter of minutes before Bash was born. She'd been anesthetized, cut open, and there he was.

Now, a different doctor in a different state had told them that by the time she looked up and saw Bash's face for the first time, the damage had been done.

As they drove down Narcissus Avenue, her guilt percolated, heating up. It didn't spring from any particular act or failure to act on her part, but a visceral certainty that she was to blame. A knowing in her bones, a maternal assumption of responsibility that stretched into the oldest crevices of a woman's DNA, ancient and echoing.

Rebecca was his mother, and if he'd been hurt while coming into the world, it was her fault.

CHAPTER 19

Sitting alone on the balcony, her laptop balanced in her lap, Rebecca scrolled through the names of local neurologists, searching for any criteria by which to judge them. Back in New York, she'd always used the same website, a clearinghouse of local doctors that you could sort by specialty and ranking. She only ever booked with providers who had at least a dozen five-star reviews. But in Florida, there was no equivalent that she could find—the Internet offered up only driblets of hardly helpful content, three-word Google reviews like "not long wait."

Okay, but did he properly treat your fucking brain? How was he at, you know, his job?

But that wasn't her only concern. In trying to determine how much a neurological assessment would cost, she had run up against the infuriating vagueness of the U.S. health-care system.

"There is no way to determine the negotiated rate until after your provider has billed. Not even the doctor can give you an estimate," the insurance rep had told her over the phone.

"So there's no way to find out how much a procedure will cost," Rebecca said.

"That's correct, ma'am," the woman had said. "You just have to get it."

The estimates Rebecca could find for neurologist appointments ranged from $500 to $1,700. The ambulance alone had cost them $7,500 out of pocket—negotiated down by her insurance company from $13,900—and there had gone their savings, wiped out in a single, terrifying afternoon. Apart from that, they just had their retirement accounts and Bash's 529 plan. They could always pull from those, but they'd take a penalty.

Thank God they had Mickey's income now, she kept thinking. The therapies referenced on the tone-deaf *What next?* card one of the nurses had given them were going to be expensive and ongoing.

Still, as her thoughts skidded into the future, there was the sobering reality that Mickey wouldn't have this job forever. The kind of work they did—writing and singing/catering—wasn't the kind for which there were plentiful, well-paying jobs in the area. And it definitely wasn't the time to be moving back to New York, the most expensive city in the world, or starting some new corporate job that would keep her apart from Bash.

All of her calculations and worries amounted to a single conclusion: they had to keep making money under their current arrangement, as much as possible.

When Mickey arrived at work, Paul wasn't in his usual spot in the kitchen preparing breakfast. Mickey busied himself setting up for the morning meal, and ten minutes later, when there was still no sign of his friend, he heard the sound of the back door opening and shutting loudly.

Through the window Mickey watched Paul trek across the grass to his cottage, head hanging, pounding his palm with his fist.

Within moments, Mr. Stone entered.

"How is your son?" he asked. "What did the doctor say?"

"He thinks it's trauma from childbirth," Mickey said. "Brain damage." Uttering the words felt like being punched in the throat.

Brain damage was not the term the doctor had used, but Mickey could read between the lines. *Neurological abnormality caused by deprivation of oxygen + irreversible = brain damage.*

"Who diagnosed him?" Mr. Stone asked.

"The ER doctor," Mickey said, thinking, *A child just out of med school.* "We're following up with a neurologist to confirm, but sounds like maybe we're lucky. It could be worse." He paused. "I think."

Mr. Stone shook his head. "No, no. I'll have my guy call you. He'll look at Sebastian."

Mickey was surprised that Mr. Stone remembered his son's name.

"He's the best," Mr. Stone added, as if he needed to say it. He hired only the best.

"Thank you," Mickey said, touched. "I appreciate that."

"In other news," Mr. Stone said. "Paul's last day was yesterday. We'll be interviewing to fill the role as quickly as possible, something you'll be expected to help with. In the meantime, are you comfortable with light cooking?"

"Certainly," Mickey said. "Whatever you need."

As soon as Mr. Stone left the room, he texted Paul.

Dude, what happened??

What do you think? He found out.

Fuck, Mickey wrote. I'm sorry.

Did he need to say that he hadn't ratted out his friend? Surely Paul knew he wouldn't do that.

Mr. Stone came through as promised. That Friday morning while Mickey was at work, Rebecca and Bash sat across from Dr. Richard Goldin in his small office on Blossom Way in Palm Beach proper. The only people in the whole office were Dr. Goldin, a receptionist, and his nurse, a wide-shouldered, blond woman named Bonnie. He wore a light blue polo shirt and cream cotton pants. His forearms were very tan; when he mentioned that he golfed with Mr. Stone, it fit.

Dr. Goldin asked a litany of questions, many more than the ER doctor had.

What *exactly* had she seen on the monitor when Bash's heart rate was racing then falling?

No, what actual numbers?

How many times did it peak like that?

For how long each time?

How close to childbirth was she at that point?

How far apart were her contractions?

Then how does she remember them feeling?

During his seizure last week, had his arms spasmed, or gone stiff?

She couldn't recall everything, especially from the day of his birth, but the specificity of the questions comforted her. Here was someone committed to gleaning a thorough understanding.

After forty-five minutes, he stopped typing up her answers and looked at her.

"I'm dubious," he said. "I don't think it's HIE."

Rebecca held her breath, not knowing whether to be relieved or more afraid.

"There is a disorder called leukodystrophy that I want to rule out." He spoke with calmness and confidence, as if the stakes were no greater than the best way to reshingle a roof. "It's a neurogenerative disease that we can diagnose with genetic testing. There are a number of leukodystrophies, so we'll have to eliminate them one by one. We'll start with the most common."

He paused to sneeze. Reading her mind, he said, "It's premature to talk steps beyond that. If he does have a leukodystrophy disorder, then the prognosis and treatment are different depending on the particular form of it. You don't want to borrow trouble, as my grandmother would say, by making plans for something that won't happen. So I prefer to start with figuring out what's going on with Bash, then we can talk about what to do with that information, okay?"

He had kind eyes, and she tried to relax.

"Okay," she said. "Question."

"Shoot."

"You said genetic. Does that mean he would have gotten it from me or my husband?"

"Or both. You could be a carrier and not have the disorder yourself, and so could your husband, in which case, Bash could have it."

She nodded.

"Or it could be de novo, meaning he could have it even if neither of you do. It just depends on the type," he said. "We'll test and see. Other questions?"

She appreciated that nothing about his tone was hurried. He wasn't trying to rush her out.

"Do you . . ." How should she phrase it? "Are you able to give me a sense of how much the tests will cost?"

He shook his head. "It's been taken care of."

She remained still, confused.

"Everything is covered. Cecil wouldn't have it any other way."

Don't argue. Don't argue. She clamped her teeth around her tongue.

"Thank you," she said, once she could trust her mouth to make the right words. She stood and buckled Bash, who was chatting happily, as if nothing bad had ever happened, into the stroller.

Dr. Goldin held open the door for her, and as she passed through it, he added, "And Rebecca, do yourself a favor and stay off Google on this. Remember what I said about borrowing trouble."

"I'll do my best," she said, meaning it.

"What do you mean you told her?" Mickey said, his hands on his head.

Rebecca hadn't yet told him about Paul in large part because she'd expected this reaction. She'd known he'd be mad about her conversation with Mrs. Stone. But in light of what was going on with Bash, it surprised her that he was *so* upset by it. Who even cared at this point?

"I just told her what I saw," she said. "Nothing more."

"You didn't even tell *me* what you saw," Mickey said angrily, pacing and wringing his hands. "But you told Mrs. Stone?"

"I didn't want to burden you with it. It would have just stressed you out."

He covered his face with his hands then let them drop to his sides.

"Why did you?" he asked, his voice full of accusation.

In truth, Rebecca wasn't entirely sure. Had she wanted to prove her loyalty to Mrs. Stone? Or her goodness or purity to herself?

"I think you did it because you just don't like him," Mickey said.

"Please," she said, though she wondered if there was truth in what he said. She took a deep breath. "I'm sorry, I should have told you before I did it. I didn't know you'd be this upset."

"He was my friend," Mickey said. "My only friend."

"He can still be your friend," she said. "Just because he doesn't work with you doesn't mean—"

"He's moving back to Jersey," Mickey said, peeling off his shirt to shower. "He's already moved his stuff out of the cottage."

She considered this as he disappeared into the bathroom. She heard the shower turn on.

"It's good he'll be closer to his son, at least," she said over the sound of the water. "I'm sorry," she said again more loudly, but he didn't respond, and she didn't know if it was because he couldn't hear her.

Children diagnosed with late infantile MLD typically live five to ten years.

Lying in the dark, Rebecca was squeezing her phone so hard that her pinkie throbbed. Next to her, Mickey's body was emitting a cloud of heat, the sheets damp on his side of the bed. He'd always been a sweaty sleeper, but since the seizure, he'd begun waking up drenched.

She'd held out all afternoon and evening, but, unable to sleep, she'd caved.

Fuck. This was why Dr. Goldin hadn't wanted her to google.

She set her phone down and shook Mickey. He grunted. She shook him again until his eyes cracked open.

"What's the matter?" he asked, closing them again.

"Leukodystrophy is very bad. Very bad. He can't have it."

"You weren't supposed to google."

"How was I ever supposed to manage that?"

Eyes still closed, he reached out and pulled her into him.

This is one thing she loved about Mickey. He was never mad for long. He always forgave her.

His chest was moist and warm, and she burrowed into it.

"Fuck," she said against his T-shirt. "Fuck, fuck, fuck."

"We don't know anything yet," he mumbled, stroking her hair.

"I'm sorry," she said after a long silence had passed.

"For what?" he asked.

"For telling on Paul. For not telling you first. For judging you for taking this job."

"It's okay," he said, now awake and alert. "Let's get some sleep."

"I'm glad you took it," she said. "Thank God you took it."

"Calm down," he said, the hint of a tease in his voice. "You're worrying me."

She turned to face the window.

"I mean it. Thank God you didn't listen to me."

After a few minutes, she climbed out of bed and crept over to Bash's portable crib in the corner—they'd moved him into their room to keep an eye on him. She felt his chest. He was breathing.

She closed her eyes and left her hand there.

Two years earlier, a miscarriage had been crushing in a way that made no sense to her. It had been early and swift but nonetheless devastating.

Rebecca, despite her concerns about overpopulation, had always assumed she'd eventually have children, but she'd never felt urgency around the idea until, one day, she had. As with most things, once she had decided what she wanted, she wanted it to have happened yesterday. She'd promptly had her IUD removed and begun logging her cycle in two separate fertility tracking apps. A basal temperature thermometer, purchased at Rite Aid for $29.99, predicted her exact day of ovulation. She'd paid for expedited delivery of the sperm-friendly lube a friend had recommended. And on her "Highest Likelihood of Conception!" dates, she'd informed Mickey that they were to have as much sex as physically possible.

He'd been happy to comply. Plus, the possibility of fatherhood excited him, too.

That first month had been fun, exhilarating—a secret they shared. Contrary to what they'd both heard about procreation-motivated sex, Rebecca and Mickey found that a common purpose made their sex life even better. There was a new satisfaction in being connected by a private goal. It all felt so in sync that she'd found it hard not to be cavalier about how quickly it would work.

By then she was immersed in forums on Trying to Conceive apps with names like Glow, Shine, and Bright. She'd learned the endless lists of acronyms used on these—TTC (trying to conceive); DPO (days past ovulation); VFL (very faint line).

But month after month, that second blue line hadn't bloomed, as hard as she peered at each strip of white cardboard, and by month four, ovulation had ceased to be a joyously intimate time of the month. The clusters of peak fertile days became frantic, mechanical. Sex became performative again, like it was when they were first dating and self-conscious, but this time, they were pretending to be casual about the whole thing—that they weren't worried that it wasn't going to work, that something in their reproductive machinery was broken.

Then, a double line.

They knew they weren't supposed to, but had been unable to resist sharing the news. Rebecca had FaceTimed three friends within the hour. Mickey had called his mother.

But four days after the positive pregnancy test, she'd risen in the night to find the sheets covered in blood.

A "chemical pregnancy" it was called. A fancy word, they'd discovered, for miscarriage.

The blood had been everywhere; their bedroom looked like a crime scene. It had awoken her while the moon was still high and bright, the bars still open, the revelers still shouting to each other in the streets below. She'd shaken him wordlessly, pointing. They'd both known instinctively what it meant, and both were sadder than they ever could have predicted, like they'd lost something real, something they'd held close for much longer than eighty-four hours.

How it was possible to grieve a mere idea, Mickey hadn't been able to comprehend.

"But it wasn't just an idea," Rebecca had said. "It was a person."

She watched Bash sleep and knew she couldn't bear losing him. She would die.

CHAPTER 20

When you can acquire affordable health care only through your employer, you're tethered to your work by your need to survive. Though
the health-care system obscures it, in America, our work is not just
how we pay our bills; it's where we are obliged to place our security
for the only thing that actually matters: our lives.

Rebecca had written and rewritten the final lines of her column a
dozen times.

She wanted to make the point, but she didn't want the Stones to
find her ungrateful.

How things had changed.

Whatever was going on with Bash remained a giant question
mark. The way genetic testing worked was that you couldn't just
decode someone's genome to find out the problems with it. The
technology was still being developed to tackle such a vast undertaking, and even if it did already exist, it would be too expensive
and take too long, Dr. Goldin had explained in a second meeting,
for it to be "scalable."

"What are companies like 23andMe and Ancestry.com doing,
then?" Rebecca had asked. She'd written a piece on them a few

years earlier, during the height of their popularity as Christmas and birthday gifts.

"They take samples and speculate what the rest looks like based on those snippets. Like if you had only a third of the puzzle pieces of a puzzle, just enough to be able to tell what it is," he'd told her. "You could predict the rest based on what you think is there—but that wouldn't mean you were accurate, and you couldn't be all that precise."

This kind of genetic testing wasn't proper for diagnosis, which required precision. To identify critical abnormalities in a genome, or "SNPs" he called them, it was necessary to sequence one little region at a time. A "panel."

Based on his suspicions, Dr. Goldin wanted to run various leukodystrophy panels on Bash, starting with the most common version of the disease and moving down the list to the least.

By the end of the first week after their appointment, Bash had been screened for the two most likely disorders. To Rebecca's relief, Dr. Goldin had ruled them both out.

They were now moving through leukodystrophy panels like a grim funnel they just had to make it to the bottom of. With each elimination, Rebecca felt like she was one space closer to winning a board game, as if Bash were inching toward to being declared a regular, healthy child. She knew this wasn't how it worked, but it was hard to avoid the magical thinking.

Fantasies of an easy answer played through her head on a loop. Low sodium? That was all? Whew! They'd go out to celebrate.

But one step at a time.

To be thorough, Dr. Goldin had also ordered a screening called a "microarray" to look for problems across the board, ones they may not have thought of yet.

That one, he'd said, would take approximately two weeks. In the meantime, he'd instructed Rebecca and Mickey to pay careful attention to Bash's behavior and physical development, noting any changes, even subtle ones.

As if they could miss a thing.

Standing over her son while he watched *Sesame Street* songs on YouTube, she sipped her coffee and did what she did every morning—scanned him for signs. Was he focusing? Was his skin a healthy shade? Were there bags under his eyes? How was his appetite, his movements when feeding himself, his temperature after napping?

All day every day, she pinned Bash on a spectrum. How well did he look compared to an hour ago? Yesterday? Tonight? Forever?

He still tried to crawl.

One afternoon, with the sun streaming through the room in slanted rays, he moved, edging his way into a beam of light as Rebecca squealed.

She texted Mickey then called Dr. Goldin, telling his receptionist that it was urgent. She was certain this was a good sign.

"He's crawling," she said as soon as he picked up.

"That's excellent," he said in a tone that told her that it didn't mean anything at all.

They passed the time walking. She and Bash were back to strolling miles a day, sometimes the same route, sometimes new ones. Street names on Palm Beach fell into two categories—floral and financial. There were Hibiscus, Rosemary, and Olive Streets. There were Worth Avenue, Gulfstream Road, and Colonial Lane. She played a sort of cracks-in-the-ground game with herself of trying to walk only on the floral ones. Whatever the route she took, she always ended up at the water.

Just over the bridge to the east were a handful of giant trees that Rebecca thought of as "the squigglies" because she didn't know what they were called. They didn't seem to belong at all, their skinny roots gathered up like a messy wedding bouquet, too natural in their beauty for the manicured aesthetic of Palm Beach proper. Their elegant trunks would be stunning anywhere, but here they stood out, magical and messy in a realm of uniformity.

She would cross the Royal Park drawbridge, waiting for it to rise and tower over her and Bash like a sinking ship, both of them looking up at it piercing the sky. The tip of a sail or two would then glide past, and the bridge would lower to become a bridge again. She and Bash would crest it and be welcomed by their familiar, magical trees, and she'd push past the speckle of magic down the palm-lined avenue that sliced a straight path to the shore. She'd arrive at the ocean, and the wind washing off the water would whip dirt-colored sand into her hair.

Everything was tender to the touch now.

She'd long possessed a sense of her privilege and corresponding obligations. This was different. It was a heightened awareness that not only what she had was unearned, but that it all—the baby laughs, the squiggly roots, the smell of salt—was borrowed.

On loan.

She'd reach the sand, the sun toasting her shoulders, and lean into her gratitude. The things she used to care about seemed silly. The size of her jeans. Whether she could be successful enough for Mickey to stop catering. Whether the eggs she occasionally fed Bash were truly from properly treated chickens, even though she only bought the cartons labeled "Certified Humane." (She'd also recently started feeding him meat, fighting off only a tinge of guilt for doing so, after reading on a crispy mommy blog that his seizures could be due to lack of protein.)

Then they'd head home for a morning nap. After the nap, they'd eat lunch, and take a second stroll to the beach, followed by playtime, reading, dinner, bath, and bedtime.

Throughout the day, Rebecca would check her phone obsessively for a missed call from Dr. Goldin's office. One week ticked to two.

She reworked the family budget. She cut subscriptions they either weren't using or were unenthusiastically using—the meal delivery kit, their three streaming services. The customized shampoo and vitamin packs she'd subscribed to on a lark after they'd moved.

She calculated what they could afford to save if they lived as frugally as possible. Looking at the fourteen hundred dollars she made for her column each month, she wondered if she should have accepted the seventy-five thousand from Mrs. Stone. The decision not to seemed shortsighted now—especially since she didn't know if she'd ever recover sufficient focus to write the damn book without a contract.

Rebecca stared at the numbers on the screen, unsatisfied.

She wanted more than just a respectable emergency fund. She wanted to avoid ever experiencing this feeling again, the feeling that Bash could suffer—or worse—because of something she had or hadn't done.

So are you coming to the Summit?

Probably not. I have a lot going on here.

Soirées to attend and yachts to board, huh?

My kid is sick. Really sick.

Oh no. I'm sorry.

It's not a good time.

I understand. I'm disappointed because I was very much looking forward to seeing you, but I understand. I hope he's (he?) okay.

She decided to stop texting with Jason Pirozzi.

The alpaca was back.

"Did you hear?" Grace, promoted to house manager after Anna was fired, asked Mickey as soon as he'd parked his bike and entered through the back of the house.

"No, what?" he asked.

"The alpaca sculpture's back. Just back where it was. Like nothing happened."

He followed her to the library where, sure enough, there it sat. It was at a different angle, but in the same spot as before.

"What the fuck," he mumbled.

"I know," she said. "So I guess it wasn't Anna, right?" She rolled her eyes. They'd all known it wasn't Anna.

"Bruce," he said, and she nodded. He'd been there the day before, boisterous and belligerent as usual. Had he snuck back to the library and returned the statue?

It didn't take long for Mickey to find out, because that afternoon, Bruce returned, seemingly sober and eager to chat.

"Hey, Bruce," Mickey said, "do you remember that alpaca sculpture that went missing from the library a few weeks ago? It's back."

Bruce snickered.

"What's so funny?" Mickey asked.

"I forgot," he said. "It was a joke. Then I left it on the floor of my car and forgot about it till Chloe found it yesterday. Did anybody notice it was gone?"

Mickey shook his head.

"What?" Bruce asked.

"Yes, they noticed, Bruce. Anna got fired over it."

"Oh, fuck," Bruce said. "That sucks. Who's Anna?"

Mickey would tell Mrs. Stone what Bruce told him, and perhaps—chances were slim, but perhaps—Anna would be offered her job back. Although Grace had told him she'd already found a position a few miles south, in Boca.

"She worked here until a couple of months ago," Mickey said. "She was in charge of the cleaning staff."

"My bad," Bruce said, his attention drifting to the far window of the room, where Chloe was barking at a squirrel and pawing at the glass. "Joke gone south."

But Mickey wasn't preoccupied for long with thoughts of Anna, or Bruce's consequential selfishness. For once, he was hardly even thinking about Bash.

A few hours earlier, Mickey had woken up and, as he did every morning, checked his voice with a low tone. Every morning for the past two years, it had been gravelly. The routine had become so predictable that he hardly paid attention to it anymore; he just made the sound out of habit while he brushed his teeth.

But that morning, there was no gravel. He'd quickly rinsed and spit, then cleared his throat. Rebecca was out on an early-morning walk with Bash, and he was alone in the apartment.

Facing his shirtless body in the mirror, he'd sung a G.

It was pure and clear.

A G-sharp. An A.

He'd climbed the scale, note by note, and his voice had cooperated, carrying across the condo with clarity and ease.

Holy shit. His voice had healed itself. All that time off—he'd unwittingly put himself on extended vocal rest, and it had worked.

And then, a thought, one that made no sense in light of everything, pounced on him like a big cat, like a dream that had been waiting: *We have to go back.*

It stunned him.

They relied on the Stones for Bash's medical care.

They had a lease, and a car, and more financial freedom than they'd ever had before: he didn't think twice before asking if she wanted to grab dinner out. He didn't check the price of a piece of fruit at the supermarket before buying it. He turned off the lights and air-conditioning when they left for the day not to save money, but just to be good to the planet. Did he really want to drag the family back to New York to scrape by? With a sick child?

He felt bad even thinking it.

Plus, there was the possibility of a fluke. He could wake up tomorrow hoarse again.

He decided not to say anything to Rebecca yet. He would wait to tell her that the alpaca wasn't the only thing that was back.

CHAPTER 21

A couple of weeks after Bash's seizure, Rebecca and Bash were out for their daily walk to pick up a vegan croissant at the bakery and head to the beach, when she took a right onto a street earlier than usual and was greeted by a hotel so grand that it didn't seem to belong in America. The Breakers rivaled Versailles in size and splendor, and she couldn't believe it had taken her eight months to run into it. It was like she'd stumbled upon a massive castle in the middle of a small island. The private drive leading up to it was the stateliest she'd ever seen, and she didn't dare cross under the tall, hedged archway through which a darkly tinted Porsche and Jaguar silently made their way, like a royal procession.

"What's a castle doing in the middle of the island?" she asked Mickey later that night.

"The Breakers. It's a hotel. We should check it out," he said. "It's apparently family-friendly."

There was no way that place was family-friendly, she thought. She learned that it was built by the man himself, Henry Flagler (or more accurately, his leased labor), in the 1800s.

The next day, she found the courage to follow a young couple on foot through the hedged archway. Pushing Bash in the stroller, she ventured into the massive, ornate lobby. Its vaulted ceilings were painted with frescoes and dotted with chandeliers that hung long like pendulums.

As Mickey had predicted, she was surrounded by families. Wearing a white sundress and accompanied by a baby, she almost fit in, apart from the fact that, unlike the other mothers, she wasn't draped in diamonds and watermelon-themed designer clothing.

In the ladies' room, soft cotton towels were spiraled into roses. Wandering into the dining area where breakfast was being served, she marveled at the perfectly speckled triangles of Stilton, and the servers—all young women—in spotless, cream, A-line dresses.

Back outside, the landscaping was impressive even by Palm Beach standards: the lawn seemed to stretch on forever, a garden reaching past the horizon like an infinite Eden. She passed through a field of fountains, wheeling Bash along.

When she somehow wound up on the far side of the property near employee parking, she came across a wooden sign that read, Breakers residents are merely steps away. Refrain from cell phone use, loud conversation, smoking, and lingering.

It took her a moment to realize that it was an instruction to staff.

"Jesus," she mumbled under her breath, snapping a photo of it. Maybe she could use it in a column later.

She made a U-turn, heading back toward the building, and came upon a café offering pastries, newspapers, and coffee. She surveyed the case of cookies and croissants.

"I'll take a Shiny Sheet," the woman at the front of the line said, ordering a copy of the *Palm Beach Daily News* by its nickname.

It was a mild day for late April in South Florida, in the low eighties and breezy. Rebecca bought a hibiscus tea for six dollars and found a seat in the courtyard. As Bash snoozed, she watched other families with children older than hers make themselves at home across the pristine grounds: they kicked balls, tossed frisbees, played chase. The children wore matching gingham clothing, the parents, navy and white cottons in expensive cuts.

There was something about it: everything thought of, no tulip out of place, no chair cushion unfluffed. It was like a dream, too perfect to be real. She didn't want to leave.

On the walk home she passed a bookstore she'd also never come across before. (She'd missed a lot, apparently, in bypassing this four-block radius.) The bookstore was tiny and whitewashed, sandwiched between two fine dining establishments on whose patios tourists sipped mimosas and munched on jumbo shrimp cocktail. Unable to resist any bookstore, Rebecca stepped inside. The vision of the shelves upon shelves, ordinarily a comfort, today felt foreign. In her old life, she cared about books. Still, she stood before a shelf of bestsellers, scanning. Maybe she would find something to distract her. In the stroller, Bash, now awake, began to rustle. He didn't like to stop once they were moving.

"Excuse me, miss?" a voice said, pulling her back into the present. "Do you mind leaving your water back here behind the counter while you browse?"

Confused, Rebecca took a moment to remember that she was still holding a half-empty water bottle from home, lukewarm and capped.

The bookstore was even smaller inside than it looked from the outside—the counter that the clerk, a young girl in glasses, stood behind was only a few feet away, but the idea of stepping forward and setting her water bottle on it overwhelmed her.

"It's a water bottle," she said. "It's not even cold." It wouldn't leave condensation rings if she set it down on a book, which she wouldn't have done anyway.

"Ma'am, please," the girl said.

And although normally Rebecca would cooperate, understanding that the clerk was only doing what she'd been told, today was no ordinary day.

Rebecca unscrewed the bottle, walked up to the checkout counter, and poured what remained in it onto the countertop. The girl watched speechlessly, her jaw hanging.

And as Rebecca walked back out onto the street, she noticed that, for the moment, she felt better.

Whenever he was alone in the apartment, Mickey sang. He sang loud and full: musical tunes from his audition book that he hadn't sung in years; pop songs he'd never sung because they'd been released since his hemorrhage. Every melody boosted his confidence. He'd forgotten what confidence felt like, to have an identity that wasn't strapped exclusively to his utility to a billionaire. And still, he kept it a secret.

He was waiting to tell Rebecca until he could be sure that his voice was here to stay, and until they knew what was going on with Bash. Because he would, of course, do what was best for Bash regardless of what happened with his voice.

And there was a niggling fear, a tiny one, but there all the same: even if Bash was okay, even if things turned out fine, that if he told Rebecca that he was recovered, that he could sing again and was ready to return to New York (he had decided that regardless of all the perks of living in Florida, he *was* eager to return to New York, if not right away, then soon), she could say no. No, because his salary was more reliable here, with a lower cost of living. No, because they'd seen that medical emergencies could arise. Or no, because she liked being enmeshed in the world she was writing about.

He didn't feel like he would have a good counterargument to these. And how disappointing would that be, for a miracle to happen only for his wife to tell him that it was too late?

So he continued to wait. As long as he waited, he could hope.

CHAPTER 22

One morning in mid-April, over a month after Bash's first birthday, Rebecca was packing up the stroller while Bash lay on his back on the floor, on a quilt covered in tangerines that Rebecca's mother had sent after he was born. The helium balloons Fran had bought for his birthday still bobbed at half-mast by the window.

Just as she was grabbing her sunglasses and keys, Bash started to whine.

"What's wrong, baby?" Rebecca went to his wriggling body, and as she realized what was happening, her heart collapsed.

There was a different way that developmental delay could manifest, one that Dr. Goldin had mentioned, and that Rebecca had half listened to, as she hadn't really seen it as a threat at the time: regression.

"Watch out," Dr. Goldin had said, "for Bash losing any of the skills he's previously demonstrated."

"Like what?" Mickey had asked, which had annoyed Rebecca for an unclear reason.

Like anything, I'm sure! she'd wanted to yell.

"Like feeding himself, rolling over, picking up toys, pointing..."

He was trying to turn over and couldn't.

Sebastian's second seizure came on a rainy day not long after. Rebecca had just left the Publix at CityPlace, their go-to grocery store because it was within walking distance of their condo, and she always preferred not to drive if possible. In a canvas grocery bag, which she'd hung on a hook attached to the stroller, were almond milk, some produce to puree for Bash, and ingredients to make cauliflower dill soup for dinner.

Fuck. Forgot garlic, she thought.

She'd just wheeled the stroller around to go back the direction from which she'd come when, as often happened in South Florida, the rain swept in out of nowhere, dropping in barrelfuls, sending people scrambling under awnings as they clutched their phones to their hearts.

Rebecca stood with the stroller under the black-and-white-striped Sephora awning when a stranger, a woman her mother's age wearing a low-cut sundress that exposed ample, sun-spotted cleavage, grabbed her arm so hard that Rebecca almost hit her as a reflex.

"Ma'am! Your son!"

The seizure was identical to the previous, horrible in all the same ways—the stiffening, the trembling, the interminable duration of it—except for one: this time, he'd been asleep when it started.

Breathing, she gently turned Bash on his side like Dr. Goldin had instructed.

"Do you want me to call nine-one-one?" the woman asked.

"It's okay," Rebecca said, aware of people gathering, of onlookers craning their necks across the plaza where they stood clustered in front of the macaroon store opposite Sephora.

Within moments, Bash had relaxed again and, incredibly, remained asleep. His hand gripped her finger. Her hand reflexively went to his chest. His little heart was racing like a rabbit, but at least now he was breathing normally.

She grew dizzy. She closed her eyes and gratefully accepted the woman's hand to steady herself.

"Do you want me to take you somewhere?" the woman asked, clearly having picked up on the fact that Rebecca was on foot.

"I'm okay," she said, reaching for her phone, hitting Dr. Goldin's number, and lifting it to her ear. It began to ring. It was only then that she realized that the rain had lifted as quickly as it had descended. The sun was back out, bright and high overhead, like a storm had never come.

She thanked the woman and set out toward home, redialing when it went to voicemail.

The primary indications of Alexander disease were seizure, infant hydrocephaly—a swollen head—and delayed development.

Bash had displayed two of the three, but since he'd only been delayed on one milestone, crawling, and was still in the normal realm to start walking—and since the leukodystrophy panel should have caught it, Dr. Goldin was hesitant to label it. Mickey had taken the afternoon off to join Rebecca at the appointment.

"And there was the issue he had rolling over," Rebecca said. "That's regression."

"But that wasn't—" Mickey stopped himself. Bash was turning over properly again. "That seems to have resolved itself."

"It wasn't just in my head," Rebecca said.

"You think that's what he has?" Mickey asked Dr. Goldin. "Alexander disease?"

"Especially given this possible regression, we can't rule it out," Dr. Goldin said.

The microarray test had turned up nothing unusual. Bash was now five-for-five for normal test results, including a negative one for Alexander disease, but he was two-for-three on telltale signs of the disease.

"But I thought you said we tested him for it and it came back negative," Mickey said.

"Just because a test doesn't show it doesn't mean one doesn't have it. No test is perfect," the doctor said. "It's also possible for it to be caused by an atypical SNP . . . a mutation not screened for in the standard protocol . . ."

He paused.

"But in the meantime, I want to run another test called an exome. It's similar, just with a slightly different focus. We'll need to take blood for that one and can do so today. Sound okay?"

They nodded in tandem as Bonnie the nurse appeared with a vial.

On the drive home, Mickey reached out to take her hand.

Rebecca, who'd always been the affectionate one, now flinched when he touched her—not in a recoiling way, but like she hadn't seen him coming.

That evening, as Rebecca stood stirring carrot turmeric soup after putting Bash down, it occurred to her that she didn't have anyone to call just to talk.

At thirty-four, she'd been the average age of a new mother in New York, but most of her friends hadn't had kids yet. Once she did, it had become hard to keep up those relationships in the same way. She couldn't go out at night. She would invite people over, but they'd have to find a space to sit among the nineteen baby stations and entertainment centers packed into Rebecca and Mickey's Queens one-bedroom, and then pretend not to be distracted when Rebecca had to nurse or pump in front of them. Once, she fell asleep while her friend Adrienne was talking to her. It wasn't exactly a recipe for gracious hospitality.

But greater than the physical challenges had been the mental one. Rebecca had found it so hard to care or think about anything but the baby in those first few months. When friends came over and talked about their jobs or new boyfriends or horrible mothers-in-law, she couldn't believe how little she cared to listen. She struggled to pay attention and would fight to pretend otherwise, nodding and responding while keeping an eye on Bash and wondering when he'd poop next.

Eventually it all became too exhausting—whether for her, her friends, or all of them—and she stopped trying so hard, drifting away from the people she'd once talked to daily and seen several times a week.

"Your lives will realign once they have kids," a mother from the neighborhood mommies' group back in Queens had told her. "This is a phase. Give it time."

But then she and Mickey had moved.

Her friend Heidi, also a journalist, had a son Bash's age, and they'd texted a lot at first. But Rebecca had inadvertently withdrawn once Heidi had begun sending videos of Charlie walking. She didn't want to feel competitive, but it stirred in her heart a small fear she now recognized would be with her forever: *Is my child behind?*

She texted Heidi. Hey! How's it going?

doing bath call u later Heidi wrote back a few minutes later.

She texted her friend Matt. Want to catch up soon? Miss you!

Yes! going into Orangetheory, text you after xo, he wrote.

Standing above the flame, she wondered if she should call her mother. Along with the new depths of fear, Bash's situation had fostered in her a desire to maintain a better relationship with her own parents. They'd surely feared for her at times in the same way she feared for Bash, and realizing that filled her with empathy. Opening her phone, she looked at her call history and saw that she hadn't spoken to them since January, apart from a few short texts.

Damn. That was a long time. Rebecca hit Call. Her mother answered after one ring.

"Rebecca?" she said, concern in her voice. "Is everything okay?"

Rebecca swallowed. *No, Mom, it's not. I need a mom right now.*

"Just calling to check in," Rebecca said. "How is everything?"

"So you're fine?" her mom asked.

"Yes, we're good," she lied.

"Good. That makes one of us."

"What do you mean?" she asked.

Her mom laughed nervously.

"Ohhh, things here are not great. The farm got foreclosed on last month, and—"

"Wait, what?"

"Dad had taken out that second line of credit on the farm? And after we lost so many animals in the flood last April, we couldn't keep up? We had to move."

"Oh my God, Mom," Rebecca said. "Where did you move to? Why didn't you tell me?"

"We got a place in Murfreesboro."

"What are you doing for work?"

"Do you remember Warren Donelson?"

"No."

"He owned the Sprint when you were little? When there was still Sprint?"

"There's still Sprint."

"Anyway, now he owns some T-Mobiles. He hired your dad."

"Dad works at T-Mobile? Like, selling phones?"

"No. Well, yes. He works there. But he sells mainly to businesses."

"But, like, in a store? Wearing a T-shirt and a name tag?"

"Yes, why are you asking it like that?"

"Mom, that's crazy. I'm so sorry." Rebecca stopped stirring and sat.

"It's fine. Don't worry about us. How is Sebastian? Is he saying words yet?"

"Not yet," she said. "He's still young for that. Where do you live now?"

"I told you, Murfreesboro."

"But where? You got a house there?"

"We're renting a condo. It's small but fine."

"Jesus, Mom."

"What? We're fine, I said! How do you like Florida? Are you happy?"

Rebecca swallowed. She wasn't going to burden her mother with the news of Bash's illness until they knew more.

"It's great," she said. "I wanted to say I'm sorry."

There was a long pause.

"Sweetheart, for what?"

"For not calling you more."

"Oh, please, you're busy!"

"I'm really not."

A long pause. It was what neither had said aloud before.

"I would have called if I thought you wanted me to," her mom said finally.

"I know. I have to finish making dinner now."

"All right," her mom said. "Thanks for calling. Send more pictures of my grandson, please, for Pete's sake."

Rebecca filled a large mug with the steaming soup. *Foreclosed?*

Her parents had always seemed invincible . . . although now, thinking about it, of course they weren't. Here they were approaching retirement age, and her father was working at T-Mobile. Her mother had never done work off the farm.

Rebecca sat on the sofa and opened her laptop. She navigated to Vanguard and logged in.

In addition to their retirement accounts, she now had a third, a brokerage. She'd created it two weeks earlier, the day of Bash's second seizure.

Money wasn't going to grow in a savings account, not fast enough.

She sat quietly for several minutes, then, telling herself she was simply curious, she opened a private browser and googled "Buy Aura stock."

It cost $204/share. She did a little googling.

On average, stocks pop between 14 percent and 18 percent after positive earnings reports.

Last month at dinner, Catherine Priest had said she'd make the company's earnings announcement in May—it could come any day now. At the low end, that would be an increase of $28/share.

They'd saved $125,000 for retirement, which of course she wouldn't hesitate to drain for Bash's medical care if necessary—if she invested all of it, she could buy six hundred shares.

At an increase 14 percent, that would become $143,000 overnight.

But market expectation influences this number. If a lower rise is expected, the actual rise will be higher. If a higher rise is expected, a lower rise is likely.

Aura had been performing poorly the year prior, and while Rebecca was no finance expert, she knew from her stint with the personal finance team at GMA that it was true—when a company was performing poorly and, therefore, the earnings report was *expected* to be negative but turned out to be positive, a larger increase in stock price was common.

That scenario would leave her with $175,000, a $50,000 profit. She'd need to sell quickly afterward to lock it in. But that would be easy enough.

No one could trace it back to her—she didn't work for the Stones in any on-the-books way. She and Mickey didn't share a last name. And Catherine Priest had been a guest at the Stones' home only that one evening.

The more she thought about it, the more doable it all seemed. Not just doable, but smart.

Rebecca clicked open her account.

CHAPTER 23

The third seizure came as Rebecca was dressing him. The now-familiar flexing grabbed hold of his small body, and she thought, *This is why they call it seizing.* Because the body is seized by an external force, something mighty against which it cannot defend itself.

This time, more than terror, it was anger that coursed through Rebecca's veins as she held Bash's tiny arms and screamed through the indifferent apartment, "Stop! Stop it!"

He came out of it hushed, his eyes vacant, and she stroked his blond head and sang the silly, half-sensical song she'd made up when he was born after he'd splashed through his first baths, while he lay on her, skin to skin: *There is a boy Sebastian. He's funner than a bash (tee-on). And boy he loves to splash (tee-on). I'll love him till I'm ash (tee-on).*

They had an appointment that morning anyway. She held him and gathered their things, while phoning Dr. Goldin's office to let him know they were headed over early.

Dr. Goldin was ready to name the diagnosis. Alexander disease, one of the rare types of leukodystrophy. He got there by process of elimination.

"I'm confused," Mickey said. "I thought we'd ruled this one out."

"We'd ruled out the most common cause of it. He doesn't have that particular genetic mutation. But just because he doesn't have the GFAP mutation doesn't mean he can't have Alexander disease. There are other mutations that can cause it. They're just rarer."

He was the rare among the rare.

And I'm the one percent who lost my voice after surgery, Mickey thought. More rare of the rare. He instantly felt bad for making the comparison.

"What mutation does he have? Is there anything we can do?" he asked. Rebecca had gone white.

"They're unclear mutations. We don't know what they do. What we do know is that he's unlikely to live past the age of six."

So based on nothing actually scientific, Mickey heard, his son was being diagnosed with a terminal disease.

What Rebecca heard was: die before six.

As a girl, Rebecca had an active fantasy life. She'd envisioned herself as one of those lady lawyers on TV in a skirt suit and heels, bringing bad guys to justice. As a teenager she created a boyfriend whom she met at summer camp and who lived in New York. This boy *did* exist—she'd really met him at camp, Kevin really was his name—but not only was he not her boyfriend, he'd spent the whole summer confusing her with another camper and calling her Renée.

The fantasizing had carried into adulthood. Before she'd ever moved into her beautiful Manhattan studio apartment—the one she'd given up for Mickey—she'd visualized it. Before she'd gotten pregnant, she'd pictured herself with an adorable little bump, bopping around the city, decaf soy latte in hand. Once she was pregnant, she'd imagined herself as a new mom: the calm kind one might describe as low-maintenance chic, her infant snug against her body in a soft, organic wrap.

And here was the thing with Rebecca—it wasn't that when the

"real" thing arrived, and looked different from the fantasy, she was disappointed. It didn't make a difference. She'd already moved on to imagining the next stage, the next piece of her future.

But when they were given Bash's diagnosis, Rebecca stopped seeing the future. It was there—she sensed it, like a person you wish would leave the room—but she couldn't look at it.

And in its place, a new need: she needed to step out of this life.

This life had become suffocating, heavy and wet. She had to shed it, she had to step out from the place where it puddled around her and into some place where she could breathe.

Weeks earlier, she'd stopped responding to Jason Pirozzi's texts, but she'd kept the dates of the Digital Media Summit in her mind: May 3 through 6.

"It would be good for me to go," she told Mickey. "To network."

Mickey, in his own state of shock, didn't seem to find it the slightest bit strange for Rebecca to have a work conference out of state so suddenly after their child was diagnosed with a terminal illness.

"Okay," he said. "When is your flight?"

They sat on plush stools at the W Hotel bar in downtown Austin. She ordered a Manhattan, up.

Jason looked the same as his more recent online photos, but with even more hair than in the photos, not less—in the way men in their late thirties who still have hair grow it out to show it off.

Rebecca wore a silk wrap dress she hadn't taken off the hanger in months. When she put it on, it revealed to her just how much weight she'd unintentionally lost—the irony of finally shedding those last seven pounds of baby weight not lost on her. Now that she didn't give a fuck. It had been so long since she'd worn makeup that seeing her reflection in the mirror was like looking at a former version of herself, one with eyebrows and lashes.

She'd decided not to tell Jason about Bash's diagnosis; that was not why she was here. She did not want to talk about her baby; she did not want to think about her precious son; she did not want the sympathy of any more strangers.

"How old is your son now?" he asked.

"One," she said. "Tell me about Paris. The only time I've ever gone I was pregnant and sick the whole time, so it's one big blur. What was it like living there?"

"Decadent," he said. "And the health care is excellent, and cheap. Even for visitors."

"Sounds terrible," she said.

"Remember horrible Tommy Doolittle from college?"

"Of course," she said. Tommy Doolittle was their ambitious classmate whose drive was off-putting.

"He ended up staying with me for a while there."

"Oh, boy," she said.

"It was a bad idea, but he needed housing."

"Did he talk about his dual degree the whole time?"

"Only every other day," he said. Then he told her more stories from his Paris days; she told him old stories from the *Good Morning America* set. They both avoided the topic of where she'd come from and who was waiting for her back home.

After two hours, they were reaching the bottom of their second round. Rebecca hadn't felt what she'd wanted. Instead of drifting toward distraction, every conversation about something other than Bash seemed to buoy him back into her mind. Was this what it felt like to be in a play—pretending your mind and voice were in sync when it couldn't be less true?

"We should toast," he said. "To your new column. I'm proud of you." He raised his glass.

She inhaled as a rock formed in her belly.

I'm proud of you?

How could he be proud of her when he was a stranger? He didn't know her. The years they'd spent apart sat on the table between them like a boulder: the life she'd made; the way Bash looked at her out of the side of his eye and then eased into a smile; the way he wiggled his toes when she asked where his toes were; the way he squeezed his eyes shut when she tickled him.

And Mickey. Mickey had said the same words after Bash came into the world via C-section. After holding her leg up as she tried to push Bash into the world, then holding her hand when it turned out he'd have to arrive via surgery. Her husband, back in Florida, was probably sitting on their balcony, alone. In the morning, he would slather Bash in sunscreen and take him down to the shallow end of the pool, where he'd float their son in his tiny inner tube before the sun climbed too high in the sky and they'd have to go back inside.

"What are you thinking?" Jason asked.

"It's been nice to see you," she said, opening her purse, relieved to see she had two twenties and wouldn't have to wait for her card to be run. She placed them on the table. "Thanks for meeting me for a drink."

They hugged, a hug that felt distant and that she nonetheless didn't want to end.

She was a mother of a dying child. The sadness came in, and it was all sorrow, and it was all air.

Mickey and Bash were waiting for her at the airport when she returned.

On the flight, she'd contemplated asking her doctor back in New York to increase her dosage of Lexapro. She could tell him to max her out. Make her as light as a balloon.

She climbed into the car after peeking through the back window at Bash, who was snoozing peacefully in his car seat. She closed the door and leaned over to lay on Mickey's shoulder. No one was waiting behind them, shooing them forward with an angry honk. No crowds, no grumpy traffic guard in a yellow vest.

"I can't handle this pain," she finally said.

The diagnosis had been devastating for Mickey, but it wasn't the pivot point it had been for his wife. From the first seizure, Mickey had feared the worst. He'd known in his gut that Bash wasn't okay. Now there was a more concrete hypothesis as to why, and concreteness was progress. Perhaps, in giving a name to the problem, something could be done.

"You will," he said. "Because we have no choice."

He put the car in drive, reaching over to squeeze her forearm.

CHAPTER 24

"Do you still want to go?" he asked two days before her birthday, the first week of May, after spoiling the surprise. Before the diagnosis, Mickey had booked the two of them two nights at the Breakers as a surprise to celebrate Rebecca's thirty-fifth birthday.

"I mean, it's a sweet idea but I'm not leaving Bash," she said.

"Of course not," he said. "We can take him. I was going to suggest we ask Bonnie to come sit in the room with him if we, you know, want to go out to dinner after he's down."

Bonnie, Dr. Goldin's nurse.

Why not? she thought. Nothing mattered now, so why the hell not?

The morning of her birthday, Rebecca sat on a bench at the rear of the hotel's beachfront terrace with Bash in her lap. Mickey was working out. Since the news, he'd been running miles and miles and miles, then coming home and lifting weights until he collapsed. He'd always stayed in shape, but this had stretched into mania. Rebecca said nothing. To each his own.

She watched another thirtysomething mother dressed in a flowy pair of peach pants chase her toddler and sweep him up into her arms, only to set him down and chase him again.

"Martin!" the woman called as Martin fled over and over, deter-mined to round the corner to the pool.

Bash, slumped against his mom, was the same size as Martin but had the posture of a much younger child.

The mother made eye contact with Rebecca and smiled.

"How old is yours?" she asked.

"Fourteen months," Rebecca said. The spark of pity on the wom-an's face triggered a wave of rage. "Fuck you!" she wanted to yell. "Fuck you!"

A middle-aged couple passed, covered from head to toe in match-ing sun-protective gear and wearing ergonomic sandals. A trio of teenage girls posed for photos in front of the surf for forty min-utes, puckering and swapping, puckering and swapping. An old couple, hunched and clutching each other for stability, inched their way out of the residence to the bench next to Rebecca, where they fell asleep, the man's chin buried in his chest, her face turned up to the sun.

Mickey appeared, glistening and grinning. One hand was be-hind his back.

"Hi," he said.

"What?" she said.

He revealed what he was holding—a red Cartier box. She'd spot-ted a Cartier store in the lobby of the hotel, along with a Tom Ford, an Escada, and a Prada, but she hadn't planned to set foot in any of them.

"What's this?"

"Happy birthday," he said. "Obviously I just bought it. I was go-ing to get you a surfboard, and then, you know."

"Mickey. What on earth?"

"Just open it."

She did. It was a thin gold chain. From Cartier. It probably cost five thousand dollars.

"We don't need to be buying things like this right now."

"I know, but one necklace seemed okay, right?"

"Mickey, why are you giving me fancy jewelry?" It came out as a plea.

He looked off.

"I don't know," he said. "Wanting things to feel normal for you on your birthday, I guess."

"Our kid is dying," she said, resisting the urge to whisper it. Bash could understand a lot these days, even though he couldn't yet speak.

Mickey continued to look out at the ocean.

"I know," he said quietly.

She was being ungrateful. He was struggling, too.

Put on the necklace, Rebecca. Put on the fucking necklace.

She handed Bash to Mickey, unclasped the necklace, and fastened it around her neck.

That evening, with the baby monitor propped between Rebecca's place setting and her water glass, they sat at a candlelit two-top in the hotel dining room. Even with Bonnie upstairs, she preferred to keep watch over Bash while he slept, just in case. What if he seized while Bonnie was in the bathroom?

Their cocktails arrived, a scotch for Mickey and an Aperol spritz for her. They tapped glasses silently.

"How're you feeling?" he asked.

"Fine," she said, eyeing the monitor. Was that a squirm? Or had she imagined it? She picked it up, peered closely. Bash was still. She put it back in its spot. "Why?"

"We haven't really talked about it, and maybe we should."

"What do you mean?"

"I mean we literally haven't talked about it since Dr. Goldin told us," he said. "You left for your conference and came back, and we haven't talked about it once."

"What's there to say?" she said.

"We could . . . I don't know, share our feelings?" She took a warm slice of sourdough bread from the breadbasket and tore off a piece. After a second, she grabbed the butter knife, cleaved a chunk of butter, and smeared it across the bread. Mickey raised his eyebrows. She ignored it.

"When I was in Austin I had coffee with an ex-boyfriend," she said when she finished chewing. "Actually it wasn't coffee. It was drinks. I don't know why I just said coffee."

His eyes locked on hers.

"Just drinks?" he asked.

"Yes," she said. "I dressed up for it, though. I wore makeup."

She was dressed in the same wrap dress now, was also in makeup now. It had all happened mechanically: put on dress, put on mascara.

"What are you telling me?" he asked.

"I wanted to be someone else. I wanted to go back in time and have made different choices so that I wouldn't have to feel like this."

Mickey nodded slowly. If there was anything he understood, it was pretending. He'd learned it young. Mickey at twelve, just like Mickey at thirty-six, possessed a singular charisma, a good ear, and perfect pitch. He'd shone onstage at his local performing arts center. Somewhere deep in his subconscious, the logic had gone like this: if he danced well enough and sang well enough, one day his father would show up to watch.

Acting had evolved for him, often becoming a kind of therapy in his adult years; it got him out of his head, and he found that, bizarrely, he could embody a character's emotions more easily than his own. If they felt joy, well, so did he. When they hurt, so did he. Mickey onstage was Mickey experiencing the full range of human emotions. And Mickey offstage? Was waiting to get back on.

Until he met Rebecca. With her, for the first time, he felt alive even when he wasn't pretending to be someone else.

"I understand," he said. "It's okay. Is that all?"

"But it's not okay," she said, grabbing another slice of bread and ripping it in half. "I don't know how to do this. I don't know how to feel this all the time. It's like my body can't take it. I'm going to die if I have to feel like this all the time." She stuffed the bread in her mouth.

"What do you need?" he asked.

She shrugged, mouth full.

"There's more," she said after the swallowing.

He shifted in his chair.

"I bought Aura stock." She paused, letting him put the pieces together.

"When?" he asked.

"Before the earnings announcement this week. We made a lot. Almost forty grand."

"Have you sold it?" His eyes danced with fear. He never looked at the accounts. He had no reason to.

"Yes," she said. "As soon as it went up. I know, it was dumb. I won't do it again." She spoke the last part like she was a scolded child who didn't actually feel sorry for what she had done.

"It wasn't *dumb*. It was—" he stopped.

"I know," she said. "Criminal. I just wanted—"

"It's okay," Mickey said, grabbing her hand and squeezing it too hard. "Don't do anything like that again, okay? It'll be okay." But they both knew it wasn't true, not in the grand sense, and the soft *shhh* sound of the monitor on the tabletop suddenly sounded like a roar.

Through the rest of the meal, they talked about things neither of them cared about, things that in some other lifetime, one in which they had a healthy child, might matter: her parents' foreclosure; Paul's new job in a Newark restaurant; the looming hurricane season. Meanwhile, Bash's little body radiated from the small screen between them.

They skipped dessert, relieving themselves of the obligation to pretend any longer, and went upstairs with a bottle of champagne as a thank-you to Bonnie, who had refused to accept payment.

That night Mickey couldn't sleep. Why did smoke detectors in hotel rooms have such bright blinking lights?

He lay in bed, his mind spinning. Despite himself, he was almost impressed by his wife's financial strategizing. At least she was doing something. Taking action, which was more than could be said for him.

He was sure that they shouldn't resign themselves to Bash's demise. He had to believe that something could be done to save his son. Why he had this kind of faith, he wasn't sure . . . maybe because, these days, he was constantly surrounded by people for whom anything was possible? Had their energy rubbed off on him? He just didn't know what to do.

Five years. So much could happen in five years—advances in technology, in medicine, in genetics. Medical breakthroughs abounded. If just one brilliant research team, a funded one, turned its attention to Alexander disease . . .

It hit him. How had he not thought of it before?

He reached for his phone, dimmed the screen to the lowest setting, and typed his idea; he knew he wouldn't forget it, but he wanted to record it anyway. For the rest of the night he tossed, that speck of light still dancing behind his lids whenever he closed them. He couldn't wait to tell Rebecca over breakfast.

As soon as the hotel restaurant opened at six a.m., the three of them, already up since five, joined the other handful of early risers in the vast dining room. In the harsh sunlight it looked different than it had the night before, colder. Mickey stood at the omelet stand awaiting his made-to-order dish as Rebecca sat at the table sipping a delicious cup of coffee and shielding her eyes; she'd taken the seat with the glare.

That coffee could still taste this good didn't make sense.

Bash giggled.

When would he lose his ability to laugh? Would that stop?

Mickey appeared, setting a plate of fruit and muesli in front of her. "You want some bacon this morning?" he teased.

"Shut up," she said, embarrassed. They both knew that eating butter might not have been a big deal to many people, including vegans having a momentary lapse, but for her, it was. Rebecca's veganism was her value system. Her eating the butter had been a kind of self-sabotage he'd never witnessed from her before.

"I had an idea last night," he said, taking a seat in the Victorian armchair. "Want these?" He handed her his Ray-Bans.

"Oh?" She put them on.

"You know how the Stones are always assembling smart people to discuss things over lunch? When it's not, you know, the Webers or the book club, I mean."

"Yes," she said. It was one of the few perks of being a billionaire that she actually envied. The Stones could call up seemingly any-one on earth and convince them to show up in Palm Beach in per-son for a single meal, even if it required flying across the world. Money, man.

"He's done one on the economy, on China, on the election . . ."

"I know," she said. "And Henry Kissinger comes to all of them." She could still make jokes, apparently. "What about them?"

"What if I see if he'll do one for Alexander disease?"

She sipped her coffee as if he hadn't just flipped her upside down, as if her hope wasn't rising like water in a flood zone.

It was a long shot—but she had to tell herself this. Because her first thought was: *Yes, yes, this is how we will save Bash.*

"Should I call Mrs. Stone right now?" she asked. Behind his shades, her excitement was hidden. He waited for her reaction.

Rebecca hadn't seen Mrs. Stone in person since Bash's diagnosis, but Mrs. Stone had started to text, addressing and signing her texts as if they were emails. Her first had read, Dear Rebecca, Between Cecil and Mickey I am being kept abreast of the news. I am thinking of you. Please let me know if you need anything. Affectionately, Astrid

It had touched Rebecca that Mrs. Stone had checked in, and that she'd signed her text "affectionately." In the days that followed, she'd found herself sharing more with Mrs. Stone than she ever would have guessed.

Rebecca, How is Sebastian feeling? —A

She always called him Sebastian, never Bash. Rebecca remembered that the name of Mrs. Stone's son had been Sherman, similar to Sebastian.

He's been fine recently, actually, no seizures.

That's so good to hear.

"I'll ask him in person tomorrow," Mickey said. "I think it should be in person."

"Okay," she said, her skin tingling. "Good thinking, Mickey. Good idea."

CHAPTER 25

Mr. Stone arrived from his flight home after a quick business trip to New York in the late afternoon. Even on the private jet, which tallied to one hundred fifty thousand dollars each way, Mr. Stone's legs were swollen after a flight, and so Mickey had an ice bath waiting. He was laying out a towel when his boss emerged from his dressing room in his boxers.

"Thank you, Mickey," his boss said, standing in his socks. He reached out to balance himself on the counter as he stripped one sock off at a time.

Mickey's heart raced. He'd never before asked Mr. Stone for a favor, and the stakes of this one were . . . well, everything.

But before Mickey could utter a word, Mr. Stone asked, "What's it called again? His sickness?"

"Alexander disease," Mickey said as Mr. Stone climbed onto the counter. For a man of his age, he was quite agile.

"I see. I assume Richard would know if there's an experimental treatment or clinical trial we can get him into." Richard was Dr. Goldin.

"He hasn't mentioned anything," Mickey said.

"Well, look," he said, slipping his feet into the icy water. "I don't want to step on your toes, of course, or give rise to any false hope.

But what if we had a lunch? I can talk to George, get names of the best people."

That's what Mr. Stone called assembling the world's best and brightest to tackle an insoluble problem: having a lunch. George, another close friend, ran a pharmaceutical empire.

"That's really generous of you," Mickey said. "I'd love that."

"Schedule it as soon as possible—we leave, you know, shortly." At the end of May, the Stones would depart to spend the summer in the Hamptons, and Mickey would stay in Florida to hold down the fort. They had fewer than two and a half weeks to make it happen.

Mickey held out a plush gray bath sheet.

Rebecca wasn't going to believe it. He hadn't even had to ask.

Rebecca, I gave Richard the name of a seizure specialist in LA. Pioneer in his field. He'll be reaching out. Follow up if you don't hear soon. —A

Rebecca, Me again. If you have any issues working with Richard on the lunch, let me know. I felt this went without saying but then decided I should say it anyway—there is absolutely no reason to settle for less than the ideal guest list. Money doesn't solve everything, but it helps with this. Let me know. —A

Empowered by Mrs. Stone's texts, Rebecca called Dr. Goldin, who'd been charged with organizing the event, and offered to help. To her relief, he seemed more than happy to involve Rebecca in composing their A-list, inviting her to his office to plan.

"Here's what I'm thinking," he said. "We want a clinician. We want research people. And we want genetics people. Cecil is the money person, but it might not hurt to have another money person there. How does this sound?"

"Good," she said. "And I have a few ideas, too."

Rebecca had dusted off her research skills and gotten to work, tracking down names in relevant fields who struck her as worthy: innovative, think-outside-the-box people.

After two days, they'd assembled their first, second, and third strings of invites and formally set the date: Saturday, May 19, giving the guests just over a week's notice.

They'd decided that a group of seven was optimal and six, acceptable. With the addition of Dr. Goldin, Mr. Stone, Mrs. Stone, Mickey, and Rebecca, they would make twelve.

Nine days before the event, Dr. Goldin sent out their eight first-round invitations, and as the replies came in, Bonnie texted Rebecca updates.

The head of the National Research Institute for Leukodystrophy was a yes. So were the Finnish research scientists studying stem-cell treatments, an expert in the gene alteration process CRISPR, and a clinician from Oregon who treated leukodystrophy patients and who was anecdotally known for having an unusual number of surprisingly positive outcomes.

They were still waiting to hear from the head of a research hospital in Berlin doing work with antisense oligonucleotides, also known as ASOs, which blocked the effects of the mutations that typically caused Alexander disease. And Dr. Goldin's medical school classmate, an oncologist who didn't have anything to do with leukodystrophy directly, but whom Dr. Goldin respected for his ability to see beyond obvious or standard approaches, was on board. Mrs. Stone's seizure specialist was a yes, as well.

They hadn't yet had a single no, which Rebecca saw as auspicious as she turned her attention to how the conversation should be facilitated. It was an important piece of the precious few hours they had with these people, and it had to be right. Bad moderation could render the whole endeavor futile.

"How do you plan to structure the conversation?" she asked when Dr. Goldin called to let her know that his classmate wasn't going to be able to make it after all—their first decline. He had a wedding.

"Not sure. Why, do you have specific questions in mind?" he asked.

Indeed, she did.

"As a journalist, I've spent a lot of time studying interview techniques, and I think we should keep it open to start. Maybe ask people to come prepared with answers to some basic questions, like, What is going to cure Alexander disease? How do we most quickly get there—what needs to happen, where will it happen, and who will do it? And, finally, how do we save this one boy?"

The third was the most vital to her, of course, and she didn't care that it was shamelessly specific to her son.

"You could begin by going around and hearing everyone's responses to the primary questions, then move into a discussion focused first on questions of clarification and understanding, then moving into next steps."

"Do you think we have time for all that?" he asked.

She paused. "How long do you think we have?"

"I don't think we can keep people for more than a couple of hours."

"I mean, we have to take all the time we need, right?" she said. *They may have a wedding,* she thought bitterly, then snapped back. People were coming. She would remain optimistic.

"Researchers tend to be long-winded . . ."

Rebecca felt a surge of panic.

"But that's why they're coming . . ." she said.

He must have heard the fear in her voice, because he said, "Of course. I'll do my best."

When Mickey arrived home that night, Rebecca had drawn a seating chart on a lined page in her notebook.

"This is what I'm thinking," she said, showing it to him before he'd even taken off his shoes.

The diagram showed people seated around a round table.

"You know the dining table is rectangular," he said.

She frowned. "I know. Can we not get a round one? How are twelve people going to have a conversation at a long table?"

"Do their best, I guess."

She glared at him.

"I know we both are nervous about this going well," he said, "but we have to remember that this is a favor *for* us."

"Okay," she said, closing her notebook. "You're right."

But after he went to sleep, she texted Mrs. Stone.

The next day, Mickey's first duty: securing a round table for the lunch.

CHAPTER 26

"Manatee!" Rebecca said over and over. "Manatee."

Bababa, Bash said. *Gagaga.*

The lunch was in two days. The Stones had left town for a three-day art show in Miami and were staying at the Four Seasons to spare themselves the back-and-forth commute. Since Mickey had a little time off, he and Rebecca had buckled Bash into the car seat and headed a few miles north to a manatee preserve. With their legs dangling off the pier, they passed him back and forth, pointing down to the giant creatures floating by underneath.

Seated between them on the dock, he pointed and babbled.

"You know," Mickey said, sipping a lukewarm Coke Zero, "we should keep our expectations in check." He glanced at her before continuing. "It's unlikely they're going to come up with anything."

"I know," she said as an especially large manatee appeared beneath her feet.

But how was she to resist having all the hope in the world?

"Do you wish we'd never had him?" Mickey asked so quietly she barely heard him over the waves and nearby chatter.

"Shh," she said, covering Bash's ears. "Of course not."

"Do you wish you'd never married me?" Mickey asked, a vulnerable tease in his voice.

"No," she said, shaking her head. "Stop it."

They sat for a while.

"My voice is back," he said out of the blue.

She turned to him.

"No way."

He spread his arms and sang a note, loud and vibrant. A family nearby turned and stared.

Rebecca started laughing. Mickey joined in.

"For fuck's sake," she said, her eyes watering as she rubbed them. "Are you kidding?"

"I know," he said, waving at the young boy down the pier who was still gawking. "I know."

The final count for lunch, not including Mickey, Rebecca, Dr. Goldin, or the Stones, was six. The Oregon doctor and one of the Finnish scientists had both been unable to make the trip last minute, but everyone else would be there.

The morning of the lunch, Mickey had already left for work when Rebecca rose, splashed water on her face, and fetched Bash, cheerfully spouting gibberish in his crib. She warmed him a bottle and started the coffee.

She put on the yellow sundress from Anthropologie and a cream blazer—she wanted to look professional, but it was still South Florida in the early summer—and drove to the Stones', Bash in the back seat. Bonnie had offered to watch him, once again, in the now-vacant cottage during the event. Rebecca had told her that she didn't feel comfortable leaving him with anyone who wasn't a medical professional, and this time, they'd insisted on paying her.

Rebecca pulled into their driveway half an hour before the scheduled start, and Mickey came out to greet them before she'd turned off the engine.

"Hi," Mickey said, opening the back door to get Bash out of his car seat. "You feeling okay?"

She nodded. He always asked if she was okay when *he* was nervous.

"Bonnie is almost here," he said. He scanned the property and seemed to consider something. The late-morning sun was bright, already bearing down on them.

"He's not wearing sunscreen," Rebecca said, instinctively raising a hand to shield Bash's face.

"Let's go inside," Mickey said. They crossed the veranda to find Mr. Stone in a teal button-down and white shorts waiting just inside the French doors.

"This must be Bash," he said. Mickey angled his son so that Mr. Stone could see his face.

"Hello, little one," said Mr. Stone stiffly. He reached out and gave their son's bare toe a pinch. (Bash fussed when she put shoes on him, and even on an occasion such as this, Rebecca wasn't going to make him do anything he didn't want to do. His little life—abbreviated as it may be—would be as comfortable as she could possibly make it.)

Through the open door they heard another car pulling in, and Mickey headed out to guide Bonnie to the side parking lot, leaving Rebecca alone with Mr. Stone.

"Thank you for today," she said. "We're so grateful."

"Anything we can do to help," he said.

"But he doesn't have the GFAP mutation. It's VUS," said the leukodystrophy specialist.

The lunch conversation had taken on a life of its own. Within minutes, the prompts Rebecca had come up with had been quickly jettisoned as they'd dived right into discussing Bash's case.

They all understood precisely why they'd been called: not to cure Alexander disease, but to save this child.

"If it's VUS, is it still—wait, how do we know it's Alexander then?"

"Demethylation."

"But its origin is unknown so it's in some ways more like ALD, no?"

"ALD doesn't typically manifest this early in infancy."

"Either way, if it's methylation, it could be that stem-cell treatment could make a difference. No?"

Rebecca followed as best she could.

"How old is he again?" one of the researchers asked.

"Fifteen months," she said.

"I think it's worth considering," said Dr. Goldin's classmate, who had been able to make it last minute.

"It wasn't effective in a trial for Alexander," said the researcher.

"But that was GFAP."

The medical school classmate was the most enthusiastic person present, pushing the others to get concrete about what might work. As Rebecca listened, she was relieved that he had come, and she wondered whether he was skipping the wedding. While the others didn't visibly share his optimism, they didn't seem cynical either. Just cautious.

"If the boy's symptomology bears resemblance to ALD—which it does—then, in the absence of evidence to the contrary, there's no reason to conclude it won't be responsive to ALD-responsive treatment," he said.

"At this point there's little to lose, I would think," said Mrs. Stone, reading between the lines. Rebecca hadn't seen her since the diagnosis, and the woman's demeanor at the table was new to her: feverish, fidgety.

This is bringing back memories for her, Rebecca thought. Astrid was afraid.

"Would a compassionate use request be necessary then?" asked Dr. Goldin.

Rebecca had been researching "right to try" policies—state laws allowing experimental treatments prior to FDA approval when someone's life was on the line. She'd learned that opponents worried about patients being lured into spending huge amounts of money out of desperation on questionable therapies that insurance wouldn't cover. But none of these people had dying children, she felt certain.

No one knew the answer to Dr. Goldin's question.

"I'm not confident that stem-cell treatment will address the Rosenthal fibers," the leukodystrophy expert said.

"I didn't see any Rosenthal fibers on his scans," Dr. Goldin said. The table was silent as several of the guests exchanged meaningful looks that Rebecca struggled to decipher.

"When was the last scan?" the specialist asked.

"What kind of fibers?" Rebecca asked.

"Rosenthal fibers are abnormal proteins present in the brains of Alexander children," the specialist said. "I just don't think they'll be responsive to stem-cell treatment. Which isn't to say we shouldn't try it . . ."

"We haven't done an MRI since he was in the ER," Dr. Goldin said.

"He must have the fibers though, if it's Alexander. If he doesn't have them, it's not Alexander," the specialist said.

For several loaded moments, no one spoke.

Rebecca's heart leaped into her throat. What was he saying?

"We ran the genetic tests for the other leukodystrophies," Dr. Goldin said. "And his presentation isn't congruent with what we typically see of those . . . bladder issues, vision and hearing problems, respiratory issues . . ."

"So maybe it isn't leukodystrophy. If he doesn't have the fibers, it's not Alexander," the specialist said again.

"What is it then?" Mr. Stone asked, sounding a bit impatient.

"I was thinking, actually," the seizure expert said, speaking up for the first time since the introductions, "that this case, to me, has indications of Dravet syndrome."

"What?" Rebecca said. "What's that?" She was leaning so heavily into the table that she was barely touching her chair. Mickey, seated at the table for once while Grace waited on them, placed a hand on her thigh.

"Epilepsy," Dr. Goldin told Rebecca, then turned back to the specialist. "But he didn't have the SCN1A mutation."

"One in five don't," said the specialist, "maybe more. If it's not GFAP and he doesn't have the fibers, his symptoms are as easily that, no? Developmental delays and seizures. And she said he's crawling..."

"He is," she said.

"I think Dravet is as logical a diagnosis as Alexander."

"Why didn't you say so before?" Dr. Goldin said playfully, always expert at lightening the mood. "You all were so confident in Alexander!" he continued, and the others laughed. *He'd* been the one to conclude it was Alexander.

"Let's all slow down . . . that's *if* he doesn't have the fibers," the leukodystrophy expert said. Then to Rebecca, he said, "The fibers can develop. Just because he didn't have them before when you went to the ER doesn't mean he doesn't now."

"If he has Dravet, what does that . . . ?" She didn't finish her question, gripping Mickey's forearm under the table so hard that he pried her fingers off and held them.

"There are seizure medications he'll need to take, and he'll need the developmental therapies," said the seizure expert.

"How long will he live?" Mickey blurted out, asking what Rebecca couldn't.

They both held their breath.

"Oh, it's typically manageable. Dravet patients tend to have generous life spans. With proper treatment, he could live as long as anyone here."

The corners of Rebecca's eyes stung, and then she couldn't help it. She was crying at the table.

"How do we find out if he has the fibers or not?" Mickey asked.

"A simple MRI," the leukodystrophy expert said, "is all we need."

CHAPTER 27

The following morning, Bash was sedated with an oral medication called chloral hydrate that Rebecca had to feed him via syringe—nothing new, since that's how they administered baby Motrin when his teething pain was bad.

But unlike he did with the purple Motrin, he started screaming the instant she dripped the thick, orange syrup into his mouth.

"It tastes god-awful," said the nurse, a southern woman in jungle print scrubs. "We're forever out of grape."

Bash lay on a medical cot in the wing of the same hospital they'd brought him to the day of his first seizure. He wore a tiny hospital gown, and this time, the patient's bracelet that matched the one on Rebecca's wrist—*Sebastian Honeycutt-Byrne. 3/5/17*—was placed around his ankle.

"Don't be alarmed," the nurse said. "Once it hits, he's going to conk right out."

It took about ten minutes for the anesthesia to kick in, but when it did, Bash didn't conk out like the nurse had predicted. His eyes stayed open even though he was unconscious. It was eerily like his seizing. Rebecca stroked the soft bottom of his foot with her finger.

When it was time for him to be taken to the scanning room, Rebecca and Mickey were given a plastic buzzer like they were waiting for a table at Red Lobster. It would alert them when Bash was done, in anywhere from forty minutes to an hour, and they'd be permitted to come back to the same room to sit with him while the anesthesia wore off.

In the meantime, they were ushered back to the waiting room.

The children's radiation wing was busy, and as Rebecca observed the other children, she ached for them all. She watched a teeny baby—only a couple of weeks old—be carried beyond the double doors into the medical area by frightened parents. A little boy in glasses who couldn't be older than four went on his own and waved at his dad, trying to be brave. A girl who was five or six sat in her mother's lap intently watching the same children Rebecca was watching as, one by one, they disappeared through the doors, like she was memorizing what to do, preparing herself for what was to come. The girl had no hair.

"They apparently have donut holes at the nurses' station down the hall," Mickey said. "Want one?"

He waited.

"Oh, you're serious?" she said. "No."

He shrugged and exited, returning moments later with a paper coffee cup of glazed donut holes.

The minutes passed like hours: ten, twenty, twenty-five.

At thirty, Rebecca's nose started running uncontrollably for no reason, and Mickey left to find tissues, coming back with a wad of stiff toilet paper.

"You know the drill," the little girl's mom said to her daughter. "Get all your wiggles out."

The little girl and her mom both started doing their wiggles.

Shortly after, a little boy who'd just arrived asked the girl if she wanted to play. In the waiting room, there were only a few books and a wooden abacus-like device for much younger children. The kids sat down next to it, and Rebecca eavesdropped on their conversation.

"Have you done this before?" the boy said.

"Yes, don't worry," she said. "It just sounds like a police car. You know how a police car sounds?"

The little boy nodded.

"Do you watch *Paw Patrol*?" she asked.

He shook his head.

"What do you watch?"

"*Daniel Tiger.*"

"Mom! How many *Daniel Tigers* will it take?"

Rebecca leaned over to Mickey and whispered, "If I hear much more, I'm going to jump off this building."

He chuckled and said, "Donut holes help."

An hour and ten minutes after Bash had gone in for the exam, their Red Lobster buzzer lit up and shook, and they jumped to their feet. The receptionist buzzed them through the double doors, and they followed giant blue monster footprints on the floor to the curtained area where their son was silently sleeping, a nurse by his side.

"He did great," the nurse said. "All smooth."

"Yeah?" Rebecca said. "How does it look?" she asked, even though she knew the nurse couldn't tell her the results of the MRI, most likely hadn't even seen the scans. The question had just come out.

It took almost two days for the leukodystrophy specialist to get the results from the lab, and every minute of those forty-eight hours was the longest of Rebecca's life. Despite the pressure the doctor said he was putting on the hospital to release the scans, claiming urgency, he could do only so much to expedite the process.

By the time the images were finally transmitted to his office in New York and he reviewed them, Rebecca and Mickey had both imagined so many worst- and best-case scenarios that they were slaphappy and delirious from lack of sleep. Rebecca had eaten nothing but a few Cheerios and a bite of pasta. She couldn't even trust her stomach to keep down coffee.

They'd watched a marathon of *Unbreakable Kimmy Schmidt* on Netflix. Mostly it just played for hours, ticking automatically from one episode to the next, while they stared into space and submitted silent prayers to the universe, but fourteen episodes in, they couldn't stop laughing. Every scene was the funniest thing ever written.

Finally, on the third day, while Rebecca was pumping and Mickey was doing his two hundredth push-up of the morning, Dr. Goldin called. They placed the phone on the counter so they could talk to him on speaker.

"I have good news," he started. "No fibers."

Bash didn't have Alexander.

They held eye contact, neither saying a word.

"And there was no atrophying or any other degradation of the brain. I spoke with Tim and Charles . . ."–the leukodystrophy and child seizure experts–". . . and we think we should proceed in treating this as Dravet syndrome."

"Okay. Meaning . . ." Rebecca asked, interrupting.

"We'll want to get him on some anticonvulsants right away. From this point you should work directly with Tim. He's the best there is, so you're in good hands. He's already mentioned something about a vagus-nerve-stimulation treatment once Bash is old enough. But he can tell you more about that."

"Of course," she said. "Oh, God. Oh, God. Thank God." Mickey was still, his hands on his head. She was shaking her hands like they were wet.

"Hey guys, I'm happy for you," Dr. Goldin said. "I know Dravet is still scary, but this is, to say the least, a preferable outcome."

"Fuck, yeah, it is," Mickey said, and they all laughed.

"Thank you for everything," Rebecca said to Dr. Goldin, unable to find more words.

"You guys made all this happen," he said. "But you're welcome."

The second they hung up, Mickey launched into song—"Brand New Day" from *The Wiz.*

"Can you feel a brand new daaay!"

He grabbed her into a tight hug that loosened into a ballroom dance. Rebecca followed along, still stunned, the fatigue of the previous three days crashing into her.

"Where should we go for dinner?" Mickey asked. "To celebrate."

Bash was still sick, but he was going to live. *He is going to live.* Rebecca had to keep repeating it to herself.

"Where do you want to go?" she asked.

"I mean, this calls for something special. Outback?" He winked. Outback was where her family used to go for steaks on special occasions, much to her disapproval.

What does one do to celebrate getting life back when you'd thought it was lost?

It wasn't that nothing sounded worthy of this moment—it was that *everything* seemed worthy of this moment. Brushing her teeth, she'd do joyfully. Filing her taxes.

"Restoration Hardware?" she said. When they'd bought the sofa, they had briefly ventured to the top of the four-story designer furniture store to check out the rooftop restaurant. They'd glanced at the menu and the view, then left.

"Done," he said. "Bash is dying to check out their summer chaise collection."

They sat on the outdoor patio under a giant yellow umbrella, and Bash played peekaboo with the hostess while Mickey and Rebecca shared the most delicious salad she'd ever eaten—a citrus fennel and celery concoction that made her lips pucker.

"This makes my mouth sing, good God," she said. "Is it really this good, or is it the circumstance?"

"I think both," Mickey said. "I've eaten some fucking good salads, and this is pretty killer."

They both thought of Paul, since he'd recommended the Restoration Hardware restaurant in the first place months earlier.

"Have you talked to Paul?" she asked. He nodded.

"He has a restaurant job. Gets to see his kid every week."

She nodded.

"You know, he really thought he was doing the right thing for his son," Mickey said after a moment. "I know he's a misogynist and yada yada. But he didn't work for the Stones because he was some father who didn't care. In his head it was how he made the most money, and making the most money was how he could be a good father."

"I know," Rebecca said. "I get it." She felt nothing but compassion for Paul now. She felt nothing but compassion for everyone.

"Do you feel like we just got on the lifeboat leaving the *Titanic*?" Mickey asked.

She pressed a fist to her lips, just having sipped her prosecco.

"This is a fancy-ass lifeboat," she said, looking around.

"You know the sayin': better to break your toe on a yacht than at the bus stop."

"*Is* it, though? You're stuck on a boat . . ."

"Yeah. A *yacht*."

"I've never heard that before," she said. "Are you sure it's a saying?"

"Or I made it up. Anyway, I kind of feel like that. We really fucking won the lottery for people with a sick kid."

She looked out to the horizon. Over the ocean, there was a rainbow.

It would have been cheesy if she weren't so raw, but it wasn't. She saw Mickey see it, too. She almost opened her mouth to say *rainbow* for Bash's sake, but she didn't.

"Yeah, we're lucky," she eventually said. "We're on the yacht, for sure."

"Are you scared?" Mickey asked.

Of course she still was scared. But more than scared, she was grateful.

"It's not my dominant emotion at the moment," she said.

They had now. They had Bash, they had the waves cracking shells against the sand in the distance, they had the tangerine sun on their faces.

And they had each other, a boat of three making its way through life. In this moment, under this particular sunset, their eyes reflected the light, and it seemed to promise: *No matter what tomorrow holds, here, little family, is today.*

As soon as they returned from dinner, she phoned Dr. Dixon, the seizure specialist, who'd given her his cell number. It was still early on the West Coast, before five.

Like most of the medical professionals who'd attended the lunch, he was a concierge provider offering "precision" medicine, not taking insurance from patients, only cash. Dr. Dixon's patients were seizure sufferers who could afford to have the country's foremost expert on speed dial.

By the end of their hour-long conversation, they'd planned a trip to LA, with the exact date to be determined but soon, so that Bash could undergo further genomic testing in order to design the optimal treatment plan for him. In the meantime, his initial seizure medications would be delivered by a boutique pharmacy within twenty-four hours.

"And the cost?" Rebecca asked.

"My assistant will send over the pricing sheet," he said. "Once you look it over, you can let me know if you have any questions."

The pricing sheet arrived early the next morning in her in-box. The estimated costs were so far beyond anything that she'd imagined that her mind went blank, short-circuiting when she tried to crunch the numbers in her head.

The testing itself started at $5,000—that was the only number in a range she'd expected.

Being a patient of Dr. Dixon's at all was $4,000 a month. Medications that were proven to be most effective for Bash based on his genetic makeup could range anywhere from $1,500 monthly to *$16,000 monthly*—nearly $200,000 a year. As the sheet explained, these medications were considered "experimental" and thus weren't often covered by insurance plans.

All together, Bash's treatments alone could cost them $250,000 annually—more than Mickey's gross salary.

"I wonder if the Stones will work with us," she said over coffee while Mickey heated up water for tea. He liked to drink hot tea after his runs, which she made fun of him for.

He shrugged.

"You know," Mickey said, "we also don't have to use Dr. Dixon. There are plenty of great doctors out there, I'm sure, who treat Dravet."

"But they're not him."

"Right. That's my point. They're probably affordable for normal Americans. We don't have to use a concierge doctor."

She scowled. "If not for concierge doctors, we would still think our son was dying."

"But if we don't have a choice . . ."

She knew he was right. They couldn't count on the Stones' generosity forever, even if his employers were willing to extend it for a time.

"Let's do this. I'll talk to Mrs. Stone about the cost of the initial testing and the medicines, and we'll take it from there," Rebecca said. If they eventually had to transition to a regular, insurance-covered provider, so be it. But she wasn't ready to settle yet when, if not for the most expensive medical practitioners on earth, they would still be wrong about what was the matter with her son, and he wouldn't be getting the proper treatment. "Maybe you can work it out for them to factor it into your salary or something."

Mickey's eyes cut to the window and back.

"What?" she said.

"Are we staying?" he asked.

It took a moment for his question to register.

"In Florida?" she said.

"Yeah . . ."

"Why on earth wouldn't we be staying in Florida?"

"Because my voice is back," he said quietly, insistently.

Rebecca sighed, loud and long.

"Mickey . . ."

"Bash is okay," he said. "His condition is treatable. 'Manageable' they said. He can get perfectly good treatment in New York."

"Mickey . . ." she said again. "You can't leave your job right now. Not with the bills we're going to get. Not when the Stones are currently *paying* those bills."

"Why not? We can go to the fucking Mayo Clinic. It's free, I read."

She stared at him.

"Think about your *son*," she said. "You want to sacrifice his health so you can go back to singing?"

"We won't be sacrificing anything! You don't know that Dr. Dixon is better than other doctors in New York just because he costs a fortune. New York has excellent doctors."

"I don't think that quitting your job, picking up, and going back to New York is a good idea right now."

Mickey stood, walked across the room, and kicked the wall.

"Your voice is back," Rebecca said. "But you didn't work for *months* before it was even gone. Remember? Remember how we snuck our own tequila into restaurants because we couldn't afford a fucking margarita? You want the margarita to be Bash's medicine next year? How will that feel?"

"I didn't sign up to fucking cater forever," he said.

"I'm not saying forever," she said, although she wasn't sure what she was saying.

"How long then?"

"Until we're in the clear."

"How long is that? It's a lifelong illness."

She shrugged.

"I honestly don't know how to answer that."

He shook his head.

"What?" she asked.

"You know, Rebecca, nothing's stopping you from becoming the caterer. Why don't you fucking pick up an old man's dirty underwear off the floor every day and count out his pills?"

She'd seen Mickey this angry only one other time—after his vocal surgery failed.

"I get it," she said. She'd barely started drafting Astrid's book. "I'll get a job. I'll contribute to our bottom line. Now that we know what's wrong with Bash, we can, I guess, find childcare that we feel comfortable with . . ." Even as she said it, she wasn't convinced she'd ever be able to leave Bash every morning with someone when he could seize at any moment.

"Let's be real—this is only partly about Bash. You would never deign to do work that you felt was beneath you. You're just fine with me doing it."

A tripped wire.

"Are you *kidding*? I've wanted you to get out! I'd love to be able to get back to New York and for you to be able to sing again! I'm thrilled your voice is back! I've been working my ass off to build my career so you can pursue whatever the hell you want. All I'm asking for is a little time to make sure things are stable."

"I'm almost thirty-seven, Rebecca. In the acting world, that's like a hundred."

"I just think it's the right thing—"

"Oh my God." He slammed both palms against the wall. Bash, who'd been napping in his room, awakened at the sound and started to cry. Rebecca went to get him and brought him back, whispering "shhh" while glaring at Mickey.

Calmly, Mickey said, "I wish you would stop thinking you have a monopoly on what's right and wrong."

"What does that mean?" she said.

"Just because you think something is right doesn't make it right. It's not immoral for me to want us to find a different fucking doctor. It's not immoral for me to want to go back to New York so I can have a career. So I would appreciate it if you'd stop casting this as a moral issue."

"Am I doing that? I think *you're* doing that," she said.

"You're judging me for wanting to go back to New York. Admit it."

"Okay! I'm judging you! I think it's fucking selfish! Okay?"

Mickey's eyes narrowed. "But you made an illegal trade and that's okay."

She let out a sharp laugh.

"What does that have to do with anything?" she asked.

"You have a monopoly on right and wrong until it's inconvenient," he muttered.

Because Mickey was clearly inconsolable, she didn't say what she was thinking, what she'd thought all along, which was that the legality of what she'd done was beside the point.

Insider trading seemed like one of those strange creatures of the stock market, an arbitrary designation to prevent an exploitative system from imploding out of its own greed. It certainly didn't seem any more unethical than making billions of dollars on the backs of people who couldn't even afford quality medical care—like her and Mickey, soon enough.

If anything, the only part of the trade that she felt the slightest bit bad about was the fact that she participated in the stock market at *all*.

They passed several minutes in silence as Rebecca nursed. Mickey rose and started to lace up his running shoes.

"I'm going for a jog," he said.

"You just ran," she said.

"I know."

"I guess I'm just confused because I thought you didn't hate your job," Rebecca said.

"Of course I hate it!" Mickey shouted. "I just know how to roll with the circumstances."

"So you were rolling fine a day ago. What has changed, really?" she asked as he opened the door.

"The fucking circumstances!" he said before letting it slam.

An hour later, Rebecca was folding laundry and Mickey was doing crunches on the balcony when she heard a phone buzz. In the living room, where hers was on the coffee table, she found a text from Mrs. Stone: Oh darling, so relieved for you. Cecil and I, both.

But that text had been received ten minutes earlier. It wasn't her phone that was buzzing; it was his.

Tracing it to their bedroom dresser and seeing that it was from a blocked number, she slid open the glass balcony door and handed it to him just as it stopped ringing. The device dinged, indicating that the caller had left him a voicemail.

"Here," she said. "Blocked number."

He didn't even look at it as he set it on the ground and continued his workout. He still wasn't speaking to her.

She returned to stacking clothes while Bash gnawed happily on a teething biscuit and unfolded every garment she'd just stacked before him on the carpet. After a minute, Mickey entered and dropped his phone on the coffee table as he went to the kitchen to refill his water bottle.

As soon as he set it down, the phone began to ring again.

"Who keeps calling?" she asked

"I don't know," he muttered, turning around to pick it up.

"Hello?" he answered. "This is Mickey."

And it all came crashing down.

CHAPTER 28

Mickey paced, listening. After a moment, he stopped in front of the glass door, his free hand on his hip as he stared out at the ocean.

"No . . . no, I prefer now," he said.

His voice had an edge, and she could tell by his body language that something was terribly wrong.

Please let it not be about Bash, she thought. But if it was, wouldn't *she* have been the one called? She was the primary number listed on all of his medical forms, the one corresponding with all the doctors and insurance providers.

"Why would I need one? Can you not give me a sense of what this is about without . . . why would I need a lawyer?"

Rebecca picked up a towel and nervously folded it as Mickey turned to her, wide-eyed. He put the phone on speaker and held it between them facing up, like an offering.

A stranger's muffled voice filled the room. Later, Rebecca would think about how youthful he sounded—not like a government official at all, but like a friend calling to catch up.

"Hello?"

"Yes, I'm here. Sorry, would you mind saying that again?" Mickey said.

"Mr. Byrne, it's Shawn Reed with the SEC. We're conducting an investigation into a trade you made in April of this year. Can you tell me about how you came to have an interest in Aura Beauty Incorporated?"

Mickey closed his eyes and opened them slowly.

Fuck, she mouthed.

"Actually," Mickey said, "I do think it's best for me to get a lawyer before we speak further. Can I get back to you later today?"

Hand trembling, he wrote down Shawn Reed's contact information with a pen Rebecca frantically pulled from her purse and, after promising to be back in touch by the end of business day, hung up.

"You did it in my account," he said. "Thanks."

"I did it in both," she said. "I was just going to do mine, but then I thought there was no way they'd connect the dots . . . I mean, we don't even have the same last name, and how would anyone know about that dinner . . ."

Paul? Had Paul ratted them out somehow? But he didn't know about the trades either.

"How much of what we made was from my account?" he asked, all business.

"Um . . ." She shushed Bash as if he was crying even though he wasn't. She picked him up and began bouncing him and rubbing his back. "Yours was twelve, I think? Fourteen?"

"So we're going to have to get into it with the SEC over twelve fucking thousand dollars?" He shook his head. "The lawyer alone is probably going to cost that much, for fuck's sake. Anything else you want to tell me? While it's all coming out?"

"No," she said softly. "And I'd already told you about it."

"You hadn't told me it was in my account."

"Both accounts," she corrected. "So we should probably expect them to call me next. What do we do?" she asked. "Do you think— can we just say we didn't know?"

He took a deep inhale, held it, then let it out.

"Okay, I'm going to get a lawyer. We'll do whatever the equivalent of a plea deal is with the SEC."

"We can't afford that," she said.

Mickey ignored her, pulling on a T-shirt and grabbing his keys. "You should have thought of that before, Bernie Madoff."

"Where are you going?" she asked.

"To find us a lawyer," he said.

The next morning, Mickey and Rebecca sat in the wood-paneled office of Jordan Baptiste, J.D., with Shawn from the SEC on speaker.

"I made the trades," Mickey said, "based on conversations I overheard while working at the home of Cecil and Astrid Stone. I didn't at the time realize it was illegal."

They'd decided that it seemed more feasible that he, an actor and caterer, wouldn't know what was illegal, while she, a journalist who had covered financial matters, would be less credible in that role. They'd gone ahead and spilled on the trades in Rebecca's account, assuming it was just a matter of time before those came to light as well.

Rebecca said nothing—no one on the other end of the call knew she was in the room. ("If anyone asks, you're *both* my clients," Jordan the lawyer had said. This way, her presence wouldn't waive his attorney-client privilege with Mickey.)

Jordan, the lawyer, had told them that most likely they'd have to pay back "disgorgements," or what they'd made on the illegal trades, times two.

Rebecca had underestimated the earnings from Mickey's account by four thousand dollars—they'd made eighteen thousand on "his" trades, meaning, if the lawyer was right, they'd owe the government thirty-six thousand dollars.

When their attorney stopped speaking a bunch of legal gibberish about disgorgements and whatnot, Shawn from the SEC said, "Josh, you there?"

"Yep, here," another voice chimed in.

"Josh is our colleague at the FBI," Shawn said. Upon hearing *FBI*, Rebecca bit her lip, and Mickey stopped tapping his foot.

"Hi, Mickey," a deeper voice said. "As Shawn mentioned, I'm with the FBI. What I'm about to say is confidential. Violating this confidentiality could invalidate any arrangement we make with you. Is that understood?"

"Yes," Mickey said.

"We're currently conducting a parallel investigation into an unrelated matter, one in which you could potentially be of help. Cecil Stone is under investigation by the agency. If you're willing to cooperate with us, our friends at the SEC might be able to be more generous in terms of penalties. That's up to them of course."

"One moment," Jordan said, before punching the mute button on his '90s black phone. "This is great," he told Mickey and Rebecca, striking her as a little *too* pleased. "This is what I suspected. They don't care about you. They care about your boss. They're about to ask you, I'm guessing, to wear a wire. We can probably knock down the penalty. You may just have to pay disgorgements." He unmuted the phone before either of them could respond.

"What kind of cooperation?" Jordan asked the FBI guy.

"They're leaving for the Hamptons on Monday," Mickey said. "I won't be going with them."

"We know," the FBI voice said. "But there's a meeting tomorrow. We need you to wear a wire. That might be it. Or there might be more."

"My client and I need time to discuss this," Jordan said.

"Sure. Keep in mind we'll need time to prep him, so get back to us as soon as you can."

"We won't be long," Jordan said before hanging up.

"Well?" he said, looking at Mickey. "Done deal?"

"What will happen to Mr. Stone?" Mickey asked.

"You heard everything I did. Could be a fine, could be jail time. The FBI doesn't take it this far unless something stinks to high heaven. He'll pay one way or another, whether you cooperate or not, so his fate doesn't hinge on you, if that's what you're asking. At least, I doubt it."

Rebecca had begun shaking her head.

"No," she said. "We can't. We need them."

"Need them for . . ." Jordan said.

Neither of them answered. Mickey leaped to his feet.

"I need to take a walk," he said.

"Uh, okay, but can you make it fast?" the lawyer said.

"I have time for a fucking walk," Mickey snapped, yanking open the door and stepping outside.

Like everything in West Palm, the lawyer's one-room office was close, only a mile from their condo, and so they'd walked over, both needing the fresh air. As Rebecca pushed Bash home in the stroller, she considered what she saw as their options.

They couldn't afford to lose the Stones' financial support, but she didn't see why they had to.

First, there was no way Cecil Stone was going to wind up in prison—the lawyer had only said that because he didn't know how much money Mr. Stone had. Billionaires didn't go to prison, not unless they did something far worse than a little white-collar number fudging. They'd issue a fine, it would be negotiated down by his own twelve-hundred-dollar-an-hour lawyers, whose law school buddies ran the SEC, and he'd pay it, and that would be that.

If Mickey agreed to wear the wire under pressure, however, he would, of course, lose his job the moment Mr. Stone learned of it, and there's no way he wouldn't find out.

She knew her husband. He wasn't the type to turn down a federal agent. (Although she knew it was cynical and tried not to think it, she also wondered if he would view this as an opportunity to get back to Broadway—"Now I'm unemployed, so we have to go back to New York!")

But Mickey's cooperation wouldn't mean that she had to burn her bridge with Mrs. Stone. Hadn't Astrid Stone herself hammered home that a husband and wife were different people with different values? Hadn't she made clear that she would do anything to prevent Rebecca from having to suffer, as she had, the loss of a child?

Anyway, Mickey had been forced to agree to confidentiality over the phone, but not her. She'd promised nothing to anyone.

Dear, What do you mean urgent? I'm at the 4 Arts. Come by. —A

Rebecca didn't stop by the condo; she headed directly over the bridge to the Society of the Four Arts, where she found Mrs. Stone in the sculpture garden overseeing the installation of a sculpture she had donated to the institution. It was a modern piece—an enormous green apple the size of a school bus, held by a red-fingernailed hand.

"It's called Eve's Temptation," Mrs. Stone said as a team of six men carefully lifted it off a trolley and onto a green patch of earth. "It's by Charles de Gaulle's granddaughter. Isn't it fabulous? Scarlett is a good friend of mine. Her health is not great unfortunately. She turns eighty this year."

"May I talk to you privately really quickly?" Rebecca asked. "I know it's not an ideal time, but it should only take a minute."

Mrs. Stone looked around.

"This way," she said, leading Rebecca across the bright grass into a cavernous archway on the other side of the garden. She stopped under a floral canopy. Roses in vibrant jewel tones enveloped them. They were alone, just the two women and the baby.

"The FBI is investigating Mr. Stone. They want Mickey to wear a wire tomorrow," Rebecca said.

Mrs. Stone blinked.

"I see. Why are you telling me this?" She crossed her slender arms.

"I think Mickey's probably going to do it, and I wanted you to know." She paused. She'd rehearsed on the way over. "I'm so, so grateful for all that you've done for us."

"And you need me to pay Tim," Mrs. Stone said, referring to Dr. Dixon. She sounded almost bored, like she'd seen this coming and wanted to get back to tending to her own business.

Rebecca hesitated before saying, "We can't afford him."

"Tim's services are not an issue," Mrs. Stone said abruptly. "I'll take care of it."

"Thank you," Rebecca said, blinking hard.

"But Rebecca, I need you to finish the memoir. Do you understand?"

They stared at each other for a few long seconds.

We keep our finances separate.

I've never had anything to do with his dealings, dear.

I've always stayed out of Cecil's business.

"You knew this was coming?" Rebecca said quietly.

"I'm old," Mrs. Stone said as quietly. "Little surprises me these days."

"The memoir is . . . your defense?" Rebecca asked.

"Mmm," Mrs. Stone said. "More like a sheen of credibility. A gloss. By a highly reputable reporter." Was that a wink or just a blink?

The sun had snuck higher and started to pour into the canopy, blinding Rebecca. She lifted her hand above her eyes.

A sheen of credibility? With the FBI? It seemed far-fetched. But then, as Bash squealed and she pulled down his stroller's canopy to shield him from the glare, it struck her: perhaps it wasn't about the FBI.

"Is this about Elle?" she asked.

Mrs. Stone's eyes shifted beyond Rebecca and back.

"She knows I am who I am," Mrs. Stone said with practiced nonchalance, "but, you know. It doesn't hurt to hear it from one of your own."

The truth took shape in Rebecca's mind. Mrs. Stone wanted her daughter to hear from an objective party that her mother wasn't involved in Cecil's affairs—not just that she'd been absent from his illegal dealings, but that she'd had no part in any of his work. The project had been about preserving Elle's respect. She didn't want to lose her daughter, too.

"I see," Rebecca said.

"Rebecca, I hope you understand that I want you to write the book that you want to write. You don't have to make me out to be perfect by any means," she said.

"Okay," Rebecca said.

"But for God's sake, do me this much." She pivoted just slightly, signaling that she was ready to go. "Make it juicy."

CHAPTER 29

"Just disgorgements for both of you," Jordan the lawyer said, throwing up his arms and punching the air. "Damn, I'm good at my job."

The SEC would garner the twenty-three thousand dollars Rebecca had made, in addition to Mickey's eighteen thousand.

The agreement was swift, and the FBI began issuing directives immediately: Mickey was to show up at work the next day, as usual. Agents would arrive at Mickey and Rebecca's in the wee hours of the morning to wire him and issue his instructions.

At three thirty a.m., Rebecca and Mickey were both already awake (who could sleep at a time like this?), when a man and woman, both in black suits, knocked on the door. They waited on the couch while he showered and dressed, then carefully hid the mic on his body and showed Mickey just how to orient his torso so that the mic could pick up conversation. They made him practice while Rebecca and Bash sat in the nursery stacking blocks in the starlight.

They wouldn't allow him to remove the mic once it was placed, and so then there was nothing to do but wait.

Rebecca made everyone coffee. Mickey and the male agent snoozed on chairs. The woman watched an action movie on her phone. Rebecca let Bash sleep in her lap, leaning against his bedroom wall.

At five thirty a.m., Mickey's alarm went off. He bolted up to sitting, a patch on one shoulder white with drool.

"Here goes nothing," he said, as the agents checked the settings one last time.

Riding his bike over the bridge, Mickey was relieved. He knew he wasn't supposed to be. It wasn't what Rebecca wanted.

A part of him felt bad, too, of course. He owed Mr. Stone a tremendous amount—but he also believed the lawyer had been right; if Mr. Stone was going to be prosecuted, it would happen with or without Mickey's cooperation.

Mr. Stone was a reasonable person. He would understand that when the FBI approached him, Mickey hadn't actually had a choice but to do what he was asked.

As he glided onto their street, he wondered whether Paul had been the one to alert the authorities or not—if he'd been that vengeful.

Already, his and Paul's texts had trickled to next to nothing. They'd drifted as quickly as they'd bonded, and the brief period of their intense, truncated friendship felt almost like he'd imagined it—the way weekends with his dad had felt growing up after he'd returned home. A dream.

Since Paul's firing, Mickey was always among the first staff to arrive, along with a couple of the cleaning crew and a yard worker or two.

He parked his bike in the back and entered the house. There was an eerie silence; even with no staff present, it felt quieter than usual.

Entering the dining room, he saw why. On the table was a handwritten note.

In Mrs. Stone's elegant penmanship, it read:

Dear All Staff,

We will no longer be needing your services.

Sincerely,

Astrid Stone

It took Mickey a moment to accept that he was included, that his tenure at the Stones', while short, could come to a halt so impersonally. But "All Staff" left no question.

This was the end for him—a catchall firing. Not even a goodbye.

Just as he was about to leave for the last time, Mickey heard footsteps approaching from the back of the house—footsteps that weren't Mr. Stone's but were slower and heavier. He fought the impulse to flee. Where would he go?

Bruce appeared, sans Chloe, in jeans and loafers, with his keys dangling in one hand. The first thing Mickey noticed was that he looked great. The whites of his eyes were clear, and his cheeks weren't their usual splotchy red.

"Sorry about the bad news," Bruce said, sounding sober but not especially sorry. "I assume you did not expect this." He glanced down at the note.

"It's a surprise, for sure," Mickey said.

"Well, you can remind the FBI that Cecil is often one step ahead of most people."

Puzzled, Mickey said nothing, waiting for Bruce to say more. How did he know about the FBI?

"I turned him in," Bruce said, only a little sheepish, like he was admitting to spilling his drink or getting into a fender bender. "Had to get out of my own little snafu with the SEC. That's how it goes, these things."

"I see," Mickey said, moving to leave, aware that the agents were listening in on their conversation. "Well, I should get going. See ya, Bruce."

"Me, too. Just came by to get Piggy." He held up a pink rubber piglet whose facial features had been gnawed through. "Chloe loves this fucking thing. Hey, Mickey, real fast—"

Mickey turned back to face him.

"Sorry if I made your life here miserable. I made a lot of people miserable." He chuckled. "I'm doing this thing where I say sorry to everybody I fucked over. So, sorry."

"It's okay," Mickey said. "Don't worry about it."

The last person on Mickey's mind was Bruce and his hollow interpretation of the Twelve Steps. Apologizing to Mickey while turning his brother into the FBI didn't add up in Mickey's mind, but Bruce had never made much sense to him.

"I do love my brother, you know," he said. "I hope he's okay."

"Well, if you're right, he's one step ahead, I guess," Mickey said. "Bye, Bruce."

"Oh, I don't mean this SEC shit," he said. "You think I'd have turned him in if I didn't think he could handle that?" Perhaps Bruce *didn't* know the FBI was listening.

"I meant the cancer."

"Huh?" Mickey said.

"You didn't know? His cancer's back. It's all over his body. That's what that shit on his legs was. Best fucking doctors in the world and they didn't see what was right in front of them." Bruce shook his head. "Cancer's smarter than everybody, I think."

Rebecca sat at the bistro table with her laptop open before her, holding her phone up to her ear.

You have reached the cell phone of Gwen Honeycutt. Please leave a message.

Rebecca hung up just before the beep. It was the third time she'd tried to call her mom that morning, and every time, it had gone to voicemail.

The agents had accompanied Mickey out. Left alone in the quiet, after the drama of the previous twenty-four hours, Rebecca had taken a long shower while Bash sat in the bouncer on the bathroom floor watching Elmo on the iPad, which was propped precariously on the side of the tub. She'd stood under the hot water until her fingertips grew pruny, tuning out the sounds of *Sesame Street* as she tried to channel her creativity. In spite of everything, she was up against a deadline: she had a column due.

After getting dressed, she'd reached out to Samantha, who'd switched to the day shift part-time and had several mornings off a week. Luckily, she was free. Rebecca left Bash with her for the remainder of the morning, giving herself two hours to knock out a draft.

But as soon as she'd sat with her cup of Earl Grey, instead of opening her computer, she'd picked up her phone and called her mom.

She wasn't sure why. Perhaps it was discovering Mrs. Stone's motive was the connection to her own daughter. Perhaps it was just that she was tired and could use a mom.

When her mother didn't answer on the first or second ring, Rebecca decided to stop procrastinating and get done what she'd come to do.

At first, she wondered if there was a way to write about her experience somehow—it was a story of means, and lack of them, after all.

The problem was, Rebecca saw wealth differently now. She didn't know which view was more correct—old Rebecca's or new Rebecca's. All she knew was that she couldn't write from her former vantage point, the one that had scored her the column in the first place and garnered her "Likes" and retweets and texts from an old flame. That place in her mind had become outdated overnight. It felt almost embarrassing now, like her high school jeans, her '90s dark lipstick, and those elastic chokers.

She thought only of everything she *couldn't* write.

She couldn't write how deep her fear ran; how she'd discovered a self within herself that was capable of more, for better or worse, than she realized. (The column wasn't about *her*, after all.)

She couldn't write how grateful she was to have found the Stones, because they had rescued her—not Bash, but *her*—and that she didn't care if that made her a hypocrite.

She drummed her fingers on the table, wondering if she should roam the island for inspiration. She picked up her phone.

Again, it rang once, twice.

You have reached the cell phone of Gwen Honeycutt. Please leave a message.

She set the phone down and sipped her tea.

Maybe, if she was honest, it wasn't a *couldn't*. Maybe it was more of a *wouldn't*—what she wouldn't write, because it was not what her readers wanted from her, nor what Henrik expected.

Or maybe it wasn't how she wanted people to see her.

She would not write that she'd gotten to know the people behind the money, and that they were kind of terrible in all the ways she'd expected, and kind of okay in other ways, and that regardless of it all, they were the reason she was no longer living in terror. She wouldn't write that even though Cecil Stone had made his fortune by screwing over the world, the fact that he had paid to save her son was all she could see now. She'd shown her true colors, flashed them before herself and Mickey and a handful of others. She could take dirty money and make dirty money if the reason was important enough. And the part that only she knew, that surprised even her, would remain her secret: she felt no guilt about it.

She suspected that one day, when Bash was older and, God willing, healthy, when time had passed and the critical state of their lives had eased into normalcy again, she'd be able to see the nuances of the situation. Come that day, perhaps she'd feel some sense of responsibility, some accountability to the values she'd professed in all the years leading up to this one. Perhaps then, she would be able to write about what happened that spring with some degree of objectivity.

But not now. Not today.

EPILOGUE

Eighteen Months Later—December 2019

Mickey and Rebecca sat at their gate in LAX munching on Chipotle salads while Bash ran back and forth along the rows of chairs, giving high fives to anyone who would oblige him. An older man, a teenager, and a pretty pilot all happily complied as the toddler passed, hand raised, for the fifth time, then the sixth.

"You don't have to keep doing that," Rebecca said to them all. "He might never let you stop."

"High five!" Bash yelled at the teenager, who lifted a limp hand cooperatively.

"Hey," Mickey said to get Rebecca's attention. He cocked his head toward the TV screen above them, playing the evening news.

There was Mrs. Stone, polished and smiling in an emerald blazer, in a recap of that morning's morning show on which she'd been interviewed about Rebecca's book. (It paid to have contacts from all those years at *GMA*.)

The biography had just come out—a tell-all covering the three marriages, two businesses, and record-breaking game-show winnings of Mrs. Astrid Martin Stone, acquaintance of Elvis, friend of the Churchills, and daughter of a Tupperware queen.

On the screen, Mrs. Stone said, "You'll have to ask the senator that question," eyes gleaming.

Rebecca shook her head.

"Were any of these stories shocking to your friends and family?" the host asked.

"My daughter couldn't believe I'd never shared the Elvis stories. Turns out, she was impressed by it, which is silly since all I did was bat my lashes . . ."

"Is it okay," the pilot asked Rebecca, "if I give him some wings?" She held up the bronze piece of plastic.

"Sure," Rebecca said.

The pilot leaned over to pin the wings on Bash's T-shirt—it was a red-eye, and he'd sleep on the flight—while Bash allowed it, skeptical. The pilot leaned back, and Bash considered the gift, decided he hated it, and rushed over to Rebecca while yelling, "Off! Off!"

"Thanks anyway," she said, removing the pin.

"What takes you all to Palm Beach?" the pilot asked.

"Work," Rebecca said.

Mrs. Stone had invited Rebecca down to lead a discussion about the book—but this meeting was bigger than a book club. Two hundred people had registered for the talk, which would be held in the auditorium at the Society of the Four Arts.

Mr. Stone had been charged with nineteen counts of securities fraud, mail fraud, and wire fraud. He'd hired lawyers who had immediately negotiated a settlement, and a crisis control team that had somehow, so far, limited the media coverage of the story. Rebecca had seen only a couple of headlines. But he hadn't yet conquered the cancer, not this time. His treatments were ongoing, according to Astrid.

"You live here in LA?"

Rebecca nodded.

It hadn't been in the plan. They'd traveled to Los Angeles thinking they'd be there a month, long enough for Bash's tiny genome to be tested further so that he could be prescribed a treatment plan tailored to it. They'd rented an Airbnb for a month. A week in, Mickey had gone in for a commercial audition just for kicks.

He'd booked it. The campaign, for Freedom Insurance, turned out to be built around his character, a folksy, cynical type whose tagline—"Whatcha sellin'?"—ended every ad.

Once it became an ongoing gig, they decided to stay for a while, and within months he'd booked more projects—a couple of indie films and a small recurring spot on a network prime-time show. After his folksy character's Super Bowl ad was one of the season's favorites, he was suddenly recognized everywhere they went.

"Whatcha sellin'?" strangers would yell at him, and he'd politely smile and wave.

It wasn't musical theater, but it was acting—and he was making good money.

For the first seven months they'd accepted the Stones' financial support in covering Bash's treatments, but after that, they'd been able to afford them on their own.

The treatments seemed to be working. Bash hadn't had a seizure in over a year. He was running, kicking, trying to jump. He knew most of his letters. He was obsessed with bunnies.

Rebecca tried to settle in to the reality that her child was okay, that he was, it seemed, going to be okay. But the whiplash of the whole experience felt too recent to move on. Whenever she tried to accept that the worst was over, fear shot through her.

And shouldn't it?

One day, she would be gone. One day, so would Mickey. And one day, so would Bash.

They'd already heard several "Whatcha sellin'?"s since arriving at the airport, so when a man approached Mickey and said, "Excuse me, but are you—" Mickey didn't even let him finish before saying, "That's me."

But then the man said, ". . . Mickey Byrne from the *Mamma Mia* tour, 2008?"

Mickey studied the stranger.

"Wait . . . Jimmy, right?" he asked.

"Yeah! Hey, man!" They shook hands. Jimmy had been the physical therapist on tour—Mickey's third national tour, at twenty-eight. He hadn't seen the guy in ten years.

"You haven't changed at all," Jimmy said.

"Right," Mickey said. "But honestly, you haven't either."

"Got to go catch my flight back to the city—good-looking family you got there."

"Great to see you, man," Mickey said.

"You're still a baby-faced twenty-eight," Rebecca said. "Hear that?"

"Mm-hmm," Mickey said, visibly delighted.

He had changed, though—that was the thing. He'd been brought to the brink, then pulled back. He'd been spared, and every day, he was aware of it. He still got to be a dad. He got to be a dad, and he was going to nail being a dad. "Bash!" he called. "Come count!"

Their latest father-son project: counting to twenty.

"Are you a passenger on this flight?" Rebecca asked the pilot, who was in uniform.

"I am," she said. "Going to spend the holidays with my parents."

Rebecca nodded.

"What do you do for work?"

"I'm a journalist," she said. "I wrote a book about that lady—" She looked up at the TV, but the segment was over. "Well, she was on the screen a second ago."

"What's it called?"

"*She Made It Herself*," Rebecca said.

"What'd she make?" the pilot asked.

"Mainly money. A whole lot of it."

"Ah. So it's like a how-to book or something?"

Rebecca shook her head.

"Just a biography," she said. "The life story of an interesting person, if you like that sort of thing."

The pilot nodded, losing interest and gazing down at her phone.

"There's supposed to be weather over the Rockies. I anticipate a bumpy flight," she said after a few minutes. "Let's hope we can sleep."

Across from her, Bash and Mickey counted up from ten. *Ten. Eleven. Thirteen.*

He always forgot twelve.

"Yes," Rebecca. "Let's hope."

ACKNOWLEDGMENTS

Thank you to Emily Griffin, Micaela Carr, Katherine Beitner, Erin Kibby, Megan Looney, and the entire team at Harper. I'm so grateful that I get to work with you. Thank you to Joanne O'Neill for the gorgeous cover design. Enormous thank you, as ever, to my wonderful agent, Claire Anderson-Wheeler, and to her lovely colleagues at Regal. It's always a joy. I relied on the expertise of a number of people in writing this book, including my husband, Lucas Richter, and the other Genetic Counseling students at Vanderbilt. Thanks for taking the time to weigh in on my fiction questions, friends! Big thanks, as well, to other friends who provided insight into the other worlds of this book: Adam Bloomfield, Wes Hart, Christine Cornish Smith, Jeremy Hays, Kathleen Hays, Dave Schoonover, Rachel Fischer, Dana Cote, Raquel Look, and Schuyler Hughes. Eliza Moreno, you were such a fantastic assistant on this project, and I owe you so much for helping me to manage drafts of this manuscript. Heléne Yorke, you're a dream writing partner but also make a great fashion terminology consultant. My writing group offered such valuable input on this book: Kate Tellers, Ophira Eisenberg, and Stephen Ruddy—love you guys. To Jennifer Kenter, Karen Kudelko, and Emily Stirba, thank you for being wonderful friends, supporting me through the writing of this book and others. To my community of writing students, I live for meeting with you each week and talking about resistance. Finally, Lucas and Finn, love you to the moon, whether we're in Florida, Nashville, or Mars.

ABOUT THE AUTHOR

MARY ADKINS is a writer whose work has appeared in the *New York Times* and the *Atlantic*. A native of the American South and a graduate of Duke University and Yale Law School, she also teaches storytelling for The Moth. Her debut novel, *When You Read This*, was published by Harper in 2019.